THE ABOMINABLE MR. DARCY

A PRIDE & PREJUDICE VARIATION

J. DAWN KING

Quiet Mountain Press

Cover Design: JD Smith – Design

Cover Photography: © JD Smith – Design

Interior Formatting: Sarah Johnson, Peculiar World Designs

Published by: Joy D. King

EBook ISBN-13: 978-0-692-67190-0

EBook ISBN-10: 0-692-67190-0

Library of Congress Control Number – **2016909060**

❀ Created with Vellum

ACKNOWLEDGMENTS

My sincerest thanks go to Christina Boyd, editor extraordinaire. I appreciate your diligent efforts to corral my head-hopping writing style but fear I had to insert a few character points-of-view after your last edits. Yes, I had to. I LOVED working with you and hope to do so again and again. My heartfelt desire is that you feel the same.

Anji Dale, you are brilliant. I'm just saying.

As always – thank you to David James Gandy, the Mr. Darcy in my stories.

Finally, to the many readers who left hundreds of comments and reviews on fanfiction.net. Almost 1,000 reviews! You really know how to inspire an author to write.

To Dan and Debbie Fortin, whose early marriage paralleled many of the events in this story. Who knew you two lovebirds had such a beginning?

"OH! THAT ABOMINABLE MR. DARCY!"

JANE AUSTEN, PRIDE & PREJUDICE

*W*ednesday, 2 October 1811
Meryton, Hertfordshire

He was by far the handsomest man she had ever seen—tall and broad-shouldered with dark, wavy hair, curls flirting at the back of his collar, and sapphire eyes that sparkled in the myriads of candles lighting the assembly. Elizabeth Bennet, like the others in attendance, watched his progress as his party entered the room. His clothes were of the finest materials, and the fit was excellent. She wondered whether he was a fastidious man. He looked the part.

Elizabeth glanced at her sister Jane to determine where her eyes rested. *The red-haired gentleman. Good!* She loved her sister dearly. If Jane was interested in the taller man—who the whispers of the assembly announced was Mr. Fitzwilliam Darcy of Pemberley in Derbyshire—Elizabeth would gaze at him no more. Since this was not the case, her eyes again drifted his way as the group walked through the crowd.

Besides *Mr. Divinely Attractive* and the red-haired man, two other men and two women accompanied the party. It was simple to surmise one of the pairs was married by their deliberate movements to ignore each other.

"Eliza, I believe you will have to restrain your two youngest siblings when they spy the officer's red coat." Charlotte Lucas, who was seated on the other side of Elizabeth, had a practical mind. They were long-time friends in spite of the seven-year difference in age. She too was surreptitiously studying the newcomers. Any unmarried man would be ideal prey for the abundance of maidens in attendance.

Elizabeth's eyes alighted to the officer behind *Mr. Heavenly Visage.* He had a pleasant, welcoming smile with a touch of sardonic. Like *Mr. Stately Sculpted,* his brow was furrowed. Elizabeth could not help but wonder whether he had seen action on the continent. The colonel was ruggedly handsome with bronzed skin, indicating many hours spent out of doors. He was not as tall as *Mr. Overtly Gorgeous,* yet the shoulders of his uniform were just as broad. Neither man looked as if they needed padding to enhance their physique. Elizabeth watched the officer's easy smile as his eyebrows rose at something *Mr. Sublimely Appealing* said. She immediately judged him as a man whom she might find much delight in knowing. *Was he a second son to have chosen the military as a career?*

"Yes, Charlotte, I believe you are correct," she said sighing. Her younger sisters, Kitty and Lydia, were uncontrolled, ill-mannered, and far too young to be out in public. Nonetheless, their mother insisted they be let loose at age fifteen to hunt down and capture a husband. The girls had long been fond of a man in uniform. The colonel would undoubtedly become the object of their attention.

Elizabeth turned to look closely at her friend, only to find Charlotte's eyes lingering on the colonel. She smiled to herself. *It was as she had hoped! No interest in Mr. Fabulously Elegant.* Sweeping her eyes around the room, she spied Charlotte's father headed in their direction, most likely to retrieve his daughter for an introduction to the new arrivals.

"I believe you are about to be summoned, Charlotte. Now, as Mama would say, 'Stand up straight with your shoulders back.'" Both young women chuckled. Yet, both knew with clarity why their mothers acted so. Only if their daughters married or sought work as a governess or companion would their families be relieved of their support.

As her friend walked away, Elizabeth again looked around the room. An interesting drama unfolded. The set had ended so the noise had diminished as the dancing couples moved to find refreshment or their next partner. Voices carried across the room.

"Come, Kitty and Lydia. Jane, smile, he's looking your way. Mary, oh where is that Mary?" said a flustered and frantic Mrs. Bennet. "Lizzy can meet them later. Girls! Come! Our neighbours from Netherfield Park have arrived. Come!"

"The lack of fashion and good taste is appalling," said the young lady in the puce dress to the woman who was endeavouring to keep up with her. They were two of the new arrivals. "How could Charles possibly want to settle in Hertfordshire? There is no one here of quality. Even a moment of time spent in their company would be a hardship."

"Unless our brother and his friends stand up with us, I fear I shall not dance this evening as Gilbert has gone to the card room. I shall not be able to roust him out." The speaker had features similar enough to the young woman in puce and the red-headed man to identify them as brother and sisters. *They must be the Bingleys.*

Elizabeth watched as Sir William Lucas, accompanied by his wife, two daughters, and two sons, approached the Netherfield party. His voice boomed to the far corners of the assembly hall. "Mr. Bingley, might I introduce you to my family?"

As he brought forward his wife and children, Elizabeth spied her mother herding Jane, Mary, Kitty, and Lydia to a spot behind Sir William, a position where she would be noticed. Elizabeth edged back into her seat, wishing she was in any other location to avoid witnessing her mother's antics to promote her own daughters to the gentlemen. Furthermore, she detected regret on the faces of Mrs. Long and Mrs. Goulding that they had been outmaneuvered.

As Elizabeth anticipated, both of Mr. Bingley's sisters acknowledged the Lucas and Bennet ladies with barely a nod and then looked away with practiced ennui. In fact, the two were twittering behind their fans. Elizabeth's ire grew as she saw the embarrassed blush creeping up her eldest sister's neck at the supercilious sisters' slight. Jane Bennet was above reproach and therefore, in Elizabeth's opinion, entirely undeserving of their condescension.

Elizabeth's anger was lessened as she realised Mr. Bingley's attention was solely for Jane. However, *Mr. Sublimely Appealing* looked straight ahead to the opposite wall, giving a trifling bow once all the individuals had been presented. *Was he above the present company? Was he shy? Perhaps he is mute, or has he difficulty with his tongue? A stutter maybe?* He was an interesting riddle to be puzzled out in her own mind.

Once the social niceties were concluded, Mr. Bingley led Jane to the dance floor as the colonel did the same with Charlotte. Conversation flowed between the latter couple, while the former gazed at each other with infant feelings of admiration.

Before Elizabeth could return her own gaze to the handsome gentleman, she heard her mother's voice with a dread that made her quiver.

"Mr. Darcy, I have another daughter who is not presently dancing. I am sure you would not neglect the young ladies who are without a partner?"

Sure enough, Elizabeth realised Kitty and Lydia had been claimed for the next set and her quiet sister Mary had returned to her book on a bench in the corner. Her mother had turned and was pointing in her direction, wagging her handkerchief at her. Elizabeth was seated with three other young women who had not been claimed by a dancing partner for the current set. She felt the heat as her face flushed. *Why? Oh, why does my mother have to embarrass me so?* Possibly the man would not realise which of the four ladies Mrs. Bennet was attempting to draw his attention to. She could only hope.

Elizabeth glanced up at the gentleman and gratefully realised his eyes had not moved from the point he had focussed on since he had entered the room. Curious to determine what had captured his interest, she looked behind. *Bare panels of wood!* There was not even an unusual knot or burl in the planking to attract the eye.

Elizabeth knew in her heart that his reaction to the matriarch of the Bennet family would be telling as to the type of man he was. Therefore, when he offered her mother a bow and walked away without saying a word, Elizabeth suspected he had been repulsed by her mother's blatant attempt to coerce him to favour one of her daughters. From Elizabeth's vantage point, it was not a flaw. Even she knew her mother's conduct had been vulgar.

Elizabeth foretold what was coming next as if she had written a script for their actions. As soon as *Mr. Practically Perfect* decamped, Miss Bingley followed. Where she went, her married sister followed; two shadows attempting to move in harmony with the reality.

As Elizabeth turned her attention back to the dance, she heard Charlotte's laughter and realised the colonel was exactly as she expected him to be—pleasant company. Mr. Bingley's grin radiated satisfaction with his partner, and Jane's pink cheeks were now from joy, not embarrassment. They made a lovely pair, all smiles and blushes. Watching them made Elizabeth smile as well.

ELIZABETH HAD no way of knowing how the candlelight danced in her eyes as she appeared to find pleasure in the interest Mr. Bingley was showing his partner. However, Mr. Darcy noticed. To him, she was a mystery, and he wondered to which family she belonged. He appreciated that she was seated regally, overseeing her little kingdom. Rich, golden highlights from the chandelier above danced in her dark hair, leaving her in a pool of brilliance—as if the heavens were nodding their approval.

Darcy drew in a breath, wondering how his attention had been caught so quickly by a country miss. Yet he assured himself he would soon discover her to be as inane and superficial as almost every other unmarried, young woman he met—more concerned for his estate and his family name than himself. The company thus far gave credence to his thoughts. He shook his head at the conduct of the last woman who had approached him. Mrs. Bennet's insistence that he favour one of her daughters with a dance was obscene. Most likely her progeny were merely younger versions of herself. It would not do for him to condescend to partner anyone from *that* family.

* * *

WHEN THE DANCE ENDED, both Mr. Bingley and the colonel escorted their ladies to where Elizabeth was seated. She stood at their approach and curtsied deeply as Charlotte and Jane introduced the gentlemen.

"Miss Elizabeth, if you are available for the next set, it would be an honour for me to stand up with you." Upon closer inspection, the colonel was older than she had first presumed, or his experiences in the military had prematurely caused lines around his eyes and mouth. Elizabeth was determined to find out.

When the music started, it was a slow country dance which would allow them to converse during much of the set. Elizabeth was pleased at the realisation.

She had not a clue she was being observed.

"Miss Elizabeth, you were not with your sisters when we were first introduced. You have yet to meet my cousin."

"I have not had the privilege, sir." Elizabeth's own eyebrow lifted as she spoke. She speculated that a close bond existed between the two cousins. Her first impression suggested the two men were opposites— the colonel was pleasant and comfortable in unknown company, while Mr. Darcy was not. "You are speaking of the man with the quizzical brow?"

"I see you are a young woman who is not intimidated by my cousin's stern manner." The colonel chuckled. "Is that how you would describe Darcy?"

"It is all I know of him."

"You have heard no rumours of his wealth? His status? Even I have been confronted with the loud whispers of 'ten thousand a year with a large estate and a house in Town.'"

"For a certainty, Colonel Fitzwilliam, I have heard my neighbours." Elizabeth paused as they moved away from each other in the dance. "'Yet wealth stays with us a little moment, if at all. Only our characters are steadfast, not our gold.'"

"Sophocles?" A befuddled furrow crossed his brow.

"Euripides."

"Ah, the great playwright from ancient Greece." They both laughed as both authors were ancient *and* Greek. "You have quite caught me by surprise, Miss Elizabeth. I know of no woman of my acquaintance who quotes ancient writers." In a blink, the colonel's countenance changed from jovial to one of earnestness. "Nonetheless, my cousin is the finest, most honourable man of my acquaintance. His character is to be valued far more than the King's coffers."

Elizabeth could not help but mutter under her breath. "Which the Prince Regent is currently spending like water through a net."

He heard. It caught him completely off guard. *She knows politics and the events of the monarchy as well?* Miss Elizabeth would have much in common with Darcy. He turned to look at his cousin and found him staring at them...at her. *Ah, the young lady has his interest.*

"Miss Elizabeth, I will be dancing the next with Miss Bennet—and Miss Bingley the set after. Might I introduce you to my cousin before the evening is over?"

Elizabeth had allowed her fertile imagination to mold this Mr. Darcy into the man of her dreams. To remain unknown, was to keep him perfect, a knight in shining armour, unblemished and unflawed. She spent the remainder of the dance pondering the introduction to come.

Until that night, Elizabeth felt she knew herself well. Her father was proud of her reasonable, inquisitive mind. She had been as well. Nevertheless, since the entry of the particular gentleman from Netherfield Park, her flights of romantic fancy had been reminiscent of her youngest sisters. *She had best take charge of herself!*

"Yes, Colonel Fitzwilliam, I would be delighted to welcome your cousin to Meryton." Elizabeth could see this pleased her partner, who seemed to continue the dance with a lighter step, inconsistent with his size.

Mr. Darcy danced once with Miss Bingley and once with Mrs. Hurst, the sisters of his friend. He spent the balance of the evening walking about the room or leaning against the wall, speaking occasionally to one of his own party. What motivated a gentleman to hold himself separate from company? Surely, with his rumoured wealth and stature, he was an accomplished man who could perform the steps needed to dance more than twice. Elizabeth wondered again; *was he shy?*

Whatever the answer, it was a disappointment to more than one young lady, as gentlemen were scarce, and several had to sit out each dance due to lack of a partner, including Elizabeth.

Elizabeth was seated with her good friend Charlotte amidst other ladies when Mr. Darcy, the colonel, and Mr. Bingley stopped adjacent to them and commenced speaking.

"Come, Darcy," said Mr. Bingley, "I must have you dance. I hate to see you standing about by yourself in this stupid manner. You had much better dance."

"I certainly shall not. You know how I detest it, unless I am particularly acquainted with my partner. At such an assembly as this, it would be insupportable. I have already danced with your sisters, and there is not another woman in the room whom it would not be a punishment to me to stand up with."

Mr. Darcy ignored the glare from his cousin. Elizabeth easily recognised that look as her mother often directed the same towards her when she was displeased.

"I would not be so fastidious as you are for a kingdom!" cried Mr. Bingley. "Upon my honour, I never met with so many pleasant girls in my life, as I have this evening; and there are several of them, you see, uncommonly pretty."

"*You* are dancing with the only handsome girl in the room," said Mr. Darcy, looking at the eldest Miss Bennet. He turned to his cousin.

"You, Richard, would welcome any female as a partner as long as they have two legs."

"Darcy!" The colonel hissed. He was appalled at his cousin's contemptuous attitude, though he was not surprised. It was always so at large gatherings. He gave his cousin a censorious look then walked away.

Mr. Bingley failed to note the exchange between the two men. He only had eyes for Jane. "Oh! She is the most beautiful creature I ever beheld! But there is one of her sisters sitting down just behind you, Miss Elizabeth, who is very pretty, and I dare say very agreeable. Do let me ask my partner to introduce you."

"Which do you mean?" Turning around, he looked for a moment at the small group of young ladies sitting on either side of the woman he had noticed earlier. Focussing on the maiden whose features were somewhat similar to Miss Bennet's, he said, "She is tolerable; but not handsome enough to tempt *me*; and I am in no humour at present to give consequence to young ladies who are slighted by other men. You had better return to your partner and enjoy her smiles, for you are wasting your time with me."

Bingley longed for the floor to open up and swallow him and Darcy completely. By the pained expression on Miss Elizabeth's face, she had heard every word uttered by his friend. He raised his eyebrows in alarm. Darcy merely stiffened and walked away.

Elizabeth gasped at his insult. *How dare he speak about me in such a manner...to be overheard by my neighbours?* In her lifetime, she had never been the focus of such rudeness, disdain, or arrogance. His character was now decided. *Mr. Blatantly Offensive* had fallen from his white stallion and tarnished his shining armour. He was the proudest, most disagreeable man in the world, and everybody, most especially Elizabeth Bennet, hoped he would never again be in their company. She was grateful Colonel Fitzwilliam had not yet performed an introduction.

Mr. Darcy was an enigma...until he spoke. *Then* he was the enemy.

Covered in mortification and enraged at his disparagement, Elizabeth's cheeks glowed a flaming red, and fire was shooting from her eyes. Charlotte reached over and put her hand on Elizabeth's forearm when it looked like she would stand. Seeing the mixture of ire and hurt on her friend's face and hoping to gain Elizabeth's attention before she did something foolish, Charlotte asked, "Eliza, what do you think of our visitors now?" It would not surprise any person in attendance if Elizabeth stood toe-to-toe with the gentleman and shared her personal view of his character flaws. That was her way.

Nonetheless, what was also known about Elizabeth Bennet was her unfailing kindness and her ability to laugh at the ridiculous. Charlotte knew how best to placate her friend. Though there was a difference in their upbringing and education, they both appreciated the keen intellect of the other. Charlotte was much more practical than Elizabeth, who was a romantic at heart—though Elizabeth would not likely admit that to herself or anyone else.

"Does he not remind you of Farmer Glenn's peacock?" Charlotte whispered.

Elizabeth spun her head to look directly at Charlotte, the sparks turning into a twinkle. "Why, Charlotte, I do believe you are correct." Elizabeth snickered. "At any moment, he might start shaking his tail feathers and squawk. Insolent man!" The last was said with the same dour expression currently on the man's face. Both young ladies laughed with delight.

Elizabeth cared not that he might have heard her comments. She had certainly heard his, and she only regretted they were breathing the same air in the enclosed room.

"My father gave that peacock to Farmer Glenn, Charlotte." Elizabeth's smile was mixed with a hint of mischief. "Papa claims they are a vain, proud bird whose only virtue is their outer appearance. I would not be surprised if Mrs. Glenn served the miserable bird for Sunday dinner."

At that, Elizabeth looked up from where she was seated and caught his eye, refusing to look away first. He must have had the same determination. Eventually, as the music changed and the next set queued, her attention was diverted by her next partner. Mr. Darcy was off the hook—for now.

Darcy groaned to himself. She had heard, and she was the daughter of *that* woman. He moved with purpose through the crowds of dancers to the far wall to take up position in the corner. His mind could not contemplate how the lovely beauty could possibly be from that ridiculous family. He sought her face and found she had turned to her friend, paying him no more attention than she did any other in the room. He dropped his head and wondered why he felt such a loss. They had not yet been introduced, and he sincerely doubted she would welcome it now. He knew his actions had not been that of a gentleman, and he felt disappointed with himself—a feeling that made him most uncomfortable.

With a genuine smile, Elizabeth stood to join Mr. Bingley on the dance floor. How this man could be friends with *Mr. Sour Puss* was a conundrum.

"Miss Elizabeth, I am delighted you had this set free. Your sister, Miss Bennet, is a wonderful partner." He then blushed to his ears and cleared his throat. "I meant, a wonderful *dance* partner."

Elizabeth was charmed and vowed to think of *Mr. Exceedingly Frustrating* no more. During the dance, Mr. Bingley spoke of how much he relied on *Mr. Knows Everything* for guidance on estate matters. She realised that he might likely rely on him for personal matters as well. Nor did she know how easily Mr. Bingley might accept and follow such counsel.

This left Elizabeth with a dilemma. Her vow to hate *Mr. Ridiculously Rude* must be shelved as she did with the stacks of books she filed away in her father's library. She wanted nothing to come between Mr. Bingley and Jane. Nothing, not even her injury.

While Elizabeth's dance partner was distracted by Jane's progress throughout the set, she contrived the perfect strategy. Espying Miss Bingley's attempts to garner *Mr. Proud and Prejudice's* attention, Elizabeth realised her best weapon was distraction. If she could throw Miss Bingley and *Mr. Perfectly Presumptuousness* together, they might be too occupied with each other to interfere with Jane's fledgling romance.

Seconds after that decision was made, the set ended and Bingley escorted her back to Jane. The colonel stepped in front of her with an apology for his tardiness. He may wear the uniform of a soldier; however, it was Elizabeth who was headed for battle. Placing her hand on his arm, she recalled a quote on war strategy from an ancient Chinese philosopher. *Pretend inferiority and encourage his arrogance.*

CHAPTER 2

*N*etherfield Park, Hertfordshire—after the assembly

"For a fact, Darce, you were hard on Miss Elizabeth." The relationship between Darcy and Colonel Richard Fitzwilliam, second son of the Earl of Matlock, was more like brothers than cousins. He was elder to Darcy by only two years. "If Bingley noted the insult as well as I noted the attention you paid her, others might have also." When his cousin started to shake his head in denial, the colonel continued. "I caught you watching her several times, my man. No sense denying the obvious, William."

"Humph!" Darcy stared into his empty glass of brandy as if the answers to the world's problems were at the bottom of the small vessel. He intended to ignore his cousin until he either changed topics or went away. *Foolishness!* The colonel never let him get away with anything he disapproved of, but rather, let him dangle until Richard received the response he desired. Darcy ran his hand through his hair.

"Fine!" Again, he looked into the glass, still finding it empty. Darcy dropped his head to the back of the high back chair and closed his eyes, recalling her open look, quite devoid of artifice. "I thought she was lovely."

"Then, why in heavens did you insult her? In public no less?"

Richard fell easily into commander temperament. Daily, he dealt with immature boys who refused to think for themselves and were unrestrained in their conduct and decisions. Darcy had always prided himself on upholding proper decorum, so this was most unlike him. Frankly, it embarrassed the colonel when Bingley related the entirety of their conversation from the assembly; Richard was outraged at his cousin's comments.

Darcy did not answer directly. Instead, he stood, walked to the decanter, and refilled his glass. Holding it up to eye level, he caught the light playing through the amber colour and realised it reminded him of the luxurious colour of her tresses. He put the glass on a side table and sighed.

"Did you hear her mother?" Even now, hours later, Darcy could not believe the two women were related. When Bingley had whispered immediately after his caustic statements that it was not the fair-haired woman seated against the wall who was Jane Bennet's sister but the dark-haired woman who had caught his eye, Darcy was stunned and horrified at his own disregard for good ton.

"Yes, I believe few did not."

"Then you understand." It was a statement, not a question. Nevertheless, even to Darcy's ears it sounded weak. There was no excuse which could be offered to justify his bad conduct, and he knew it. He also knew he did not like having his sins exposed and discussed like he was back in the nursery.

"Not at all." Richard Fitzwilliam was frustrated following Darcy's reasoning. "You were attracted to Miss Elizabeth so you offered the worst slight you could give a woman? You remarked on, nay, *insulted* her looks, William. Even a woman with little vanity could not help but be hurt and offended. No, I do not understand at all."

The colonel knew his cousin had little experience with the fairer sex. The early loss of his mother and almost complete isolation with his reticent father, left Darcy uncomfortable around women. Only Richard was privy to an event from their university days which also impacted Darcy's attitude. One of Darcy's classmates, the future baron of a large property in the southwest of England, had a beautiful, younger sister. Darcy was immediately captivated. He was on the verge of going to his father to request support when he overheard the lady speaking to her brother about the wealth Darcy would bring to their family's reduced coffers. She cared not for him as a man. Even though Darcy exemplified perfect aplomb, Richard knew better. For him to show any interest at all in a lady was shockingly uncharacteristic of his cousin.

"See the mother? See the daughter in twenty years," Darcy quipped. "There can be nothing else to add."

"Then, why did you stand and stare at her all evening? Why could you not look away?"

"Because I did not know she was a Bennet!" Again, Darcy ran his hand through his hair, a habit he thought he had broken. "For the most part, she was seated alone. She was not *with* any of her sisters, and she was obviously pained by Mrs. Bennet's exclamations and the conduct of the younger Bennet daughters." Darcy started pacing the length of the carpet that ran in front of the fireplace. Back and forth. "I heartily approved of her discomfort with their impropriety. It showed insightfulness and highlighted her own good conduct at the gathering. Her expectations, and most likely, desire to participate in the dancing did not lessen her joy in observing others. She seemed regally content. Richard, it served to add to her dignity." Darcy maintained his even stride. "Yes, there is something very taking with her features, of that there can be no doubt. And, the stellar qualities she displayed provided other evidences into her character which greatly appealed to me. Yes, I was staring at her. And, oftentimes, I caught her staring back. It was wondrous that such a woman was curious about *me!*"

At this, he came to a halt directly in front of his cousin. "I only need remind myself of what I owe my family name. How could I possibly pollute the shades of Pemberley with the likes of a Mrs. Bennet? How could I bring my dearest sister in close contact with those younger daughters? It would be a degradation!"

"How quickly you went from admiration to love, from love to

matrimony, Darcy. I am all astonishment!" The colonel's tease had an undertone of seriousness. "Do you want me to wish you joy?"

"Richard!"

"Fitzwilliam Darcy, sit!" It was not a request.

There were some boundaries that even family did not cross. Fitzwilliam Darcy knew his place in the world, and he was not intimidated by a colonel in the King's army. Yet, he respected the man in front of him—deeply. No one else would have been allowed to address him in such a manner. Reluctantly, he obeyed.

Once his cousin sat, the colonel continued. "First, let us return to your statement about daughters growing to be like their mothers. Is that always the case?" Before Darcy could reply, he added, "That is rhetorical, Will." Once Darcy closed his mouth, the colonel began again, thinking this was good practice should he ever abandon the military for the law. "What of your own sister? Is she, at almost six and ten years of age, at all like your dear mother? Georgiana is timid and shy and will forever be so. Your mother moved in society with grace and delighted to be in company, gathering people to her like a hen with her chicks."

Richard saw he had Darcy's full attention. "And, never would your mother, at any age, have contemplated climbing into a carriage with a servant for the purpose of an elopement. They are and will forever be two individuals with two entirely different outlooks on what is required of them."

"How dare you bring up Ramsgate!" Darcy was livid, no longer thinking of Miss Elizabeth. "As her guardian and brother, I failed my sister. You, as her other guardian, failed her as well." Darcy stood again, rapidly approaching his cousin with his index finger pointed at him threateningly. "We—you and I—are solely responsible for what could have happened. Georgiana is innocent!"

Richard was not intimidated. "Cousin, you are wrong." The words were softly spoken. This caught Darcy's attention sooner than had the colonel bellowed his response. "Again, would your own mother have acted as she did?" When Darcy did not reply, he released the arrow into the center of the shield. "Then, why would you assume Miss Elizabeth is anything like her mother? The salient point is that you do not know her, and she does not know you." He paused for effect. "This is most unlike you."

"I felt the threat. I felt danger. Once I looked at her—truly looked —I could not look away. I have never been so captivated by the sight of a woman." Again, Darcy put both hands up to his head but stopped himself before he pulled at his hair. His voice, too, had softened. He thought of all his cousin said and realised what he had done. His head dropped. "I have erred grievously. I deserve no consideration; no forgiveness. My discomfort with being in a room where I knew so few, trying to fend off the advances of Miss Bingley, and being approached by Mrs. Bennet in such a vulgar manner are the reasons I give for my conduct." Before the colonel could respond, he held up his hand to stop him. "I understand this is no excuse, as there could be none." Darcy resumed his pacing. "I have likely wounded a most innocent woman. That is not the actions of a gentleman, which is what I was raised to be."

Then it hit him at once—Miss Elizabeth Bennet had reminded him of his own mother, not hers.

He sank down in the chair across from his cousin. "Richard, how shall I make amends?"

Military strategy was what the colonel knew best. *Surely it was not much different from personal relationships?* He pondered the situation and the current attitude of his cousin before he answered.

"It is my belief, Darcy, that two actions are incumbent upon you. First, you need to humbly apologise. And second, you might want to look beyond her family, her circumstances, to know the woman herself." The colonel chuckled. "You already have much in common."

"How do you mean?" At that, Darcy lifted his head, his brow furrowed.

"While we danced, we spoke of ancient Greek literature and politics. It was the most intelligent conversation I have ever had with a female, my own mother included—and yours." He chuckled at the pleasant memory. "What quick wit." Richard sat up straight in his chair. "You will not be able to impress her with your wealth and property, Darcy. Miss Elizabeth values character above gold. So, I believe, my man, you are in a spot of trouble. Big trouble."

"Thank you for stating the obvious, *Dickie*."

"You are welcome, *Fitzy*." Richard laughed aloud. "Good heavens, I just thought of something."

"What might that be?"

"From what Miss Elizabeth observed, you, for the most part, stood silent as a statue, holding up that wall by your leaning on it. She may think you kept your mouth closed because you have bad teeth."

"I do not find that at all funny."

"Well, if you cannot get back into Miss Elizabeth's good graces, there is always Miss Bingley. I do not think it would matter what you say or the condition of your teeth. She would want you all the same."

"Hold your tongue, Richard!"

The colonel laughed even harder.

* * *

LONGBOURN, Hertfordshire—after the assembly

"Jane, what did you think of Mr. Bingley?" The sisters were burrowed under the bedclothes, avoiding the midnight chill. Elizabeth giggled at Jane's response to her question. Jane's face, even in the soft candlelight, was brilliant red.

"Oh, Lizzy, he is everything a gentleman should be. Sensible, good humoured, lively; and I never saw such happy manners. So much ease, with such perfect good breeding." Jane's expression softened. "He is so handsome. And, he listened to me, Lizzy. He paid rapt attention and responded properly."

Far too many men chose not to see more than Jane's serene beauty. She had learned to discourage further contact if a gentleman seemed only interested in a lovely woman to grace his arm and his home. That a gentleman looked beyond the superficial to ask more than her opinion of the condition of the roads was unusual. Elizabeth was delighted for her sister.

"And, what of his sisters, Jane? Would you want them to be your sisters as well?"

"You move too fast, Lizzy!" It was hard to imagine it was possible for her blush to deepen, though it did.

"They do not approve of us, Jane." Elizabeth's tone brooked no argument. Jane's reputation, which was deserved, was to look beyond the negative aspects of someone's character. "I believe Miss Bingley and Mr. Darcy are the same. They weighed and judged the Bennets this evening and felt only disdain." Elizabeth rapidly reviewed the events at the assembly and continued. "Of Mrs. Hurst, I do not know. She vacillated between following her sister, who was following Mr. Darcy, and watching her brother, who she appears to hold in affection."

"I am sorry, Lizzy, but I paid scant attention to both women. My interest was elsewhere."

They giggled as if they were children again. Their ebullient tête-à-tête stoked the feeling that some sort of a turning point, a change in the direction of the winds, had occurred from the actions and reactions at the Meryton assembly.

"Mr. Darcy should not have said what he did, Lizzy." Her sister's humiliation was felt in the depths of Jane's heart.

"I know, Jane." Elizabeth's response came out as a whisper. Her emotions were battered from his words. After the initial response of intense, fiery anger, came hurt… and disappointment.

She would not tell her sister the plan she had devised as surely Jane would not approve. Her heart was too good to bear malice for Miss Bingley and Mr. Darcy. Therefore, to preserve peace and promote a match between Mr. Bingley and her beloved sister, Elizabeth would swallow her retort, not giving anyone even a hint of her eventual goal.

"The simple truth, dear, is that I can do nothing about Mr. Darcy's comments. He is free to behave as he would like. Do I regret that he made them so public? For a certainty, I do." She reached over and patted Jane's hand. "One cannot wonder that so fine a young man, with family, fortune, everything in his favour, should think highly of himself. Nonetheless, I shall make a resolution to overlook his pride so I can be in his company without using my vocabulary to strip pounds of flesh from him with my words. I will be genial. I will be kind. I will do all I can to change his poor opinion of the Bennet family."

"Oh, Lizzy, can you do that? Will you do that?" It was more than Jane had hoped. She knew her younger sister's capricious temper. Yes, she was aware of other people's flaws even though she chose not to dwell on them, and Elizabeth had much to recommend. "A man as kind as Mr. Bingley would certainly not befriend a man who was not a gentleman. There surely is inherent good in Mr. Darcy and Miss Bingley."

"You are undoubtedly correct, Sister, dear." Even though her choice of words was agreeable, Elizabeth suspected that Jane was anything but accurate. "Tomorrow night we shall gather at Lucas Lodge, and Charlotte told me the Netherfield party has accepted the invitation. My resolve will be put to the test. However, I am determined to rise above."

Elizabeth likened herself to a warrior in a battle she was determined to win. The same Chinese philosopher had said, "Keep your friends close, but keep your enemies closer." She would be as friendly as possible to both Miss Bingley and Mr. Darcy to determine how best to pair them off and keep them away from Bingley and Jane.

She had set herself a task which would require all her faculties. Leaning over, Elizabeth blew out the lone candle, plunging the bedchamber into darkness. With no one to witness her expression, she smiled with wicked glee.

CHAPTER 3

*T*hursday, 3 October 1811
Longbourn

Rain began to fall the next morning, cutting short Elizabeth's typical jaunt out of doors. It was where she did her best thinking—or her best plotting. Returning early meant she arrived back at Longbourn, her family's estate, prior to any of the other females coming down to break their fast. Before Elizabeth headed upstairs to change into a proper morning dress, she decided to visit her father's study. Mr. Thomas Bennet was in his usual position, relaxed in his leather chair with a book open on his lap, his eyes peering through the spectacles resting low on his nose.

"Papa, are you well this morning?"

"I might ask the same of you, Lizzy." He looked up at his favourite daughter. "Your mama invaded my bookroom last night to tell me you were insulted at the assembly by one of the visitors to Netherfield Park. Do I need to ride over and call him out this morning?"

Elizabeth loved her father dearly. Her most precious memories were of the time spent curled up in the small chair he kept close to his desk, reading or playing chess with the man who encouraged her to improve her mind. She had been an apt pupil. Nevertheless, she recognized his imperfections. His comment was like a thorn under her skin. He was an indifferent parent, remaining separate from his wife and daughters. Their special bond did not protect Elizabeth from his biting comments.

"Do you want to do so, Papa?"

As a precocious ten-year-old, she had asked her father why he bothered to have children if he did not want to spend time with them. "I needed a son," was his reply. Elizabeth realised then that she would always be lacking in comparison to the son who never was. Even now, she hoped he would at least stir himself to do the right thing to protect his daughters from harm. Her desire proved fruitless.

"Now, would you really expect your father to do such a thing?" Mr. Bennet snorted. "If I was unsuccessful—which I assure you I would most likely be—you, your sisters, and your mother would be cast out into the hedgerows by my heir. Because of the entailment on Long-bourn, you would be without a home and any support. That would be a heavy price to lay upon your conscience for a few bruises and blue devils, my daughter."

Elizabeth keenly felt the disappointment of his reply. What daughter did not want her father as a protector, as a knight on a white horse charging to the rescue? And, his indolence spurred Elizabeth to believe she must protect her family. If she did not, who would?

"Papa, I need to ready myself for the day. We are invited to Lucas Lodge tonight. Will you be attending along with your family?" She was not aware she held her breath, awaiting his answer.

"I think not, child." He had returned his eyes to his book. "You go and skewer the young man with your wit. Do what you must. You have my consent. That will be good enough for me."

"You may count on me to do exactly so, Papa." Her father's pride in her ability to conquer a worthy opponent with her wit warred with the loss Elizabeth felt that he had left her to fend for herself. Climbing the stairs, she lifted her chin. She was a warrior.

* * *

"GIRLS! Hurry to dress and break your fast!" Mrs. Bennet's tone was determined. "Ready yourselves quickly. Assuredly the gentlemen from Netherfield Park will be here soon."

However, the only arrivals were the gossiping hens of the neighbourhood. What news did they bring? The insult.

Mrs. Prichard, the vicar's wife, the mother of twin nieces who were recently out in society, spoke first. "He said Miss Elizabeth was the last woman on earth he would ever marry. How cruel!"

"Tell me it is not true? He would not dare say that he found you boorish and nonsensical, would he? A vicious comment, dear Miss Elizabeth, as we know how proud you are of your own intelligence. Why he sat next to me above a half hour without saying one word. Cruel man!" said Mrs. Long, one of her mother's dearest friends and the mother of three maiden daughters and aunt to one unmarried niece also under her care.

Mrs. Fielding, who was married to a tradesman in Meryton, with two daughters unmarried, added, "I heard the man described you as homely a woman as he had ever seen! Of course, I do not believe a word of it, Miss Elizabeth. You are not nearly as pretty as Miss Bennet or Miss Lydia, but you have a measure of health and sturdiness to your looks, dear."

Flame and smoke appeared to erupt from Elizabeth's eyes as silence settled over the room, the occupants waiting for her response. She knew these women. They pretended to be kind but were looking out for their own advantage. To have daughters with little or no prospects was frightening for a household with minimal funds set aside. The daughters and nieces, who accompanied their relatives, feared being a burden.

The mantel clock ticked the passing seconds. Discomfort was setting in on the women like an itchy, wool coat.

"My, what creative imaginations you have," Elizabeth said with a smile, hoping it appeared genuine. "I shall have to remember these comments word-for-word and pass them on to the gentleman for his entertainment and enlightenment. I am certain he will appreciate knowing the care and concern the women of the neighbourhood give to those they have known for a lifetime. That way, as a newcomer, he would not suffer if he did not receive the same, no?"

The barbs flew straight, and it was no time before the mothers shuffled their charges away from the Bennet drawing room.

Her youngest sister snorted. "Oh, what a joke. The hens think Lizzy is homely." Kitty joined in her giggles.

"Hush!" Jane looked them directly in the eye, her heart aching for Elizabeth.

The Bennet females remained seated as Elizabeth stood and walked to the window, presenting her back to them all. She heard the soft rustle of Jane's skirt as she moved to stand close behind her.

"They do not mean what was said, Lizzy."

She swiveled her head to her favourite sister. Elizabeth's raised brow said more than words could have done. Turning back to stare out of the window, Elizabeth gave consideration to her situation and her plans.

Resolution grew in her breast until it threatened to boil over. "Do what you must. You have my consent," her father had said. Elizabeth resolved to take him at his word. She would not allow anyone to distract her from her task. Yes, their words smouldered and burned into her chest like embers, festering. Her first inclination had been to run to her bedchamber and curl up under her grandmother's quilt, seeking comfort and solace from the ache. But she had a task to do, one that started right at that moment.

Spinning around, she caught Lydia and Kitty snickering behind their hands, in a manner reminiscent of the Bingley sisters the night before. The fire in her bosom rapidly turned into a conflagration.

"Lydia, Kitty. You have no need to prepare for Lucas Lodge tonight as Father said you are too young and unruly to appear in public." Elizabeth's posture was fierce and unrelenting. "If you can behave without complaint tonight, possibly he will allow you to attend the card party at Aunt Phillips' tomorrow."

Their appeals to their mother fell on deaf ears. Mrs. Bennet was already fluttering her handkerchief, wailing her discontent, and on her way to make her case to her absentee husband.

"Mama!" Before she could leave the room, Elizabeth moved to the doorway stopping her mother's momentum. "Mama!" Elizabeth repeated, finally gaining her attention. Both were on a mission. "Papa said if you complain to him, he will withhold the carriage so you may not attend. He will also hold your pin money for the month so you will have no more ribbons and lace."

Mrs. Bennet stomped her foot in vexation but said nothing. None of them had reason to doubt Elizabeth. They knew her habits well and how she was her father's favourite. All of them assumed she had stopped in his room that morning—which was the only truth in the past few minutes.

"Lizzy," Mary hesitantly asked. "What about me? Must I attend?"

Elizabeth's voice softened. "Do you want to?"

Mary was stunned. No one ever consulted her opinion. "I do not."

"Then it appears only Jane and I are for Lucas Lodge tonight." Elizabeth caught each sisters' eye before moving to her mother. "I pray you enjoy the evening's peace, Mama." With that, she vacated the room without looking back.

* * *

UPON ARRIVING AT LUCAS LODGE, Elizabeth knew she had never been in better looks. The gown she had worn at the assembly was her newest, however, the pastel yellow gown with a narrow, light green stripe she wore that night was her favourite. Wearing it, she felt like sunshine on a summer day. Her hair had been washed and brushed until the curls were soft and manageable. They were pinned with white pearls which had been a gift from her aunt and uncle Gardiner. Her pale green shawl had also been gifted to her by the same relatives.

Without the distraction of the younger sisters preparing for the night, their lone maid was able to give time and attention turning out Elizabeth and Jane to their best advantage—not that Jane needed such help.

As they stepped carefully up the footpath to the Lucas home, Elizabeth pondered her plan. The first defence enacted successfully that afternoon in the drawing room had greatly increased her confidence. She had spent the afternoon formulating her words and actions for the gathering, carefully tucking away the day's insults, until she knew exactly what she hoped would take place.

The butler opened the door and announced them, peering behind the two Bennets for the rest of the party. When he saw no one else alight from the carriage, he lifted his brow, cocked his head, and announced the two who had arrived. Miss Lizzy was no stranger to Lucas Lodge. She was well-liked by all the staff.

Elizabeth could not help whispering on her way by the elderly man. "Are you thinking we might have misplaced something, Mr. Burt?"

"Or someone?" was his soft reply.

Elizabeth snickered. It was a wonderful start to what she expected would be an exciting evening.

* * *

NETHERFIELD PARK

Bingley's sisters were late. While the other gentleman waited in the entrance hall of Netherfield Park, Fitzwilliam Darcy paced nervously back and forth. He had spent hours in his room writing down every humble word he could think of in a manner that might appease a young woman who had been slighted. His final draft was carefully folded, resting snugly in a small pocket in the front of his pale green and yellow striped waistcoat. It was his favourite, reminding him of summers spent at Pemberley, racing Richard across the grassy fields under the hot July sun. He wore it when he needed confidence. Tonight was such a night.

"Bingley, where are your sisters?" Darcy's frustration overflowed.

"I am anxious as well, old man." A boyish grin spread across Bingley's face. "Miss Bennet is an angel. Yes, perfection is what she is."

"I say, Charles, are you in love again? Did I miss this monumental event last night while I had a successful visit to the card table?" Gilbert Hurst had crowed at least six times about his winnings since the men broke their fast, and Hurst noticed Bingley had called Jane Bennet an angel almost twice as much.

Bingley fired back. "I will not have anything ruin my evening, Gilbert." He walked right up to the man and poked him in the chest. "You cannot say or do anything to temper my excitement at seeing Miss Bennet again. Am I in love? I am not."

At that, there was a general sigh of relief.

"Yet!" Bingley added, chuckling at them all.

The teasing and ribald laughter common to men continued until Mrs. Hurst and Miss Bingley appeared at the top of the stairs. Bingley rolled his eyes when he noted the height of the feathers adorning his younger sister's headpiece. *Would she even fit inside the carriage? Possibly she would have to ride up top with the driver?*

The colonel leaned over and whispered to his cousin, "Should I draw my sword and clip those feathers?"

They tucked their smiles away and feigned interest in the black and white marble floor tiles until the ladies had descended the staircase.

Caroline immediately moved to capture Darcy's arm. He sucked in a breath and put paid to his irritation as he had pledged after the assembly to improve himself, to become a better man. That he would have to start with Miss Bingley was unpalatable, but he would do so.

"Miss Bingley, might I help you to the carriage?" Even to his own ears, his voice sounded weak and insincere.

Caroline Bingley relished appearing on Darcy's arm. Since the first day her brother brought the great man to their house, she wished to become the next mistress of Pemberley, and the thought influenced her every decision. She had not failed to notice the attention Darcy paid Miss Elizabeth at the assembly. As he had watched the second Bennet daughter, Caroline Bingley watched him. She would stop at nothing to achieve her goal. Whether it meant stepping on country chits like Eliza Bennet while they rusticated, Caroline would allow nothing to dissuade her from her course.

Colonel Fitzwilliam stood back as they filed to Darcy's carriage. It promised to be an interesting evening. He stopped himself from rubbing his hands together in anticipation, though he could not keep from smiling.

CHAPTER 4

*L*ucas Lodge

Again, the Netherfield party was the last to arrive. When they entered Lucas Lodge, Elizabeth's smile was genuine when she spied Miss Bingley's hand on Mr. Darcy's arm.

Caroline Bingley adored a grand entrance. Being seen in company with Mr. Darcy was a boon, and she wanted the unmarried ladies of Meryton to appreciate her elevated rank. She particularly wanted Elizabeth Bennet to realise Mr. Darcy was practically spoken for.

Darcy was grateful for the opportunity to speak with the young woman who had plagued his sleep the night before.

"Miss Elizabeth," he began, only to be immediately interrupted.

"I beg your pardon, sir, I do not believe we have been introduced." Elizabeth raised her eyebrow, a bubble of pleasure bursting inside her chest on seeing him nonplussed.

Charlotte Lucas had approached the guests just as Darcy had walked over to where Elizabeth stood. "Might I present Mr. Fitzwilliam Darcy of Pemberley in Derbyshire and Darcy House in London and Miss Caroline Bingley of Netherfield Park?"

Elizabeth wondered whether Miss Bingley was aware she was

petting his arm as Charlotte spoke. Regardless, Darcy leaned away from her and pulled his elbow stiffly to his side.

"And this, Mr. Darcy and Miss Bingley, is our neighbour and my closest friend, Miss Elizabeth Bennet of Longbourn."

Elizabeth tilted her head to the side, a small smile appearing on her face. *Miss Bingley seemed permanently attached to his arm. No matter! It was time to start her maneuvers.*

"What a charming couple you are." Miss Bingley lifted her chin, accepting Elizabeth's words as both her due and the honest truth as she saw it. Mr. Darcy? His face failed to hide his surprise and his distaste.

"Miss Elizabeth, how droll you are," said Miss Bingley, obviously pleased Elizabeth had recognised her place.

"'So, hand in hand they passed, the loveliest pair that ever since in love's embraces met.'"

She quoted Milton? Darcy could not help himself. He was curious about Elizabeth Bennet, but he was not going to allow her to promote a match with Caroline Bingley. "You are mistaken, Miss Elizabeth."

"Imagine that!" Her laughing eyes met his before she moved away, leaving a preening Caroline and an antagonized Darcy behind.

Darcy was not the only gentleman wondering what Miss Elizabeth was about. Colonel Fitzwilliam knew from their conversation the night before that she was no simple-minded girl. *What woman, who had been so insulted by a gentleman, would greet him with such a smile?* Scanning the room, he found his quarry and headed her way.

Charlotte Lucas supposed the colonel to be the rarest specimen of men—one who held the fairer sex as friends! His approach was relaxed though purposeful.

"Miss Lucas, a pleasure to see you this evening." The colonel leaned in close and said softly, "I wonder whether I might have a moment of your time?"

"Certainly, Colonel." Charlotte appreciated a direct man. Her father's rambles had tired her long ago.

"Might I ask what your friend is up to?" He nodded towards Elizabeth, who was walking away from Caroline and Darcy. The look on his cousin's face made him chuckle and Charlotte grin.

"I do not know her particular plan, Colonel, but I have no doubt she has one." Charlotte looked to him instead of at her friend. "Elizabeth is never malicious. I am certain whatever she has in mind will be a learning experience for Mr. Darcy. A humbling one as well."

"Hmmm." The colonel nodded his head, contemplating her words. It was as he expected. Miss Elizabeth Bennet, underneath the offended layers, was kindness itself. *Yes, she would be a good match for Darcy.* "Then I suggest we keep an eye on whatever unfolds and enjoy the lesson learned, Miss Lucas."

* * *

ELIZABETH WATCHED Mr. Bingley move directly to Jane. Without their mother's interference, the couple was left undisturbed in the crowded room. It was exactly as Elizabeth had hoped.

When Mr. Darcy headed towards Jane and Bingley, Miss Bingley followed. Therefore, Elizabeth quickly approached the pair.

"Miss Bingley, it pleases me to see that exact shade of orange in your gown." Elizabeth suspected the colour was her favourite as it was a similar palette to the dress worn at the assembly.

"It does?" Caroline Bingley was instantly skeptical. It was not in her nature to be polite or kind to a potential rival—not that she believed she had anything to worry about with Elizabeth Bennet. The chit's gown was at least two seasons old!

"For a certainty." Detesting liars, Elizabeth chose her words carefully. "When the sun sets over the western hillside, just before it goes to a hazy darkness, that particular hue shines across the evening sky. It is glorious, is it not?"

On first introductions, Caroline Bingley had found Miss Elizabeth Bennet insipid and insignificant. That such a country nobody was able to recognise and acknowledge quality, pleased her.

She released Mr. Darcy's arm to stroke the fabric of her gown.

"Glorious it is, Miss Elizabeth." She quickly examined Elizabeth's choice that evening. "Your gown is…tolerable."

In her mind, Elizabeth was rolling her eyes, but she looked up in time to catch Mr. Darcy's roll his. She could not help but grin.

"And, your feathers, Miss Bingley!" Elizabeth's eyes smoothly moved up their full height. "I do not recall ever seeing a headdress so rare, so extraordinarily designed."

Caroline lifted her chin, so the feathers waved back and forth in a hypnotic motion, as if she were the bird who originally wore them. "I am surprisingly pleased you noticed."

Elizabeth tucked her hand into the vain woman's arm and gently pulled her in the direction of Charlotte and the colonel. As expected, Mrs. Hurst followed. Elizabeth looked back to see Darcy's direction. Had he moved towards his friend, she would have had to change her actions. As it was, he found a position against the wall close to the large fireplace and remained. Elizabeth smiled to herself. *All was going according to plan.*

Once Elizabeth had her pawns in position, she spent the next part of the evening diverting anyone approaching Bingley and Jane. If someone started in their direction, she moved in, engaged them in conversation, and coolly walked them away from the couple.

Colonel Fitzwilliam was highly amused. He turned to Charlotte and said, "Ah-ha! I see the plan. Miss Elizabeth is intercepting the enemy to protect the prince and princess's tête-à-tête."

Charlotte laughed softly.

"May I speak frankly, Miss Lucas?"

"When have you not, Colonel Fitzwilliam?" She was pleased to see a pink hue flush his cheeks.

"Touché, my lady." He bowed to her. "Are you familiar with the play of chess?"

"A little."

"I believe the king is my cousin and the queen is your friend. Are you in agreement?"

"I am."

"The king is currently leaning against the fireplace, surreptitiously looking for warmth. However, his eyes are solely focussed on the movements of the queen. Do you not agree they make a fine pair?" Mischief sparked from his own eyes.

"I do not!"

He was surprised Charlotte was so adamant. "Why ever not?"

"Your cousin's insult last evening was thoughtless and cruel. He may have wealth and property in excess of any other who has passed through Hertfordshire in my lifetime, however, Elizabeth is the kindest, most honourable of my acquaintance. Underneath that sharp wit beats a heart that begs to be acknowledged. She did not deserve Mr. Darcy's censure. She has a dignified beauty that cannot and will not be matched by any woman of elevated rank."

The colonel sighed. Her words rang true. He had witnessed Darcy's humbling of himself, but others had not. He shook his head. This was going to take more time and effort than he imagined. *Poor Darcy!*

His respect and appreciation for Charlotte Lucas grew. Her swift defence of Elizabeth spoke well of Miss Lucas. She was a woman whose unmarried circumstance—at such an age—had not embittered her. The colonel was surprised by how much pleasure that realisation brought him.

"Miss Lucas, what you have said is indeed true." He glanced again at Darcy. "My cousin's words were highly officious." He looked back at the woman alongside him. She was slight in form but great in character. "I know Darcy well. His words of regret to me last night were sincere."

Charlotte paused to consider his words. What she said next took him by complete surprise. "Will you marry, Colonel?"

Without pause, he said, "I am married, Miss Lucas," and pointed to the evidence of his rank on his uniform. "I am married to His Majesty's army who controls my every thought, movement, and my future." He could not keep the twinkle from his eye. "I thank you for asking."

Charlotte felt the disappointment deeply, though she was not surprised at his response. She recognised well enough that he was a good man to have as a friend.

"Then, Colonel Fitzwilliam, let us see how this game plays out, shall we?"

To the excitement of her parents, the second son of the Earl of Matlock took her hand and placed it on his arm for all the world to see. Charlotte understood it for what it was—a pact, a bond. Nothing more. It was good enough.

* * *

"My dear Louisa," Caroline Bingley crowed to her sister. "Did you notice the deference Miss Elizabeth showed me? Such a simple creature."

"Do be cautious, Caroline. I think we may find out she is smarter than you give her credit."

"I agree that she has some intelligence. Why, she complimented both my gown and my headdress. She has a measure of taste, something I did not think we would find in this county hamlet." Caroline Bingley wrinkled her nose as if a bitter odor had wafted her way.

"It is my opinion, Caroline, that she is clever and scheming." Louisa Hurst had not been gifted with keen insight. She tended to follow her sister's direction and counsel since, on her own, she rarely thought of anything better to do. However, being the sister to Caroline left her in a constant state of suspicion. She, too, wanted to advance her young brother's sphere and influence. "What woman in our circle would greet you with a smile while you stood next to such a powerful man? It makes no sense."

"Oh, Louisa, you worry too much. It is a simple case where Miss Eliza was reminded of her station, which is as it should be. Nothing more."

"She is a gentleman's daughter, Sister. Mr. Darcy is a gentleman—which makes them equals." Of one thing Louisa Hurst was clear, it was position and status. "I do not trust her."

"I do not trust any female under eighty and over eight with Mr.

Darcy, Louisa." Caroline lifted her chin and looked down her nose. "I will let nothing or no one stand in my way. I will be Mrs. Darcy, mistress of Pemberley before summer of next year—you wait and see."

Louisa knew that look of determination. From experience she knew that what Caroline wanted, Caroline usually got. She did not envy Miss Elizabeth.

Elizabeth approached the two women as if they were the closest of friends.

"Miss Bingley, I do hope I caused no embarrassment with my comment upon your arrival. I believed with all my heart that you and Mr. Darcy are well-matched. Why there is not another unmarried lady in all of Hertfordshire who carries herself with such an air, such sophistication. You must be the most accomplished woman in the room." Elizabeth had said nothing that was not strictly true by definition. Her own father's dictionary defined sophistication as "sophistry of being deceitful, altered, or unrefined." Elizabeth grabbed her hand. "Tell me, Miss Bingley, of all your accomplishments, which does Mr. Darcy favour most? We must do you a service to promote the match."

Caroline studied the guileless face of the young woman before her. "Miss Elizabeth, you would not know—having not moved in the same circles we do in Town—but a woman must have a thorough knowledge of music, singing, drawing, dancing, and the modern languages, to deserve the word; and besides all this, she must possess a certain something in her air and manner of walking, the tone of her voice, her address and expressions, or the word will be but half deserved." *Stupid, stupid woman—if you think you would ever attract someone of Darcy's position! However, whatever your reason for pushing me together with Darcy, I will gladly accept it.*

Elizabeth felt secure in achieving her goal with Miss Bingley. *"Pretend inferiority and encourage arrogance." Pawn moved into place.*

"Thank you, Miss Bingley." Elizabeth, in need of relief, called Charlotte.

"Charlotte, might we open the instrument so our esteemed, new friend can exhibit for the enjoyment of all, and especially for one in particular?" She nodded towards the tall man who had yet to move away from the wall.

Charlotte glanced quickly back to the colonel. Their eyes met in silent agreement.

"Certainly, Eliza." She moved towards the pianoforte with Miss Bingley following closely. Elizabeth remained next to the colonel while Mrs. Hurst moved to where her husband was hovering by the refreshment table.

"Pardon me, Miss Elizabeth, might I ask a question?"

"You may."

"Have you ever hoped to enter the military service as a spy, Miss Elizabeth?"

"Never!" Elizabeth looked up at him with a twinkle in her eyes. "I would be a general." After such a declaration, she walked over to stand by her sister and Mr. Bingley.

The colonel could not restrain his laughter.

* * *

FOLLOWING TWO PERFECTLY EXECUTED SONGS, Caroline Bingley stood and closed the lid over the keys, making sure no one followed her performance. She walked over to Mr. Darcy, who still had not moved.

Elizabeth had paid rapt attention to Miss Bingley as she played. Every movement, word uttered, and look spoke volumes as to the lady's desires. Miss Bingley wanted Mr. Darcy as her husband. As Elizabeth suspected, Miss Bingley would stick to Mr. Darcy like a thistle on a wool coat. There was no need for Elizabeth to give her any more attention. Elizabeth realised this particular skirmish was over. Miss Caroline Bingley had lifted the white flag and would do as "the general" bid.

Therefore, she walked towards the wall, waiting until Miss Bingley moved into place, her next pawn in sight.

"Mr. Darcy, do you not agree that Miss Bingley's performance was that of a truly accomplished woman?"

Darcy hesitated before answering. He had wanted to speak with

Miss Elizabeth alone to apologise. It would be impossible to do so with Caroline Bingley hanging on his right arm again. "It was."

He turned his attention to the woman on his right. "Miss Bingley, it looks as if your brother is attempting to gain your attention."

It was a clever ploy, however, not clever enough.

"Oh! Pray, Miss Bingley, do not move." Elizabeth put her hand on Miss Bingley's arm. "You are both charmingly framed by the window behind you. If only I had talent as a painter, I would endeavour to capture the image for your home." She added a smile for effect, aimed directly at Mr. Darcy.

Miss Bingley was pleased and moved even closer to Mr. Darcy. The man himself was bewildered. He had arrived at Lucas Lodge with a plan and had yet to accomplish the one task he had assigned himself.

Why, after almost a decade of women of every age seeking my attention, the one woman I long to speak with is going out of her way to pair me with another? It makes no sense.

"Miss Elizabeth..."

Before he could finish his thought, Elizabeth thanked them for the pose and excused herself to rejoin Charlotte and the colonel.

Darcy stood with his mouth agape, snapping it shut only after realising he must resemble a fish with a hook in its lip. Without thought to the hands still grasping his arm, he followed after his prey.

Elizabeth sensed his frustration but cared not for his feelings. In his arrogance, he had not only disparaged her but her family and neighbours as well. She was confident Darcy would never encourage a connection with a Bennet, thus she must keep him distracted.

She heard rapidly approaching footsteps on the hard wood floor coming behind her, and she knew it was Mr. Darcy. Facing him, she squared her shoulders and raised her eyes to his, again catching him by surprise and throwing him emotionally—if not physically—off balance.

"Mr. Darcy," she whispered. He leaned forward. "I believe you trod on Miss Bingley's hem, and she is in some distress."

Horrified, he turned his head, and indeed, the bottom of Caroline's dress had the mark of his boot on the hem of the delicate, orange silk.

Blowing out an exasperated breath, he closed his eyes. Behind his lids, he saw Elizabeth's smile and her dancing, dark eyes. This was the closest he had ever been to her, and she looked and smelled delightful.

"Pardon me." Darcy could only bow and return to Caroline. He knew this would end his evening. The Hursts and Bingley would be rounded up and the carriage called. The state of a woman's dress was a casualty not easily endured.

He looked back at Elizabeth's dress and had an epiphany. The colour of her dress and the colour of his waistcoat were the same. *Happenstance?* He shook his head to throw off the thought. *Fanciful thinking!* He needed the clarity of Netherfield Park's male companions or the silence of the sitting room attached to his chambers to ponder exactly what had happened that evening.

* * *

LONGBOURN

Shortly after the Netherfield party departed, the gathering broke up, and Jane and Elizabeth returned home to Longbourn. The household was asleep, and the sisters helped each other ready for bed.

Jane was deliriously happy. The hours she had spent in conversation with Mr. Bingley had elevated his value in her eyes until she was sure there was no man like him in all of England. Jane joyously repeated the substance of what had been discussed, lingering over every word.

"I am happy you are happy, sweet sister." Elizabeth was genuinely pleased for Jane. There was nobody more deserving of gaining the desires of her heart than her eldest sister. For herself? The strain of pretending a jovialness she did not feel was wearing. With her back turned and her face towards the window, Elizabeth silently reviewed her evening. Never had she felt such turmoil. A lone tear trickled from her eye, tracing an uneven path down her cheek to the pillow.

The unsavory events of the past four and twenty hours haunted her. A man she briefly admired had wounded her, and the man who gave her life—which obligated him to protect and defend her—had not. Longtime friends had made sport of her, and she had lied to her mother and sisters, including Jane.

Until the day prior, with the arrival of Mr. Darcy to Hertfordshire, hers had been a serene existence. Now, her life seemed upside down, and there was only one man to blame. Mr. Darcy. He was, in every way, abominable.

CHAPTER 5

*N*etherfield Park

Miss Elizabeth Bennet frustrated Darcy.

He sat in Netherfield's library sipping brandy. He did not want to see Bingley or Richard. He wanted to see *her*. He wanted to explain and apologise and beg her forgiveness. He wanted…he wanted. He sighed.

In his adult life, Darcy had never felt such turmoil. He wished for his mother to advise him. *What do you do with a young woman who completely unsettles you? How do I treat her when she is extraordinarily different from any other female of my acquaintance?* Darcy ran his hands through his hair, pulling at the ends in his newly resurrected habit.

Normally, turmoil suited him. He relished resolving problems that arose on the estate or in business, breaking them apart into solvable pieces, researching possibilities, and coming to a beneficial conclusion.

What exactly did he know about Miss Elizabeth Bennet?

First, he had been attracted to her fine eyes.

Second, he had studied her movements and expressions at the assembly. But what had he learned? She cared enough about her sisters to attempt a guiding hand.

Third, according to Richard, she took pleasure in extensive read-ing, and she was clever, as proved by her skill in directing Caroline Bingley to her purpose. *But why?* Was it a form of amusement she used to pass the time when in unpleasant company? *It could not be.*

Fourth, Elizabeth's smile and laughter were sincere.

When he stepped close to her this evening, the desire to reach out and touch her hair was so strong his fingers tingled. He had rarely had that reaction to a woman—wanting to touch.

All of this proved to him that his attraction was not unfounded, something unexpected from such a brief acquaintance.

Lastly, he discovered she was a Bennet, related to *that* woman. His immediate reaction to this knowledge was to halt, by whatever means necessary, any attraction he felt for her—thus his horrid words. He exhaled forcefully.

His head dropped in disgust. In truth, he had made the insult before he knew for certain which young lady was Mrs. Bennet's daughter. He had assumed that whoever she was, she would have been a model of indecorum. Besides his error in desiring to take his disgust of Mrs. Bennet out on an innocent maiden, he had been uncomfort-able and under stress from more personal matters. Darcy wanted to kick himself with his own boot. He also knew he was impolitic and ungallant to disrespect any female.

He breathed deeply. Even as he heard himself excusing his conduct of impugning her unfortunate birth, he knew he was in the wrong.

In reviewing his own behavior, Darcy realised that of the two of them, it was Miss Elizabeth who acted with decorum, not himself. Therefore, it would be up to him to make amends. He needed to take action to correct her opinion of him.

When he was at home at his country estate, he hunted game for Pemberley's table and those of his tenants. He had grown up studying his prey until he had become quite adept at the sport. Tonight? He had stalked her with his eyes the whole of the evening. Their only encoun-ters were at her bidding, not his. He felt the loss of control, and it confounded him.

With the last sip of brandy, he recalled the conversation in the carriage on the way back to Netherfield—and how matters would change with Miss Bingley out of the picture.

As soon as the carriage door had closed, Miss Bingley opined, "Charles, do not tell me you are serious about Miss Bennet." It was a demand for confirmation, not an inquiry. "Yes, she is lovely, but the mother, her younger sisters! And what was Miss Elizabeth about tonight, attempting to curry my favour? The connection would be a debasement, Brother. You must put a stop to this immediately."

She then had turned to her sister for support. "We must return to London, is that not correct, Louisa?"

Mrs. Hurst had looked to her husband for any indication of his opinion. When none was offered, she conceded. "Whatever you feel is best, Caroline."

"Mr. Darcy, Colonel Fitzwilliam? Surely, you see the need to remove our brother from this unseemly influence." Caroline continued her rant, her voice rising in volume and pitch. "You must realise the harm that would come to Charles and the Bingley family name should he continue on this course."

The colonel had recognised Miss Caroline Bingley as a grasping social climber who had decided his cousin was her ticket to the first circles. Caroline was no different from hundreds of other unmarried women who sought the same. In addition, her unwillingness to respect her brother's position in the home was crass. It showed an independent spirit that flouted proper authority. He would not want to be tied to her, no matter her fortune of twenty thousand pounds.

The colonel's patience for her complaints had strained even his easy manners. After spending the evening with such a pleasant companion as Miss Lucas, the shrew across from him in the carriage had given him a headache. "Not that I want to interfere in what is clearly a family matter, Miss Bingley, but I must ask, why you feel you should be making this decision rather than your brother?"

He heard Hurst chuckle.

"You do not understand, Colonel. You are from a family who is experienced in cutting off nobodies like the Bennets. My brother does not have the same experience and can easily be taken in."

The men were stunned at her comment. Even her sister whispered "Caroline!" as a warning. Nevertheless, the words had been uttered with conviction. Caroline Bingley had thrown down the gauntlet and a response was required.

Into the hush, Bingley spoke words his sisters did not want to hear.

"Since you feel so strongly about this, Caroline, and you too claim to have plans in London, Louisa, I will expect you both to have your bags packed for an early departure tomorrow."

"But you need a hostess, Charles, if you are to remain. You are incapable of managing a home on your own."

"You are wrong, Sister." In the muted light from lantern outside the carriage, Bingley did not blink. "The gentlemen and I will be making regular calls on our neighbours. If a hostess is needed, surely one of the mistresses of the surrounding estates would be pleased to serve as chatelaine."

Before Bingley could be worked on by his sisters, his brother-in-law Hurst spoke. "I will escort my wife and Caroline to London on the morrow, returning by evening so we may continue becoming better acquainted with the fowl hidden in your fields. We will surely be able to bag a covey or two without these two banty hens interfering with our sport." Mr. Hurst laughed at his own humour.

Bingley said no more, though he nodded his head at his sister's husband.

Caroline Bingley seethed as her sister glanced uncertainly at her husband. Louisa Hurst doubted this was the result Caroline had been hoping for.

Darcy had wished himself elsewhere and was relieved he was a spectator at the same time. In the years he had known Bingley, it had been his fondest desire to see the younger man stand up to his rebellious sister. He was impressed with his friend and knew then how attached Bingley had become to Miss Bennet. In spite of such a brief acquaintance, only intense feelings for Miss Bennet could have inspired such a change.

Caroline had called her brother incapable. *How could a sister say such a thing?* Darcy thought of his relationship with Georgiana. Never could he imagine her saying such.

A thought occurred to him which made him squirm in his chair. Had he treated Bingley in the same manner as Caroline? Was the counsel he so freely offered bred from a feeling of superiority? Was his insult to Miss Elizabeth the same? Horrified, Darcy immediately vowed to change to improve his character.

What a difference three miles of good road brought to a household! The next time he was in company with Elizabeth, there would be no Caroline Bingley to distract either of them. He could not help the smile growing on his face. *This was war!* He would win her over. Miss Elizabeth Bennet would come to know him as the man his father raised. He wanted her respect—and her good opinion.

With that, he put his glass on the table, and went to his bed. Tomorrow, his campaign would begin.

* * *

LONGBOURN

"I cannot sleep, Lizzy. You are wiggling like a worm." Jane reached over and pushed her sister's shoulder. "Elizabeth Anne Bennet!" Jane whispered as loud as she could without waking the whole household. Then she heard a sob.

"Hmmm?" Elizabeth rubbed her eyes and was surprised at their wetness. Memories of her dreams flooded her heart, leaving feelings of pain and misery.

"Lizzy, you were having bad dreams." Jane clasped Lizzy's tear-stained hand. "What is troubling you so?"

Jane rolled back over to light the candle on her side of the bed.

Elizabeth stopped her. "No, I pray you." It was easier to speak in the dark. She wiped her eyes with the corner of the sheet and sat up, breathing in deeply, propping her pillow behind her. After a moment, she was able to put her turmoil into words.

"I fear even your kindness will fail me when you hear what I have done."

Jane chuckled. "How very Lydia-like, Lizzy."

The comment was so unexpected that Elizabeth gave a short laugh. Their youngest sister was reputed to create drama wherever possible.

"What have you done?"

"The conscience can be a terrible thing. It pricks at first, like a nettle. If ignored, it starts pounding until it becomes a sound so loud that you can hear nothing else." Elizabeth looked down at her hands tightly clasped on her lap. "Jane, I was not honest when I kept Mama and our sisters from attending Lucas Lodge. Papa had not said one word about them staying at Longbourn."

Jane paused before she replied. She was shocked. "What was your motive in doing so?"

The words poured out of Elizabeth like water released from a dam. "Though I love my mother and my sisters, I was ashamed of their behaviour. I found their conduct at the assembly to be offensive, not only to myself, but to those in attendance."

"But Lizzy, they have always been thus. Are you ashamed of them because the party from Netherfield—someone from outside the neighbourhood—witnessed their conduct?"

"I closely watched the response of Miss Bingley and her sister, Mrs. Hurst. They were laughing and making sport of our family, Jane. Mr. Darcy had such a look of disdain and disgust whenever his eyes alighted on Kitty and Lydia's wild behaviour—and that of our mother as well.

"The only one of their party who appeared to overlook their conduct was Mr. Bingley. He seemed unaware." Elizabeth leaned into her sister, who was also sitting up against the headboard. "For a certainty, his attention was where it should be, was it not?"

"Lizzy!"

"Sister, we have little to recommend ourselves. Our importance, our respectability in the world, must be affected by checking their exuberant spirits whilst displaying our own fine manners."

"Yes, this is true." Though Jane was inclined to seek the best in any given situation, she could see that her sister's opinion was accurate. "And that is why you wanted them away from Lucas Lodge?"

"It was."

"Then I believe you did not act for yourself, Lizzy. I believe you did what you felt necessary to keep them home in service of me. Am I correct, dear sister?"

"Oh, Jane." Elizabeth's emotions were raw, and her heart ached. "I have never seen you so affected by a young man. When I realised the poor impression that our family was making on his sisters and his friends, I vowed to do anything to prevent interference and help forward the match. Thus, the lie." Elizabeth bowed her head and breathed in slowly. "But it does not end there."

"Whatever do you mean?"

"I also contrived to pair Miss Bingley with Mr. Darcy so they might be busy with each other and could not stand in the way of you and Mr. Bingley." The relief Elizabeth was beginning to feel by confessing her actions moved her to continue. "However, my thinking was clouded by Mr. Darcy's comments about me. It was not a good plan. No matter my attempts at matchmaking at Lucas Lodge, there was nothing I could do to control the situation once they returned to Netherfield Park. I cannot prevent Mr. Darcy or Miss Bingley from speaking against the Bennet family."

"Lizzy, Mr. Darcy should not have said what he did." Jane felt her sister's pain in her own heart.

"His words hurt deeply; I shall admit." It was not a pleasant chuckle that came out of Elizabeth's mouth. "Mama has been quite vocal that I am not nearly as pretty as you or Lydia. This I can accept." She stopped her sister's instant words of protest. "Nevertheless, it is one thing to hear it from a parent. To hear it from a stranger, whose only knowledge of me, *was* my appearance, was a blow to my esteem.

"Each time Mama made light of my features, Sister, I made excuses in my mind justifying her opinion. With Mr. Darcy, I had no justification. I must accept that he was simply telling the truth." Elizabeth let out the breath she had not been aware she was hold-ing. "It was poorly done but that does not excuse me from allowing my injured vanity to become vindictive. I am deeply ashamed of myself, both for my intentions to interfere in their lives and for being critical of Kitty and Lydia when my own behaviour was reprehensible."

Silence filled the room.

"Elizabeth, it is as I suspected, you were doing this for me. Now, I will let you in on a secret, dear." Jane's voice was steady. Despite her reputation of being calm and serene, her emotions ran as deep as her sister's.

"You have a secret?" Elizabeth was stunned. She could not ever recall a time when they had not shared freely with each other.

"I do." Jane chortled, an odd sound coming from her. "Do you know that when I found out what Mr. Darcy had said, I wanted to find the heaviest of father's tomes—most likely the family Bible—and hit Mr. Darcy on the head with it? And I wanted it to hurt."

"What? You? Never!" Elizabeth laughed. "My dear, sweet, 'would do anything for peace' Jane?"

"Then I became angry with Mr. Bingley. He should never have allowed Mr. Darcy to injure you in such an infamous manner without checking him. Neither gentleman acted chivalrously."

"I had not thought this."

"Well, you should have." Jane looked down at her own hands. "Lizzy, I am almost three and twenty years of age with no prospects. I have no accomplishments other than my appearance, which is losing its bloom."

Elizabeth interrupted. "No, Jane. You are the most beautiful, young woman I know—far more lovely than Miss Caroline Bingley."

"I thank you for that, though you see me through the eyes of one who loves me." Jane sighed. "I am coming to feel very much as Charlotte does. I do not believe I can wait for a deep and abiding love. Not anymore."

"Oh, Jane. Do not speak so, I pray you."

"Lizzy, if we were in Town, I would be one of many who rely on their looks to gain an offer of marriage. This would be my seventh season since our mother launched us each in our fifteenth year. From the standpoint of society, I am on the shelf as firmly as Charlotte."

"But Jane..."

"No, Sister, I pray you, listen to me." Jane took in a deep breath to calm her voice. "Mr. and Miss Bingley and their party are clearly aware that our youngest sisters are out in society at a tender age. Therefore, it is a matter of simple math that they, too, can know how long I have tried to make a match—and failed.

"If Mr. Bingley were to overlook these obstacles and still show me interest, I would gladly accept his attentions. If he cannot, I will go to stay with our aunt and uncle in London to find a position which will support me. It is time, most likely past time, that I quit being a burden to our parents. My pride will not allow me to do so any longer."

Elizabeth was astounded. She had no idea of Jane's sentiments. "Jane?" She reached an arm over to pull her sister close. It was now her sister's sobs that filled the room.

* * *

FRIDAY, 4 October 1811

The next morning found Elizabeth tapping on the door to her father's study. She realised the events of the night showed on her face but needed to clear up the matter of the lie before she could proceed with her day. Jane was still asleep, though was equally as restless as Elizabeth had been.

Her assumption that she would meet with her father's disapprobation was correct, though it was tempered with his brand of sardonic humour.

"Why would you do such a thing to your sisters, Lizzy? You know how they look forward to such gatherings. It was unbearable for me to have them here at Longbourn. They voiced their complaints the whole of the evening. Have you no sympathy for my solitude? I had to ask Hill to refill my brandy to help dull the noise."

"Papa, I am truly sorry for spoiling your evening of quietude." Her regret was genuine.

"Nonetheless, Lizzy, I did give you permission to act as you felt necessary." He finally looked up from his book, his eyes twinkling with mischief. "You most likely did what I should have done months ago. In the future, I may follow your example." Before he had finished his comment, his eyes were again focussed on the pages of his book. Looking back up, he ended with, "Or I may not."

Lizzy walked out of his study and out of the front door. Trying to move past her dispiritedness, she started running, hoping to outpace her unease. She ran across the fields until she collapsed on the ground in exhaustion. Elizabeth knew what she had done was wrong even though she had justified it at the time, and her father had dismissed it so quickly.

Looking up at the sky from where she was seated, she felt small. Then she looked down. There, she watched an ant trying to move a small clump of dirt. The clod was so miniscule that Elizabeth could have flicked it away with no effort at all. Yet, to the ant, it was a monumental task that required much effort and many attempts. For as long as Elizabeth watched, the ant continued its efforts. The ant needed to let it go. Elizabeth wished it would. It seemed a fruitless task which would have no happy ending.

Elizabeth giggled up at the sky. She was that ant. She needed to release her own disappointment with herself. She needed to release the embarrassment of her family, and she needed to release Mr. Darcy's harsh words.

Remembering a time from many years past, Elizabeth's giggles turned into a sigh. She had been playing in the barn and found one of the cats kept there to keep mice away from the straw. She recalled sitting next to a large tabby whose curled tail kept moving back and forth—slowly. Had it been a metronome, it would have been a ponderous, steady rhythm. Elizabeth had felt quite proud of herself when she caught that tail mid-movement, grabbing onto it tightly. Unexpectedly, the feline turned on her and started scratching, claws fully extended. The more it scratched, the harder she held onto the tail. It took the efforts of two grooms to separate her fingers from that barn cat.

As Mrs. Hill patched the second Bennet daughter, she scolded that had she only let go of the tail instead of stubbornly holding on, the cat would have left her alone. It was a powerful lesson to a little girl and an appropriate lesson for a twenty-year-old woman to remember.

Elizabeth lifted her chin. She loved her family in spite of their faults—and knew they loved her in spite of hers. She was going to let go of resentment. As of this moment, she was going to no longer hate Mr. Darcy.

At least, not so much.

CHAPTER 6

*N*etherfield Park

Fitzwilliam Darcy's frustration was growing with every minute that passed. When he had arrived at breakfast that morning, Caroline Bingley was seated at the table. The absence of travelling clothes was telling. Instead, she wore one of her morning dresses indicating she would not be returning to London that day.

Sure enough, Bingley had given in to her demands.

"You have a sister of your own, Darcy." He later explained. "You know how much you want to please her and keep peace in your family, am I not right?"

Both Darcy and Colonel Fitzwilliam shook their heads. The colonel, too accustomed to the company of green recruits, was not one to hold his peace. Darcy would never have allowed such improper behaviour in Georgiana.

"Bingley, there is something missing in this household."

Charles Bingley was confused. He had spent hours with his steward and his housekeeper to ascertain all was in order. "What might that be, Colonel?"

"A backbone." Like Hurst, Richard Fitzwilliam had been relieved with the notion of the women's departure. There was pleasant enough female company to be found in the neighbourhood. They did not need a hostess. A country home, a multitude of coveys, a stocked larder, and a full wine cellar was all that was necessary.

"Richard!" Darcy felt the same as his cousin, however a gentleman *and houseguest* kept those sentiments to himself. *What a hypocrite I am! Did I not say something far worse to Miss Elizabeth only two nights prior?*

Bingley began, "I know what you are thinking—"

"—I am sure you do not," the colonel and Darcy said at the same time.

"Caroline has promised me she will be attentive to our needs as mistress of this household and cognizant of behaving properly in company." Bingley's face lit. "She has also offered to invite the two eldest Miss Bennets to our home for tea for the purpose of getting to know them better. How could I send her away when she obviously has repented of her error?"

Again, the colonel stated Darcy's thoughts out loud.

"Ah, so your desire to spend time with the lovely Miss Bennet in your own home away from her mother and younger sisters influenced your decision?"

Charles Bingley's face blushed a bright red so that his whole head looked on fire. "Well, to be quite honest...yes, you are correct." He looked down at his feet in embarrassment. Nevertheless, as much as he detested disappointing his friends, his desire to be in Miss Bennet's company was far more powerful.

After Bingley left to talk to his steward, the colonel finally asked Darcy about the odd relationship; Darcy merely shrugged his shoulders.

"He is a puppy." Colonel Richard Fitzwilliam had long been puzzled at his cousin's attachment to the young man. Both the Fitzwilliams and their aunt, Lady Catherine de Bourgh, had taken Darcy to task over his association with someone so closely tied to trade. Yet, Darcy continued to guide Bingley and help him navigate the social waters.

The colonel had been on the continent when Darcy's father had died in a riding accident. He was not able to return to England until almost two years had passed. Prior to his father's death, Fitzwilliam Darcy had always been quiet, yet he had smiled easily and had been full of energy and enjoyment with the camaraderie of his male cousins. The change to his cousin when he had finally been in his company had been shocking. Darcy's reserve had left him with a façade of stone. To the world, he was unapproachable. Only Richard remembered the caring heart that beat within. For Bingley to attach himself to such a man, spoke well of the young gentleman's tenacity.

"After father's death, when I was finally emerging from under the weight of responsibility for Pemberley, I found little joy in my daily existence. Charles was a breath of fresh air. He has never asked for anything and has greeted every adversity with a smile. How could I not do what was within my power and authority to help him?"

* * *

IT WAS close to an hour after breakfast when Hurst requested the company of the colonel to admire his latest shotgun acquisition. Darcy decided to use the opportunity to take his favourite horse for a ride. The bay mare had fine lines, a smooth gait, and a strong will. A thoroughbred with a white blaze running from her forelock to her nose, she pranced her white fetlocks on the gravel. The filly was ready to run, and so was Darcy. He had named her Katherina after the lead character in Shakespeare's *The Taming of the Shrew*—a perfect fit.

Darcy lengthened the horse's stride to a steady gait for almost an hour before he lifted the reins, bringing the animal to a stop. The same cold wind that chapped his cheeks had blown his curls in all directions. Even though it was not done for a gentleman to ride without a hat, Darcy had left his with the groom back at the stables. As hard as he had ridden, he would have lost it long ago or lost his seat whilst trying to keep the hat on his head.

Both Darcy and the horse breathed heavy puffs of steam from the exertion and the chill. Looking around the rolling hills and verdant farmland, Darcy felt the pull of home. Since he had retrieved his sister from Ramsgate in July, they had been ensconced in their London house. He had not been to his family seat in Derbyshire since the spring planting. He had missed the autumn harvest, but his responsibility was with Georgiana in their townhouse. However, at his sister's insistence, he had travelled to Hertfordshire with the Bingleys. Apparently, *he hovered,* and Georgiana did not approve. At Netherfield Park, he would be a half day away from Georgiana. Had he returned to Pemberley, it would have been a three to four day journey if he was needed.

He heard her before he saw her. Though the words of her song were not discernable, the tone was merry. Elizabeth Bennet had her arms spread wide, her face turned to the heavens, and a smile on her face that brightened the dreary day.

Darcy failed to realise that in his distraction, he had leaned forward in the saddle, rising to his full height. Katherina felt the change of weight immediately. The mare reacted far faster than Darcy. She went left, and he went right. When they parted company, Darcy flew through the air until he was sprawled on the ground, landing with a grunt. His horse snorted.

The noise caught Elizabeth's attention, and she turned towards him as he was still in mid-flight. She recognised him immediately.

"Mr. Darcy!" Elizabeth ran to him as quickly as possible over the uneven terrain. "Mr. Darcy!" As she approached, she shied away from his horse, her natural fear of the equine species heightened by the fact that the horse had just unseated an experienced equestrian.

She knelt. The gentleman was lying on his side facing her, his eyes closed. "I pray you, Mr. Darcy, please be conscious, please." Elizabeth was hesitant to touch him.

As she was pondering how to proceed, he whispered, "I am conscious."

"Your eyes are closed, Mr. Darcy. Are they injured, sir?"

"No, Miss Elizabeth, they are not." Humiliated at being in such a position in front of her, he snapped. Then he added, his voice softened, "I am hoping you are a figment of my imagination and can continue hoping so as long as I do not open my eyes."

His surly attitude was in contrast to the lightness of his words. She could not stop a grin from breaking out in relief.

"I am sorry to be the bearer of bad tidings, sir. I am, indeed, very real." She was surprised when he lay all the way back on the ground again and threw his arm over his brow. "Are you well? Or rather as well as you can be after being parted from your horse in such a spectacular manner?" she said with no little amusement.

He groaned.

Her mirth turned to anxiety until she saw the hint of a smile.

"Miss Elizabeth." His eyes opened. "I am well. In truth...the only damage to my person...is that I landed on my pride."

"*This* is wonderful news, Mr. Darcy." She could barely contain her laughter. "Then, if I understand the situation correctly, you should be unhurt."

"Oh?" Mr. Darcy understood how she found the circumstances humourous. Nevertheless, his embarrassment did not sit well with him.

"You have pride in abundance, sir. The landing would have been made softer because of it."

His eyes opened wider, and he saw the twinkle in her own before she burst into the most melodic sound he had heard in his whole adult life. She radiated joy. He could not help but join in her laughter. As he moved to stand, she stood and backed away from him. He laughed until he bent over, slapping his hands to his thighs. Amazingly, he felt his worries and responsibility pour off his shoulders as if he had shrugged a heavy millstone from around his neck.

"Mr. Darcy, I offer an apology." Those were not words he expected. "I had just made the resolution to be nice to one and all, and yet, the first words from my mouth came with bite. I pray you accept my sincere regrets along with a promise to do better in the future."

At her words, Darcy immediately started searching the pockets in his waistcoat. When he did not find what he was looking for, he checked the pockets in his jacket and then his greatcoat. He even put his hands deep into the pockets of his trousers. He felt panic rising in his chest and could hear his own breathing quicken.

"Mr. Darcy, truly, are you well?" Certainly, he had shown her a much different side of himself than she had observed at the Meryton assembly and at Lucas Lodge. His clothing was covered in mud and was askew, his hair was wild, and his face was a ruddy hue. Elizabeth worried that he had hit his head when he had landed on the ground. "Have you misplaced something of import, sir?"

Finally, he stopped his movements, apparently resigned to his fate. Darcy dropped both hands to his side and his chin to his chest. Breathing in slowly through his nostrils, he exhaled quickly, raising his head to look directly at the woman in front of him.

"Miss Elizabeth, in the matter of apologies, I beg you accept mine." Again, he stuck his fingers in the small pocket to the left of his waist-coat, disappointed again to find it empty. "I admit my words you over-heard at the assembly were not those of an honourable man. They were unkind and untrue. For this I am ashamed. To state my feelings on the matter clearly—so you would realise the depth of my regret—I put pen to paper and, after many starts and stops, wrote my humblest words of apology."

He clasped his hands in front of him, as if he needed to do so to keep from reaching out to her. He wished the paper he had toiled so long over was in his fist. "From the bottom to the top of my heart, I beg your pardon. My parents raised me to be a gentleman, to be a man of honour. Had a man spoken to my sister in such reprehensible terms, I would have called him out." He paused and drew in another breath. "I must ask. What can I do to right this wrong? I will do anything within my power upon your word."

Who was this man? Had the fall been so severe it had altered him exceedingly?

"I thank you. In spite of not having your note, your apology was well said." She could see his relief. "Nonetheless, this leaves me with a dilemma."

"How is that, Miss Elizabeth?"

"You see, sir, I vowed that night to loathe you for the rest of my life."

"I am sorry to hear that." He again dropped his head completely missing the sparkle in her eyes. His voice softened. "Very sorry, indeed."

"In spite of what you observed of my family, I too was raised with principles. I was taught from infancy to treat others as I hoped to be treated. I was taught to overlook faults and to search for the good." Elizabeth watched as he nodded his head in agreement. "My eldest sister, Jane, took those lessons to heart. Because of this, you could search all of England and not find a kinder, gentler woman. She is all that is good, Mr. Darcy." Elizabeth sighed. "And then, there is me. You see, I was not as diligent with my lessons. I am stubborn and own a temper that flares quickly. I have been known to hold a grudge with a grip so fierce, I cannot make myself let go."

"Then, neither of us performed well," he said, his voice still muted with feeling.

"No, Mr. Darcy. We did not." Elizabeth turned away from him and walked in a small circle. "You treated me abominably, sir, and I have done the same to you. It was not my place to try to manipulate Miss Bingley. So, in addition to apologising for startling you and your horse, I offer my regrets for raising expectations in Miss Bingley."

"Miss Elizabeth, no more, I pray you." He stepped closer to her. "You owe me nothing. Any slight that you perceive you have done to me is nothing compared to my public declaration of an opinion which was—simply put—an untruth. Those who may have overheard are your neighbours, your friends. I would leave the area, Miss Elizabeth, to give you peace. However, these neighbours would not know of my regret. Therefore, I ask you now, my lady, what I can do to repair the damage I have wrought?"

"I do not know, sir," Elizabeth stated, shrugging her shoulders. "This has brought to my attention a deficit in my character. Yes, I was hurt by your words. But, then I became angry. Because I had such a low opinion of your character, sir, in my anger, I plotted against you and Miss Bingley to keep you from interfering with Mr. Bingley's becoming acquainted with my sister." She looked him directly in the eyes. "I am telling you this for one reason only, Mr. Darcy. Your unkind words may have started this chasm between us, but my own actions and attitude made it grow."

"Miss Elizabeth, then may we agree that there is fault on both our parts? That neither of us acted in a manner appropriate to our station?" This woman intrigued him. Had she been a lady of the *ton*, he might have been trapped by virtue of being alone in the field with her. He would have had to speak with her father about possible repercussions. He never would have been able to express himself freely without knowing his words would be thrown back at him or made public to force him to bend to her demands. He might have been the only one proclaiming guilt. She was remarkable in that none of these consequences had been demanded by Elizabeth. Truly remarkable. "May we now agree to begin again?"

She pondered this plan. It would take some adjusting of her opinions but it would be good in forwarding a connection between Bingley and Jane. *This might work!*

"Mr. Darcy, I am Miss Elizabeth Anne Bennet from Longbourn. You are most welcome to Hertfordshire." She dropped into a deep curtsey.

"My pleasure." He bowed—*relieved*. "I am delighted to make your acquaintance, Miss Elizabeth Anne Bennet." He smiled, which she quickly returned. "I am Fitzwilliam Alexander Darcy of Pemberley in Derbyshire."

Elizabeth could not resist. "Mr. Darcy, now that we have been properly introduced, we must speak of the weather or the roads. Or, we could speak of horseflesh or lace. Whatever you choose."

They laughed. It was a new beginning. With another bow and curtsey, they both returned to their respective homes, Elizabeth's steps much lighter, and Darcy's horse, Katherina, much less burdened than before.

CHAPTER 7

*N*etherfield Park

Caroline Bingley stood at the front window, watching for Mr. Darcy to return from his ride. When he finally came into view, his appearance was wild and highly irregular. And yet, she thought he had never appeared more handsome. She would do anything to become his bride.

It had galled her to beg her brother to reconsider his decision. To promote her own plans, she needed to be near Fitzwilliam Darcy. Caroline almost choked over the words of apology and regret, only made worse by the fact that she needed to use Jane Bennet as a lure for Charles to change his mind. Now, she was committed to hosting the two eldest Bennet daughters at Netherfield Park. Thus, the invitation had been sent for tea the next day. Caroline was determined to prove to Mr. Darcy her abilities in the management of a household so he would know, with confidence, that she was well qualified for the position as the future Mrs. Darcy. Her skills as hostess would surely draw him in.

Looking at the smile on Darcy's face as he walked from the stables, Caroline hoped it was in anticipation of being in her company. He said nothing to her at breakfast to indicate his feelings about Charles being unreasonably harsh with his demands. Since he was a notoriously private man, she was not surprised.

She turned away from the window, reaching up to pat her hair and then down to smooth her skirts. Caroline wanted nothing out of place when her soon-to-be intended walked into the room. Therefore, she was disappointed when his long strides took him passed her and directly up the stairs to his rooms. He had not even noticed her presence through the doorway of the drawing room. She sighed so loudly the attending footman turned his head. Having caught the attention of a servant, her humiliation seemed complete.

Caroline Bingley knew that being the daughter of a tradesman—no matter how successful—would keep her from the first circles unless she married well. Upon meeting her brother's wealthy friend, Darcy, the ambitions of her parents had developed into an inferno in her bosom. He was her ticket to accomplishing her dreams. She was determined to let nothing, or no one stand in her way.

* * *

FITZWILLIAM DARCY MET his cousin on the stairs as he headed to his rooms to change from his muddy riding clothes. The muck that covered his greatcoat and trousers had been brushed off after it dried, but the stains were still visible. Growing up at Pemberley, the Fitzwilliam cousins were regular visitors. As was common with most healthy boys, mud was not an unfamiliar substance. However, the sheer magnitude of the marks on Darcy's clothing was notable.

Colonel Fitzwilliam stopped mid-step when he noted the smile and the sound of humming coming from his cousin. Two thoughts came immediately to mind. One, he could not recall seeing such a laissez-faire expression on his cousin's face in the last five years, and two, he hoped Darcy never intended to serenade a woman. The tune was barely recognisable.

"Nice ride?"

"Indeed." And that was it. No embellishments. Darcy continued up the stairs, his smile still in place, though the humming had ceased. Apparently, he was aware of his own weaknesses.

Had this been anyone other than Fitzwilliam Darcy, the colonel would have immediately suspected a woman was responsible for generating such a change to his somber mien. As it was, he could only assume there had been good news from Georgiana or of a successful investment. However, knowing his cousin, Darcy would have reported the news of Georgiana immediately as the two men shared guardianship. Had it been a business transaction, Darcy would be more than pleased to share information as they had invested Richard's income from the military several times, allowing the colonel to purchase a small property in the Derbyshire countryside. Therefore, it had to be a lady.

Surely not Miss Bingley! The woman, like so many of the *ton*, had nothing to offer Darcy. His estate was not entailed, and his father had been diligent in leaving his children with no financial worries. Since the death of his uncle Darcy, his cousin had continued to spend his time almost exclusively in filling the coffers. Like Richard, Darcy was the grandson of an earl who never cared for the honour of being titled. Darcy had everything to offer and would require a woman of spectacular connections to be the next mistress of Pemberley. *No, not Miss Bingley.*

Richard knew his next course of action. He must speak with Miss Charlotte Lucas.

* * *

Lucas Lodge

Charlotte's mother was cut from the same bolt of cloth as Mrs. Bennet, Mrs. Long, Mrs. Goulding, and Mrs. Fielding—they were all gossips of the highest order. Thus, it took little probing for Charlotte to learn what Elizabeth had faced at the hands of "concerned" neighbours the day before. For years she had studied the Bennet family. After all, what else was there for a lady of leisure to do with her time

61

if there was no inclination to practice music, net purses, or paint tables?

Had Elizabeth been asked which Bennet sister had the most tender heart, she would—without hesitation—answer Jane. Nevertheless, Charlotte knew the truth of the matter. Yes, Jane was kind. However, Elizabeth was the one who put herself out to help others when she learned there was a need, whereas Jane would merely express her sadness at the affliction. It was Elizabeth who sought to aid her younger sisters to act with propriety, and it was Elizabeth who would set aside her own desires to promote Jane's happiness above her own.

The family life at Longbourn, in many ways, was a struggle for recognition. Charlotte had no doubt that the Bennet parents had a measure of affection for all five of their daughters. Nevertheless, their mother showed preference to the oldest and youngest because their looks most closely resembled Mrs. Bennet's when she was a maiden. Her physical appearance, as she often claimed, had caught her a gentleman for a husband. The middle three daughters were much overlooked by their mother. Mr. Bennet had shown special interest in Elizabeth from her early years—though it appeared solely for his entertainment.

"Colonel Fitzwilliam, welcome to Lucas Lodge." Charlotte had been so deep in her thoughts that she failed to hear the butler announce his presence and had only heard her mother's welcome. She stood, blushing, at being caught unawares.

"Miss Lucas." The colonel lowered his voice as he bowed before her. "Wool gathering on a cloudy afternoon during visiting hours?"

"You have caught me out, Colonel Fitzwilliam." Her curtsey was slight, but the lift of her eyebrow was not. "To what do we owe the pleasure of your company today? It was my understanding that you and your cousin were in the area for sport?"

They both laughed good-naturedly, the camaraderie of the night before extending into the day. Mrs. Lucas, delighted in having a single son of an earl call on her eldest, left the room under the guise of ordering tea. Alas, Charlotte knew her mother was seeing hope where there was none.

"How are things at Netherfield Park, Colonel?" He was dashing in his uniform and her eyes rebelled, giving his face a quick once over, not realising he was doing the same to her.

"It is a coincidence you should ask, Miss Lucas." The colonel had sat in the chair opposite hers, edging it closer so they might speak privately. "My cousin was smiling this morning." He sat back in the chair as if those six words gave a full explanation for his visit.

"And?" Charlotte could not help shaking her head in confusion.

"Ah, you see, Miss Lucas, Darcy rarely smiles." As her brow lifted again, he began to explain. "My cousin was left the responsibility of one of the largest estates in England along with the guardianship of his younger sister but five years ago. His duties have weighed heavily on him. And from the day he inherited the Darcy holdings, he has been the focus of matchmaking mamas and their grasping daughters. He has had those he considered close friends turn traitor and others seeking association for what they could gain from him. His life has been…isolated, Miss Lucas."

"A devastating situation for any young man, Colonel." Charlotte felt empathy at his plight. "I would imagine there are many who would think the wealth that came with his position would compensate for any hardship he would face. Am I correct in assuming so?"

Richard sincerely appreciated her good sense and her compassion. "Yes, it would seem his life would be one of ease. Many young men who have inherited fortunes choose to allow their stewards to run their estates while they followed pleasure rather than responsibility. Needless to say, Darcy is proud of his heritage and is determined to continue its prosperity for future Darcys."

"How admirable, sir." Charlotte was as surprised as she had been the evening prior with his plain manner of speaking. "So, I must ask, what or *who* do you think wrought such a miracle as a smile from Mr. Darcy?"

"Who indeed, Miss Lucas?" The colonel sat forward in the chair, leaning his elbows on the arms, his fingers coming to rest under his chin. "I was hoping you happened upon your friends from Longbourn this morning, to determine whether any one of them had seen my cousin while he was on his morning ride about the countryside."

Charlotte could not help but laugh. The man knew the habits of women. "Do you have sisters?"

"I do not."

His reply gave Charlotte reason to pause. *How did he know so much of females when his occupation surrounds him with only men?* Shaking her head slightly, she dispensed with the thought. It was not—nor ever would be—her concern.

"Mr. Darcy's comments at the Meryton assembly *had* wounded Elizabeth's pride. She swore to exact revenge on the *repugnant* Mr. Darcy." Charlotte's voice dropped to a whisper. "The ladies of the neighbourhood were even more callous in their repetition of those comments. When I heard of their unkindness, I rushed to comfort my friend. It so happens that I arrived at Longbourn just as Miss Elizabeth was returning from her walk.

"Yet, like your cousin, Eliza was all smiles—genuine, happy smiles. When I commented on the change to her countenance, her only reply was, 'It is a new day, Charlotte, and I have made a new acquaintance.'"

"Do you know of whom she was referring?"

"When I asked her, she only chuckled and walked into Longbourn, humming the tune Miss Bingley had played on the pianoforte the night before."

"That is it!" The colonel snapped his fingers and pressed his lips together. "*That* was the same tune my cousin was trying to hum."

"When he was smiling?"

"Yes."

Silence filled the room as the two pondered over the similarities. Charlotte's eyes widened as did the colonel's.

The colonel muttered, "It could not be..." as Charlotte proclaimed, "She told me she hates him!"

"It would not be a good match for him. Many of our society would view her position as a degradation to him." He shook his head slowly.

"Would you?"

"Not at all." His reply was instantaneous. "There are few things that would bring me greater joy than to see Darcy happy. If Miss Elizabeth makes him smile, then she would be most welcome.

"Miss Lucas, nonetheless, I do believe I see a big problem."

"What would that problem be, Colonel?"

"The difference in their spheres is an obstacle few choose to make the effort to overcome. Darcy and I have family members who would vehemently oppose any connection with a country miss, even though she is gentry." He rubbed his chin in thought. "Since infancy, expectations as to the bride of the heir to Pemberley have been high, vacillating between either my cousin, Anne de Bourgh, or a titled maiden from the first circles."

"I understand, Colonel Fitzwilliam." Charlotte comprehended the way society worked. "However, what do you feel is the problem specific to Mr. Darcy and Eliza?"

The colonel sat back in his chair, his hands crossed on his lap, and his eyes looking directly at Miss Lucas. "I believe Darcy feels a strong attraction to Miss Elizabeth."

"And this is bad?" Charlotte was puzzled.

"Oh, no! This is good."

"How so?" Charlotte moved forward to the front of her chair, completely intent on his words.

"It is my studied opinion that Darcy and Miss Elizabeth met this morning, somewhere and somehow." His eyes lost focus as he considered what he had observed earlier. "My cousin practically grew up on a horse—actually, all of us did. Yet, he was covered in dried mud when he came into Bingley's estate. Therefore, I must assume he was unseated during his ride. Also, enough time had passed from his landing in the mud until his return to Netherfield Park that his pants and coat were dried."

"What do you believe might have caused this anomaly?"

"Do you not mean, *who* do I believe might have caused this?" His gaze returned to the woman in front of him. "My conjecture is that my stoic cousin happened upon your friend during his ride so suddenly that he was thrown off that miserable mare."

"I know Elizabeth well, Colonel." Charlotte grinned. "Seeing such a proud man, especially one she had sworn to dislike, land on his... well, wherever he landed, would provide her keen delight." Charlotte again sat back in her chair. "If they spent time talking—say enough time for his clothing to dry—if he offered an apology, Eliza would proffer the hand of friendship. It is her way."

The colonel was relieved to hear this. He loved Darcy more than his own brother. His cousin was naïve to many aspects of feminine conduct. To have such a favourable report about a lady from a perceptive friend carried much weight.

"Then I believe we are close enough to solving the mystery." The colonel started tapping his fingertips together. "We—you and I—need to help them along."

"Us, sir?" Charlotte was surprised. The last thing in the world she would have thought of the man in front of her was that he was a matchmaker. That he wanted to work with her, *together,* was also a surprise. Yet, she could see the wisdom in it. "Elizabeth is soft-hearted, though she can be a bit hard-headed."

"Miss Lucas, you have not seen hard-headed until you see Darcy in one of his moods—which is the majority of the time."

"Colonel, I will do nothing to harm my friend."

"Trust me, Miss Lucas" —the colonel stood, ready to take his leave — "this will be like taking a toy from a newborn babe."

It was not until the colonel had bowed over her hand and left that Charlotte realised her mother had left them alone the whole time he had been at Lucas Lodge. She sighed at the future of her mother's unfulfilled fantasies. It would *never* happen, not in a dozen years.

Charlotte thought about all Colonel Fitzwilliam had said about his cousin. If he was correct—and she had no reason to believe otherwise —Mr. Darcy and Elizabeth Bennet were the perfect match. Walking out of the drawing room, Charlotte caught her reflection in the hall mirror. It was only then that she recognised she was smiling in the same manner Eliza had earlier. Elizabeth Bennet had found her perfect match and she could not be more pleased.

CHAPTER 8

Saturday, 5 October 1811
Netherfield Park

It was not until the Bennet sisters arrived at Netherfield Park that Elizabeth was again in Mr. Darcy's company. For the preponderance of the visit, only the four women entertained themselves over the well-arranged repast. Apparently, this had been at Miss Bingley's design for when the gentlemen appeared after their sport, Mr. Bingley inquired whether she was *finally* prepared for them.

Miss Bingley was an accomplished hostess and was pleased to prove her diligence on this occasion. Not only was the table laden with small cakes accompanying the tea, but there were also nibbles of savory fare that were beautifully presented.

Under normal circumstances, Elizabeth was adventurous, willing to try anything new. Nevertheless, the prospect of seeing Mr. Darcy again had the butterflies in her stomach all aflutter. She accepted only one shortbread biscuit which still resided at the side of her teacup.

Mr. Hurst, a confirmed gourmand, filled his plate until some of the delicacies threatened to topple to the carpets. The colonel's plate was more conservatively filled, while Darcy and Bingley barely ate. It was a circumstance the colonel could not fail to mention.

"I say, Hurst," merriment oozed from Colonel Fitzwilliam's voice as he lifted his small half-filled dish towards the man. "What is it about the power of a lovely lady, my man?"

Gilbert Hurst looked up and compared his pile of food to both Darcy and Bingley's. He snorted. It had been a long while since he thought himself to be in love with his wife. *Had I ever lost my desire to sate my belly whilst courting Louisa?* He shrugged his shoulders. With no words spoken, the colonel received his message loud and clear.

Miss Bingley assumed they were speaking of the food and not wanting to seem negligent in her duties, pressed the men to partake. After no little encouragement, Bingley did so. Darcy turned and carried his cup of tea to the window, where he surreptitiously studied the lawns. He was grateful no one thought to ask him what he found to be of interest in the park. It was the lady seated on one end of the settee who had his attention, and he thought the rose-colored muslin dress was lovely against her skin. Yet he knew that to watch her as he desired would give rise to expectations, and he would not do that to her.

Colonel Fitzwilliam understood Darcy was affected by Miss Elizabeth's presence. Knowing his cousin's nature, he felt it was incumbent upon him to intercede, *to help things along.*

"Miss Elizabeth, I woke this morning to a cloudy, grey sky. Are you pleased it did not rain?"

"I am, Colonel Fitzwilliam, for I do enjoy a stroll through the autumn leaves." Since she was looking at the man who had addressed her, Elizabeth was unaware she had garnered the attention of anyone else. "However, 'for every cloud engenders not a storm,' so while I am pleased, I am not surprised."

"You are a reader of Shakespeare, Miss Elizabeth?" Darcy could not help but ask, no longer able to pretend indifference. In his experience, few women read the classics. Not even his sister—and she was a lover of books—though her inclination, lately, was towards romantic novels.

Elizabeth turned her attention to the man she was most anxious to see, wondering how they would act in company after their conversation in the field. "You appear surprised, Mr. Darcy, but yes, I have read 'Henry VI.' That was Gloucester's response to King Edward, I believe?" Elizabeth lifted her chin—a challenge offered.

He chuckled to himself. "Was it, Miss Elizabeth?" The challenge was received and accepted. Whether there would be a truce or not was yet to be determined. She was testing him, and he would not correct her. Elizabeth, by virtue of mentioning one of the characters in the correct act and scene of the play, had to be well aware of who spoke.

"Do you not think Clarence also expressed himself clearly on the occasion, sir?"

For the first time since he stepped into the room, he noticed how her eyes sparkled and seemed to dance with glee. He could not fail to note their beauty as he had at the assembly.

"I most assuredly do, Miss Elizabeth." There would indeed be peace. Their truce would last. "Well done."

"I thank you for your approval, Mr. Darcy. Should it be rarely bestowed, its value would be most appreciated."

Darcy caught the smile at the end of her comment. *Impertinent girl!*

Though Caroline Bingley had no inkling who Clarence or Gloucester was or what they had to do with the weather, she was acutely aware of the ease Darcy and Elizabeth had in speaking with each other. Though Elizabeth had avoided Darcy at Lucas Lodge, she was not doing so at Netherfield Park, and Caroline was not having it. She had expected animosity between the pair, not seeds of friendship.

"Miss Eliza, tell me, have you spent much time in London society? Miss Grantley has written that the counties beyond the metropolis are quite primitive." Caroline sniffed in blatant superiority. "You cannot have spent all your years in Hertfordshire?"

Caroline's comments caught the immediate attention of all in the room. Jane Bennet despised confrontation of any sort. She bowed her head, twisting her hands in agitation. However, Elizabeth welcomed it.

"I do not know Miss Grantley. Is she a close acquaintance of yours,

Miss Bingley?" Elizabeth knew what the woman was about. It was a paltry device, a mean art.

Caroline pressed her right hand to her heart as if it would stop ticking at the thought. "My dear, Miss Eliza, Miss Grantley is part of the first circles of society. As such, we think so much alike that we are of one thought." She quickly glanced at Mr. Darcy to make sure he was listening. Caroline desperately wanted him to realise how much she belonged in his sphere of friends. "If you spent any time at all with those of elevated rank, you would understand her meaning."

"Primitive? Is that so, Miss Bingley? It has been my study that every savage can dance and sing." Elizabeth set her teacup and saucer on the table in front of her. Putting her hands together on her lap, she continued. "This must be a relief to you."

Her response confused Caroline. "How so?"

"I believe Mr. Darcy's estate is in the Derbyshire, is it not?"

"Eliza Bennet, I have had the privilege of being a guest at Pemberley several times. There is not an estate in the whole of England so grand."

Elizabeth lifted her cup off the saucer and took a sip, allowing the conversation to settle in the minds of those in the drawing room. "I do wonder whether you and Miss Grantley are of one mind as she feels country living is primitive. Surely you do not mean Mr. Darcy's bucolic estate, Pemberley, is occupied by savages?"

"Never!" Miss Caroline Bingley sputtered at the perceived insult to the estate she longed to have as her home and the man she would need as a husband to achieve that goal. She missed the look of mischievous delight on Darcy's and the colonel's faces.

"Oh, I see—" Elizabeth's voice remained calm "—you are merely trying to let me know that Miss Grantley has no interest in pursuing Mr. Darcy then. She would also have no interest in your brother since he has leased a country estate."

"Miss Eliza, I am not..."

"Maybe you are endeavouring to adjust my opinion as to you and Mr. Darcy being a charming couple?"

"Miss Eliza!" The colour, which had left her face at first, returned with a vengeance. "I was endeavouring to make a point."

"Pray. How I do run on!" A small smile crossed Elizabeth's face. "I fear I must thwart your opinion of a country upbringing when I answer your original question. I admit Jane and I have spent much time in London with our aunt and uncle. In doing so, we regularly attended the theater, the opera, the museums, and Vauxhall gardens. We have strolled Bond Street, had ices at Gunther's, and shopped for books at Hatchards." With an impish grin, she added, "There. Have I sufficiently disappointed our hostess?"

Jane gave a small cough into her hand to remind her sister they were guests at Netherfield Park. Elizabeth looked to her and winked, hoping no one else noticed. Only the colonel had caught the rapid twitch of her eye. He stifled his laugh.

"Your relatives, I believe they reside in Cheapside?" Caroline sniffed in her arrogance. She had clearly underestimated her foe.

"And your relatives, Miss Bingley, what part of London are they from?"

Caroline sensed the ground shift to quicksand.

Both women heard the snort from Mr. Hurst. He had long tired of his sister-in-law's influence over his wife. Their marriage had lifted Louisa from trade to the life of a gentlewoman. The Bingleys hailed from the industrial area of Manchester, and Caroline had long striven to put those days behind her.

Caroline Bingley wanted to stomp her foot and might have done so had she not been seated. The conversation had not gone the way she had planned. Eliza Bennet was a nobody who seemed to show an abominable sort of conceited independence and her indifference to decorum was unappreciated by the mistress of Netherfield Park. Hoping to regain her elegant mien, she moved to the tea tray and offered to refill the gentlemen's cups.

She looked to Mr. Darcy with confidence. Caroline knew his opinion of Meryton society and Elizabeth Bennet in particular. She too had overheard his comments to her brother at the assembly, stating his opinion of the young woman as "tolerable" and "not handsome enough." Surely there was little danger of Elizabeth gaining favour with the man. When her eyes moved to see his reaction, she expected to see his look of condescension towards the second Bennet daughter and approval of her own comments. She was shocked! Caroline had never seen such admiration in his dark eyes—and it was not aimed towards herself.

The colonel was savouring the performance and could not wait to share all with Miss Lucas.

Bingley worried that he made the wrong decision allowing Caroline to remain. Yet, having Miss Bennet in his home was such a reason for joy; in the end, it was worth his sister being hostess.

Darcy was enchanted. He was learning more about Miss Elizabeth Bennet, and each morsel of information only added to her manifold attractions. For the first time in his eight and twenty years, he felt his heart might be in peril. He smiled at the thought, comforted in knowing he was not the cold, stern man he was rumoured to be. *Yes, they would be good friends.*

* * *

LONGBOURN

It had been a few hours since the Bennet sisters returned to Longbourn. Mrs. Bennet requested a full report with a complete description of the gowns worn by the Bingley sisters as well as the items served for tea. She was uninterested in the conversations between the hostess and her daughters, only seeking to know how Jane was progressing with her efforts to form an attachment with Mr. Bingley.

"Lizzy, you were quite bold," Jane said as she finished brushing her long, blonde locks. Elizabeth was trying to tame her curls into obedience at the same time—to little effect.

Elizabeth scoffed. "The Miss Bingleys of the world are in every respect entitled to think well of themselves, and meanly of others, Sister, dear. They cannot see beyond their own elevated opinions, so they belittle those who do not fit into their ideals. I have no desire to *better* myself or our society to be at *her* level. I am perfectly content being a country miss, something she would never understand."

"I do feel that she did not help her situation with Mr. Darcy today." Jane keenly felt Caroline's likely injury.

"Oh, Jane, I would not waste your tears on Miss Bingley." Elizabeth hopped into bed and pulled the bed clothes up to her chin, wiggling until some heat was created between the cool cotton sheets. "I am fairly certain that she has done what she needs to do to repair his opinion of her." Elizabeth giggled. "Jane, dear, I believe she was hoisted with her own petard."

"Lizzy, I do hope you do not speak of such in her hearing as I doubt she has read 'Hamlet' and would have no understanding of your meaning."

"Why, Jane!" Elizabeth burst into laughter. "That is possibly the harshest thing I have ever heard you say about another."

"It is, is it not?" Jane's snicker turned into full-blown merriment.

* * *

NETHERFIELD PARK

"What did you think of tea this afternoon, Darcy?" Richard had waited until Hurst and Bingley had retired upstairs to question his cousin. Bingley's hollow apology for Caroline's behaviour was still ringing in his ears.

"Miss Elizabeth is clever." Darcy smiled at the memory of her calm countenance as she had answered her adversary. "She was undaunted by anything Miss Bingley said."

"This is true. This is true." The colonel poured himself and Darcy another brandy. "Pray tell me, Cousin, what think you of the fair lady? You first proclaimed her as not pretty. Do you still think thus?"

Darcy walked to the fireplace and set his glass on the mantel. He looked to the fire and kicked the embers back into place. Finally, he said, "Remember, Richard, I believed her to not be a Bennet. However, I was determined to be miserable at the assembly. Because I did not want to be there, I was not guarded in my speech, which I deeply regret." Darcy paused as if to formulate his words. "Richard, when I looked at Miss Elizabeth—truly looked at her—I was drawn to her in a way I have never felt before. She is so alive, so vibrant. She does nothing to attract my attention, yet she has it all the same."

Darcy was not aware how his entire mien had softened as he spoke of Miss Elizabeth. The colonel discerned the contrast between the expressions on his cousin's face from when they had been speaking of Miss Bingley and thought to share that with Miss Lucas as well.

"We were able to speak plainly with each other yesterday and have decided to begin anew. I believe that for the first time in my life, I could have a lady as a friend."

A friend? Really? Does he truly think this possible? The colonel wished he had paper and ink to write this down, so he missed nothing when he next spoke with Charlotte. *When had she become Charlotte instead of Miss Lucas?* "Humph!"

"You doubt that Miss Elizabeth and I can be friends?" Darcy was puzzled at his cousin. He expected him to be pleased.

Richard turned his thoughts back to the discussion. *Friends indeed! Ridiculous!* "What I believe matters not. However, I do hope you and Miss Elizabeth have the start of a beautiful *friendship*, one which will last a lifetime." He painted it a bit brown. His cousin did not seem to notice.

"I, too, feel in my heart that Miss Elizabeth would be a good companion to Georgiana, and I am thinking of writing to request my sister's presence here at Netherfield Park. My only hesitation is that it would mean exposing her to the fawning of Miss Bingley."

"Would that not be a good thing?"

"How do you mean?"

"You have to admit that the contrast between young ladies would be a good lesson to our ward. She could learn how *not* to behave from the one and learn how to smile like the other."

Darcy considered his cousin's words carefully. "Yes, I believe you are right." He picked up his brandy and drained the glass. "I will write the note immediately and send it express."

The colonel was almost blinded by Darcy's smile. He had never seen the man so happy.

"This is a good plan." Darcy laughed heartily, and Richard nearly choked on his brandy at the sound. "Imagine, having two such women in close proximity—a sister and a friend. How pleasant this will be."

The colonel decided to follow his cousin's example and head to his room and put his own pen to paper. He did not want to forget any of even the smallest details when he headed to Lucas Lodge in the morning. He only hoped Miss Lucas did not mind receiving a caller at such an early hour.

CHAPTER 9

S unday, 6 October 1811
Longbourn

Elizabeth woke the next morning to the news that the militia was soon to settle in Meryton for the winter and the heir to Longbourn would be arriving to make his first appearance at his future inheritance. Both pieces of information were met with mixed emotions from the females in residence. Mr. Bennet's contribution to the melee was the dispensing of the facts as he currently knew them, then retiring to his bookroom soon after.

Elizabeth followed him into the room. "Papa, what think you of the news?"

It was a rare occurrence for her father to hurt her feelings like he had. Most likely, in his bid to find humour in the mundane, he had not realised he had done so. In fact, Elizabeth could not recall a time when it had happened before. She respected his opinion. His barbs had always been cushioned by wit and aimed at others.

Mr. Bennet removed his spectacles and rubbed his hands over his face. Then he reached in his desk drawer and removed a letter, handing it across the desk to his daughter. "I received this by post yesterday and I believe that if you were to look up the definition of the word 'buffoon' in the dictionary, you would find the name of my heir, Mr. William Collins."

In spite of their close relationship, she could not recall when he had been as seriously affected as he was at that moment. She waited for his well-chosen censure or the snicker at his cousin's foibles…but the words did not come.

Before she could unfold the letter and satisfy her growing curiosity, her father stood and walked to the front of the desk, leaning against it, his feet and arms crossed.

"Elizabeth, before you read this nonsensical missive, I want you to understand that there is a part of me which is grateful for the young man's blatant self-aggrandizement." He again rubbed his face, as if he was trying to erase unpleasant thoughts. "His father was both ignorant and illiterate. Rather than expend efforts to improve himself, he became a relentless bully. He insisted his son be educated at university, though, from the tone of his words, the son learned little."

"And you are grateful for this?" Elizabeth was puzzled. From her father's attitude, she understood this was not an exercise, an opportunity for furthering her comprehension or her education. He was seeking her opinion!

"I am." Mr. Bennet paused. "You see, Lizzy, had the son presented himself to Longbourn as a young man of five and twenty years with a desire to learn and grow, I would have felt an obligation to help him along, to befriend him, and welcome him into our household. This I would have done with pleasure." At her raised brow, he chuckled. "The pleasure would have been in knowing he would grow to love Longbourn and act responsibly in caring for my family."

His words confused her.

"Ah, Daughter, you are questioning what I am about, are you not?" At her nod, he continued. "With his character exposed with such clarity, there is no hope of relief. No hope that I can spend the rest of my days with my books knowing *such a man* would be master of Longbourn. I find I must bestir my will to secure the future of my family."

Elizabeth saw no twinkle in his eyes and no smile about to burst forth. It was almost miraculous! Her own father would no longer shun his duties. While her mind wanted to proclaim, "It *is time!*" she heard her voice say, "Then our lives are in good hands, Papa."

Though he seemed committed to his resolution, she addressed him tentatively. "I understand your words. What I do not comprehend is your purpose in sharing this information with me." She placed the letter carefully on her lap and looked him directly in the eye. "I sense you are serious, Papa, and while I thank you for your consideration of my sisters and myself, I am worried about this Mr. Collins."

"My Lizzy" —her father motioned with his hand towards the folded parchment— "please."

Elizabeth looked down to find blocked letters pressed together so tightly that it was a challenge to decipher. Quickly scanning its contents there were words, names, and phrases which stood out. In the first short paragraph the word "entail" had been mentioned five times. Lady Catherine de Bourgh was referenced no less than a dozen times on the first page, and matrimony was mentioned thrice. It was on this particular subject that one portion of a paragraph jumped out and hit Elizabeth right between the eyes.

"I am very sensible, Cousin, of the hardship to my fair cousins—and could say much on the subject—but that I am cautious of appearing forward and precipitate. But I can assure the young ladies that I come prepared to admire them. At present I will not say more, but perhaps when we are better acquainted—"

"Papa?" She could not keep the uncertainty from her voice, repulsed by the implications.

He waved his hand again. "Read on."

Elizabeth turned the page and did so. Shocked at the contents, she crumpled the paper tightly in her fist. "No!"

"Yes, Lizzy." Mr. Bennet leaned forward and removed the letter from her fingers, placing it behind him on the desk so his daughter could no longer see the offensive pages. "You understand why I cannot leave matters as they stand. Mr. Collins paints himself an absurd, little man whose sole interest is in bowing and scraping to his patroness, Lady Catherine de Bourgh."

"I do comprehend your feelings on the matter, Papa." While she responded calmly, it was not the words about Mr. Collins himself that upset her. The man wrote of the connections his patroness had with peers of the realm and large, wealthy landowners—and it was primarily the mention of Mr. Fitzwilliam Darcy of Pemberley in Derbyshire that made her most distraught.

"Papa, he says Mr. Darcy is betrothed to the daughter of Lady Catherine de Bourgh. Mr. Collins would have no way of knowing we have been introduced to the man. Yet, the whole second page is devoted to his descriptions of both the mother and daughter, the estate, the gardens, their connections, and his prospects. To state something so unrelated to us...is nonsensical." Elizabeth shook her head slowly as she continued speaking. "What does he hope to gain by sharing such information with complete strangers?"

Mr. Darcy was engaged to marry his cousin? She was surprised at the hurt she felt. In her brief conversation with Mr. Darcy in the field, nothing had been mentioned to indicate he was promised. Of course, neither had he made any promises to her other than offering friend-ship. Nor did she want any. *But, what about Miss Bingley? Surely, she would not continue her pursuit if he was out of her reach?* It was most unsettling!

"His verbosity indicates a smallness in his thinking, Lizzy. Mr. Collins wishes to promote himself by mentioning the names of those in the highest circles. He is unaware we are acquainted with Mr. Darcy. It would not be out of character for such a man as Mr. Collins to use false pretenses and stratagems to promote himself beyond his proper place." Thomas Bennet patted his daughter's knee. "Worry not, Lizzy. It is good we know Mr. Darcy's future plans. Your mother, though she already hates him for his damaging words against you at the assembly, would overlook his slight should he have shown any interest in you. Thus, you are safe from your mama's matchmaking. You need not spend any more time with that abominable man. Mr. Darcy is reputed to have an unsociable, taciturn disposition. His manners and selfish disdain of the feelings of others will undoubtedly make him the perfect groom for, as Mr. Collins states, 'the jewel of England' but never for one of my girls."

Elizabeth deeply appreciated her father's unexpected words of tender regard for the prospects of her and her sisters. She knew not how to explain meeting Mr. Darcy and the subsequent conversation in a way that would not raise the concern of her father. Long had their family been exposed to the harsh comments from the matrons of Meryton about the consequences of being alone with a single man. Even though Elizabeth was aware it was done to instill caution in their daughters, there was a measure of truth to their words. Should those same women learn that she and Mr. Darcy were in conversation in the isolated field, speculation would be rife and the potential for damage to her reputation would be great. In her father's eyes, her words about the improper conduct of her younger sisters would have been made null with her own decision to remain in the field with Mr. Darcy.

And yet, Elizabeth longed to let her father know she had agreed to put the insult behind her and start again as a friend.

"Do not worry, Lizzy." Again, her father patted her knee, misunderstanding her lack of ease. "I will not allow any gentleman, including the heir to Longbourn, to play with the affections of any of my daughters."

Elizabeth embraced her papa before returning to the privacy of her bedchambers. She sought quietude to ponder this recent intelligence. *Mr. Darcy is to be married!* Why did that make her so agitated?

* * *

Meryton

The party from Netherfield Park arrived at the small stone church in Meryton just before the start of services. Lizzy had found little peace after speaking to her father and was restless until they finally appeared. As expected, Miss Bingley was clinging to Mr. Darcy's arm. His expression was the same as at the Meryton assembly—dour and unapproachable. She wondered how much Miss Bingley's presence was responsible for his stern countenance. Gone was the friendly face from two days past.

Elizabeth followed his progress as they walked down the aisle, thinking he would make a handsome groom when he married the illustrious Miss de Bourgh. *Would he be elegantly dressed primarily in dark colours, as she realised was his custom? Would he look back at the doorway in eager anticipation as he awaited his bride? Would he speak his vows to love and cherish his wife with truth in his heart?* A sharp pang cut deep in her chest at the thought.

"Stop it, Lizzy!" She directed her gaze to the lectern. Elizabeth was determined not to let the turmoil of the morning affect her worship. She would think on the changes her father would be making within the family—that should lighten her heart. Elizabeth bowed her head, but the words of the prayer were like distant drums beating an indistinct call.

Still, Elizabeth's mind would not stop mulling the events of the past eight days. Mr. Bingley had arrived in Hertfordshire on Michaelmas. He and his friends and family had been in residence only three days when they came to the assembly. During the next five days, Elizabeth had felt the height of pleasure at seeing Mr. Bingley's attention to her dearest sister. She glanced up and found Bingley's eyes staring in rapt attention to the woman sitting on Elizabeth's right side. How could she not smile at that devotion?

Elizabeth had also felt a depth of anger and hurt she was unaware resided in her heart. She had long prided herself on her strength of character. These interactions with Mr. Darcy had caused her to question her own disposition. Her eyes moved to Mr. Darcy only to find him staring back. *Was it in disapproval?* Then she perceived a slight smile.

Elizabeth looked at her hands twisting in her lap. *What does he mean by it?* She decided that the best means of protecting her heart was to ignore him. *Easier said than done.*

* * *

DARCY WAS ENTIRELY unaware of the turmoil in Elizabeth's mind. He only noticed what he assumed was reverence for her surroundings. It was a quality Elizabeth would share with Georgiana. *They have so much in common!* Darcy forgot to maintain his mask of studied indifference as he watched the second Miss Bennet. His mind was diverted from the sermon, and he realised his cousin sitting next to him was aware of his distraction.

"She is beautiful, is she not?" Richard had leaned over, whispering so only Darcy could hear— he thought.

"Lovely."

The rich baritone of Darcy's softened voice resonated so Caroline— who was seated to his right—heard. In response, she sat taller in her seat and leaned into his side. It was a bold move, but she felt he had invited it with his observation. He thought her lovely! Caroline smiled. *Eliza Bennet had only served to make herself look uncouth at tea.* Caroline wanted to laugh out loud at the irony. She had intended to lower Miss Elizabeth Bennet in Darcy's eyes and yet, seemingly Miss Elizabeth had done it to herself!

* * *

Colonel Richard Fitzwilliam, because of the responsibilities of his office, did not attend services regularly. Nevertheless, he admitted that had he been as diverted as he was on this occasion, he would, for a certainty, attend more often. He caught the eye of Miss Lucas and winked. He wanted to rub his hands together in anticipation of sharing his observations with her. The colonel longed to get her impressions and insight. If only the sermon would end.

In the pew in front of the Lucas family, he counted the six females sitting next to the man he assumed was Mr. Bennet. *Imagine a half a dozen females in one house!* It was no wonder the man rarely stirred from his bookroom. He pondered the lengths he himself would go to in pursuit of some long-lasting peace and quiet. Richard almost chuckled aloud. It was, however, a poor sort of humor.

Jane Bennet was the beauty that Bingley claimed her to be. Her ethereal blonde locks were popular with the *ton*, though they were not the colonel's preference. The middle Bennet daughter had her nose buried in the prayer book. *Was she in need of spectacles?* The two youngest were blatantly looking around the church to see who was looking back at them. Richard passed quickly from watching them as he did not want them to think he had any interest.

Even with her head bowed, Elizabeth radiated energy that drew Richard's attention, his curiosity, and his admiration. He understood what had captured Darcy. Again, the colonel considered how she was perfect for his cousin. Darcy would benefit from Elizabeth's zest for life.

Richard rarely thought of marriage as his present circumstances did not lend themselves to a felicitous union. On the rare occasions he had reflected on the possibility, he did not believe a spirited wife would suit him. Any woman he married would need calm intelligence and maturity. She must understand a man who had lived on his own, who had responsibilities towards others, and who would not expect a grand lifestyle. He would need a woman like... His eyes moved to Charlotte. He felt something like regret.

The colonel sat up straight on the wooden pew, pressing his shoulders back. He closed his eyes, inhaling deeply. Resolution poured through him like ale from a tap. He would not marry. He *could* not marry. The life of a soldier was hard on a woman. Richard had observed the tears as husbands parted from wives, not knowing whether they would ever return. He had vowed early in his career never to cause a woman he admired that sort of anguish. To him, marriage was the most reprehensible decision a military man could make.

* * *

DARCY'S FRUSTRATION was growing until it threatened to consume him. After the services concluded, Caroline would not leave his side, though he had tried to pass her off to her brother. Bingley paid no attention at all. Mrs. Bennet seemed to steer Miss Elizabeth away from Darcy every time he attempted to get close to her, Mr. Bennet looked at him mockingly each time he tried and failed, and Elizabeth did not look at him at all.

Desperate times called for desperate measures. As soon as Darcy handed Caroline into the carriage, he stepped back and closed the door.

"Mr. Darcy, where are you going?" Miss Bingley could not imagine him not wanting to return to Netherfield Park in her company.

Darcy walked to the back of his carriage and untied the horse he had brought along for just this purpose. He noted that his cousin had already collected his mount and was standing next to Sir William Lucas. Darcy then draped his mare's reins over the hitching post in the front of the church knowing she would put him through his paces after being tied up in such an inelegant manner. He was determined to speak with Miss Elizabeth Bennet.

When Elizabeth emerged from the church, Darcy bowed to her, smiling and murmured, "Miss Elizabeth." She was wearing a dark blue pelisse which made her eyes look like the sapphires his father had purchased for his mother from a merchant ship from Ceylon when they first married. The jewels were kept in his London safe for the next Mrs. Darcy. "Are you well?"

Elizabeth offered a polite smile, though it did not quite reach her eyes. "I am well, Mr. Darcy. You, sir? Are you well?"

"I thank you for asking, Miss Elizabeth. I am well."

Frustrated by their inane discourse, he continued, his words coming out in a rush. "I have requested my sister to come to Hertfordshire. Will you allow me, or do I ask too much, to introduce her to your acquaintance?"

Elizabeth cocked her head to the side as if puzzled. "I would be happy with an introduction, sir."

Darcy looked directly into her eyes. The warmth he had been drawn to like fire on a cold day was gone. *What had happened to her? Was she in distress?* He had to know. He realised she was either upset with him or uncomfortable—and he had no idea why that was so. When she left Netherfield Park after tea she *had* smiled at him.

Elizabeth dropped her shoulders and released her breath in a huff.

She lowered her eyes to the ground, closing them briefly. She shook her head slightly.

As she took a step past him, he turned to walk beside her. Elizabeth decided to be blunt so he would leave her alone. "I am particularly curious, sir, when you were going to inform the neighbourhood of your engagement?"

"Engagement?" *Good heavens! Did she think he had an arrangement with Miss Bingley?* He shuddered. "Miss Elizabeth, I have no idea of what you are saying. I am not, nor have I ever been engaged."

"Is that so?" Sarcasm dripped from her voice. "Would Miss de Bourgh have the same response to my question, sir?"

"Anne?" Darcy was utterly confused. His eyes went to Richard, the only possible person who knew Lady Catherine's misguided hopes. She had long promoted a match between him and her daughter. Other than his cousin, no one else in Hertfordshire could possibly know. *Why had Richard talked to her about such a thing? Darcy* was going to wring his neck when they were alone.

"So, her name is Anne?" Elizabeth felt the knife pricking her heart plunge ever deeper. "Your familiar use of her Christian name belies your claim, does it not?" With that, she straightened her shoulders and climbed into the family carriage without looking back.

"Miss Elizabeth!" Darcy called after her in a futile attempt to stop her. He moved to untie his horse and follow when he felt a restraining hand on his arm.

"Do not." It was Mr. Bennet, and from the look in his eye, he was resolute.

Elizabeth refused to glance his way.

Darcy wanted to hit something, though he knew he would not. *How had things gone awry?*

CHAPTER 10

*N*etherfield Park

"Pistols or swords, Richard?" Darcy was enraged. "Choose your second. Hurst or Bingley?" He had waited hours for his unsuspecting cousin to return from Lucas Lodge. He could not begin to reason out why Richard had spoken without restraint. It was unlike him.

Richard's visit to Miss Lucas' home had been pleasant. In hushed tones they had repeated conversations and shared their impressions. Her insight had given him much to think on. He was happy to count her as a friend. Darcy's anger, after such a wonderful encounter, was completely unexpected and unappreciated. "Do be serious, Darcy." Richard put both hands up, his palms facing his cousin. He did not want to fight Darcy. They had not settled a difference with fisticuffs since their adolescent years!

Richard stood his ground. "In what manner do you believe I have wronged you?"

Darcy stood as stiff as a board; his large hands fisted at his sides.

"Miss Elizabeth was curious *when* I would let the good people of Meryton know I was off the marriage market."

"You proposed?" Richard was stunned. *Wait until he told Miss Lucas!*

"You offered for Miss Elizabeth?" The colonel paused in thought, pondering why Darcy was so livid. "I would think it a fair question then. Have you not spoken to her father? Is that what is holding you back?"

Darcy was unable to keep his voice down. In three strides he was nose-to-nose with his cousin. His words were clipped. "As I told Miss Elizabeth, I am *not* engaged!"

"You are not?" Richard shook his head. "Then, in heaven's name, why does she believe you to be betrothed?"

"Because, Richard, you told her I was to marry Anne." Darcy had leaned in even closer. Without thought, the colonel took a step back.

"Cousin Anne? Anne de Bourgh?" Richard brought his hand up to smooth the hair from his brow. "How on earth did Miss Elizabeth hear about our cousin in Kent? And why would she believe you were to marry? It makes no sense, Darcy." Richard shook his head in disbelief. "And why would you think I would speak of something so untrue to a young woman who is nearly a stranger to me? Darcy!"

For the first time since he stood in front of the church, Darcy began to doubt himself. Without realising it, he ran his hand through his hair in a mirror image of what his cousin had just done. "I do not know."

"Think, Darcy. This sounds like Lady Catherine speaking."

"But, how?" Darcy walked back to the fireplace while Richard went to Bingley's brandy and poured two glasses. "How did she know of Anne? I cannot imagine Miss Bingley saying anything to Miss Elizabeth. She has never been to Rosings. Neither has she been introduced to either Anne or Lady Catherine. She is the only one interested in driving Miss Elizabeth away, yet she could not know anything of our aunt's desires."

"But somebody does—someone who has access to the Bennets." Like Darcy, Richard enjoyed strategy, moving players until they were in their proper position. Something was out of alignment. He looked up at his cousin. "There is only one way you will know for certain, my friend. You will need to ask the lady."

The matter had appeared cut and dried before Richard walked into the room. Now, the field was muddy. Darcy looked at the mantle clock, and he had enough daylight left to ride to Longbourn and back.

"A moment, if you please." Richard's plea stopped him in his tracks, though he was now impatient to be on his way. "This is a good time to mention a decided lack in your conduct, Darcy."

"What?" It was the last thing he expected to hear from his cousin. "I was raised a gentleman where honour and duty pulse through my blood. Are you implying I am less than what I should be?" Darcy could feel his anger surging into his chest. Blowing air out his nostrils like a recalcitrant bull, he stood his ground.

Richard chuckled, but it was not a happy sound. He slowly lifted his brow until he had his cousin's full attention. "Mighty arrogant of you to say so, Darcy. Have you already forgotten your insult to Miss Elizabeth?"

"Of course, I have not." Darcy stood firm. "Since that night I have striven to make reparation to Miss Elizabeth. If this is the matter you are thinking to castigate me, you had best refrain. If there is another matter where you find me lacking, tell me now."

Neither cousin would break eye contact.

"Just speak, Richard. I am in a hurry."

Richard admired his cousin. There was not one other man of his acquaintance who could have stepped into George Darcy's shoes with such alacrity. Like his father before him, Darcy was unbending with high expectations for himself.

"When are you going to tell Lady Catherine that you will not marry Anne? It is not fair to her, Darce. Anne has waited patiently for five years for you to do your duty, and now she has no other options. And what of Miss Bingley? When will you tell her there is no hope? For as long as we have known her, she has made her preferences known—so do not say you are unaware. You leave these women dangling. It is badly done, Darcy. Badly done."

Darcy was stunned. But...Richard was right—every single word rang true. Darcy backed up until the back of his legs hit a chair, and he sank down into its comforting cushions.

He knew not what to say. Until arriving in Hertfordshire, he had been confident in the correctness of his actions and attitude. Every day he was learning unpalatable truths about himself. That he should act deplorably towards these women was unconscionable. No matter that he had no respect for either Lady Catherine or Miss Bingley, his refusal to speak up had consequences for others. These were not the actions of a gentleman. Shame washed over him. He knew what must be done. Standing, he walked back to his cousin. "I thank you, Richard."

No apology was uttered as he walked out of the library. None was expected. It was the way of men.

* * *

LONGBOURN

The din around the table at the noon meal was deafening. Mrs. Bennet, Kitty, and Lydia spoke at once.

"But, Mr. Bennet, our daughters will never find husbands..."

"But Papa. The militia are coming."

"Officers!"

Mary Bennet felt only relief. She was not of a sociable nature and despised being out in society. Her father's declaration that the two younger girls were to remain home and no longer participate in public assemblies pleased her greatly. Mary had been given the gift of choice. Her father had left it to her discretion whether she wanted to participate in gatherings.

Elizabeth and Jane were pleasantly surprised. It lightened Elizabeth's heart to know that *finally* her beloved Papa would put his family ahead of his own desires.

"But Mr. Bennet! When you are gone, we will be thrown out into the hedgerows—by your heir—before you are even cold in the ground. Unless at least one of our daughters marries well, we will be destitute."

"Mrs. Bennet!" In Elizabeth's recollection, her father had never raised his voice to his wife. The babble stopped instantly. In a much calmer tone, he continued. "With the distraction of the youngest girls out of the

89

way, you may focus your attention on finding mates for our eldest daughters. The more the Bennets are represented by proper conduct, the more elevated the gentlemen will be who come calling. This will benefit not only the older girls but the younger ones as well. They will be exposed to the sphere of society you long to reach, my dear."

Elizabeth shook her head at his reasoning. *How so?* Meryton society was Meryton society. With the exception of the Netherfield party, there was a small chance they would meet anyone from an elevated rank. Nevertheless, Elizabeth had to give her father credit as his arguments worked. Mrs. Bennet turned her focus to procuring a new gown for Jane before the next meeting with Mr. Bingley. Jane's cheeks blushed.

Elizabeth was restless, and there was only one thing for it—she needed to be out of doors. Grabbing her heavy coat, she left Longbourn behind. As Mary would say, "Reflection was the order of the day."

The fields were grassy and rimmed by trees naked of their summer foliage. The air carried a dampness that, when added to the chill of the day, seeped into her bones. Elizabeth resolved a brisk walk was the perfect cure to warm her blood.

Near the fence between Longbourn and Netherfield Park was a stone folly which had been built generations past. Designed by an architect with an apparent love of the Greek style, it was constructed by a stone mason who took pride in laying each brick into place. Over the years it had changed the colour from a light grey to a deep charcoal. In the center was a circular bench where a young girl with a vivid imagination could daydream of gods and goddesses, lords and ladies, and kings and queens.

The stone was cold, and Elizabeth was grateful for the thickness of her wool coat. Sitting in her favourite spot, she heard the hooves of a powerful horse. Seeing the tall form riding with ease, his greatcoat black against the dreary sky, Elizabeth recognised Mr. Darcy. After their abbreviated conversation that morning, she doubted he would stop.

He did.

"Miss Elizabeth." He bowed to her after dismounting from the mare. With the reins in hand, he put one foot on the bottom step, but came no further, not knowing whether his presence would be welcome. However, he was determined to find clarity from the morning's conversation.

"Mr. Darcy." She stood, waiting for him to make the next move. After experiencing her impertinence when she encountered him outside the church, Elizabeth doubted he would stay.

"May I?" Darcy motioned to the bench next to where she had been seated.

Sighing, Elizabeth said, "You may." Her hesitation was in not having shown herself to an advantage earlier that day. She had been embarrassed by her own conduct. She sat back down and waited for him to secure his horse. His approach was slow and measured, as if he was trying to think of his exact words before he arrived.

Darcy was unskilled in parlour conversation and lacked the finesse of his cousin Richard.

"Do you have family in Kent, Miss Elizabeth?"

To her it was an odd start to the conversation. Not having any idea what thread he was weaving, she answered succinctly. "My father's cousin, Mr. Collins, has the living at Hunsford Parsonage in Kent. Do you know him, sir?"

"We have not met, Miss Elizabeth, though I know of him from my aunt." In one short sentence the matter was revealed in full to Darcy. William Collins was the newly appointed parson to Lady Catherine's parish. Even though they had not been introduced, Darcy knew the type of man his aunt preferred to dispense spiritual advice to those under her care. He would be a self-righteous sycophant whose only purpose was to ingratiate himself with his patroness, following her every command.

"Mr. Darcy, though you have every reason to believe otherwise, I despise gossip." Elizabeth huffed out her breath. "Over the years, I have seen the damage one small piece of misinformation can do to a stellar reputation. Therefore, I pray you forgive me for speaking of something wholly unrelated to me—again, sir."

Darcy shuffled through his memory to recall an earlier apology. It was when they met in the field. However, his own error pushed her words of regret deep into the vaults of his recollections.

"We are of the same opinion, I believe, Miss Elizabeth. Nonetheless, I have also observed there is often a measure of truth to the tales being told—enough to make it acceptable to the listener."

Elizabeth questioned the response from her heart. At his words, the beats came faster and harder, threatening to jump from her chest. It was the same feeling when someone or something frightened her. *Why did she fear what he might disclose?* "So, the small element of truth in the information Mr. Collins wrote in his letter would be...?" She could not look at him, nor could she complete her bold question. Though it was not her concern, she held her breath until he answered, not wanting to miss one syllable.

"My aunt has long desired a marriage between her daughter, Anne, and me. Lady Catherine claims it was the wish of my parents that Pemberley and her estate, Rosings Park, be united, yet I cannot recall either of my parents mentioning it to me. Had it been their will, they would have made it known." Darcy removed his beaver and tapped it with his hands, finally settling it on his knees. They were seated next to each other on the bench, both staring straight ahead. "The fault for this misinformation is mine."

"How can that be, sir?" Elizabeth finally looked sideways at him, knowing the blame was hers, not his. That he would take responsibility caused her to realise she had misjudged him yet again.

"My cousin reminded me that I have let this go too long, Miss Elizabeth. The first time this marriage was mentioned to me by Lady Catherine was the spring after I lost my beloved father. At that time, I had much responsibility pulling at me and had no inclination or time to ponder taking a wife. Therefore, I politely rebutted her blatant insistence on a match between Anne and myself. As the demands persisted, I tired of repeating myself over and over, so I stopped. Since then, each time my aunt has commanded I bend to her purpose and acquiesce to her will, I have disregarded her comments without reply." Darcy stood and walked two paces away, his back to her. "Please accept my apologies for shirking my duties, which led to our present difficulties and confusion. I am not engaged to marry my cousin, Anne de Bourgh, nor will I ever be."

Elizabeth could not prevent the emotion that burst from her. "You take too much upon yourself, sir." At that, he turned. "Whether the information was true or not, *I* had no business propagating the story, even if only to you. I am appalled at my own bad behaviour."

"Pray, do not feel that way." Darcy sat back down beside her. "No matter the direction from which you look at this situation; it will always come back to my poor decision as the source."

Elizabeth slowly shook her head. "Mr. Darcy, I have hardly known myself this past week." When he started to speak, she raised her hand to stop him. "Please, allow me, sir." At his nod, she continued. "My father has long favoured me above my sisters. I allowed his kindness and his words to influence my opinion of my own character. I considered myself to be the most sensible of all the Bennet females."

This time it was Elizabeth who stood and walked away, though she did face him before she spoke again.

"I condemned you after the Meryton assembly for your arrogance and disdain for others. Nevertheless, did I not exhibit those same qualities in my opinion of you, sir? Hardly sensible at all!" Elizabeth took one step closer to him. "Only to you will I admit that I still feel the sting of your words from that night. Yes, I have endeavoured to forgive and forget, though my mind keeps each word intact and easily retrieved." She took one more step towards the man who had turned her world upside down. "I am sorely in need of improvement. I find I do not like myself much at all, Mr. Darcy."

"But I like you!" was Darcy's quick response. He was shocked at the words which had escaped from his mouth. Once spoken aloud, though, they danced around them both like the ballet of butterfly wings moving in harmony. There was a freedom in having his feelings in the open.

Darcy was not the only one surprised. Elizabeth's eyes widened as a blush started the journey from her neck to her cheeks.

"I do not mean to make you uncomfortable, Miss Elizabeth." Darcy stood again, this time twisting his hat around and around. "Because I have been busy with estate matters and caring for my sister, I find I am left with little experience with how to speak around a lady I admire. When I am not in your company, I think of all the things I wish I had said. This is novel for me. I have not had a woman friend before."

"We are not unalike in this, sir." Elizabeth walked over to stand in front of him. "My life in Hertfordshire has not put me in company with many gentlemen other than the ones I grew up knowing. I find my own experience for having this sort of association is as limited as yours."

At the same time, they both walked back to the bench and sat, each still looking forward.

The idea of having a "friendship" appealed to Darcy. Unbeknownst to him, it appealed to Elizabeth as well.

"Miss Elizabeth, when the colonel spoke to me about my neglect in setting things straight, it was painful to realise how far I had fallen short of how I was raised. However, because I value my cousin highly, his words—though they were not what I desired to hear—will do nothing to damage the camaraderie between him and myself." He glanced over at her. "When he sees that I have accepted his counsel and acted upon it, he will know that I value him." He hesitated before he continued. "Miss Elizabeth, to be friends, we need to act in the same manner with each other. We should not hesitate to express concerns, even if they should cause a sting, as you mentioned earlier."

"I see the wisdom of your counsel, Mr. Darcy." She smiled. "It is the same way with my sisters. There are many disagreements—almost daily—yet even though we freely express our displeasure with each other—with the exception of Jane, of course, as she could do nothing to displease any soul—we love each other dearly."

Darcy's breath quickened. *She speaks of love!* If it was not unmanly, he would have sighed.

CHAPTER 11

*F*riday, 11 October 1811
Longbourn

During the whole of the next week, the Bingleys, Darcy, and the colonel spent much time with the two eldest Bennets and their parents. Charlotte Lucas was almost always included. Overall, it was a merry bunch.

As soon as they arrived in each other's houses, Bingley quickly moved to Miss Bennet like a magnet drawn to iron. If Miss Lucas was visiting, the colonel would seek her out, and they would immediately put their heads together in conversation. Darcy would wander towards Miss Elizabeth.

Mrs. Bennet caught Elizabeth as she entered the drawing room to welcome the guests when they arrived.

"Lizzy, you are doing a fine deed by your sister."

"How is that, Mama?"

"By keeping that abominable Mr. Darcy occupied, you are allowing Mr. Bingley to concentrate on your sister." Mrs. Bennet patted her daughter on the shoulder. "Oh, I know what you are up to, Lizzy. You cannot fool me."

"Mama, I…"

Mrs. Bennet tapped her daughter lightly on the chin. "No, you cannot fool me." She walked to the entrance hall to make sure all was ready for their guests. Mrs. Bennet had to admit that it was much less work to have only Jane and Elizabeth to fuss over. *Possibly Mr. Bennet was in the right after all! How peculiar!*

Although frustrated that she had not been allowed to explain the change in her relationship with Mr. Darcy to her mother, Elizabeth's wisdom and experience indicated it was best not to try. Her mother had already drawn her own conclusion about the matter, and her propensity to hang onto her opinions, even if they erred, was legendary. *Oh my heavens! I am my mother!*

Dazed, Elizabeth walked into the drawing room and dropped into the nearest chair.

"Lizzy, are you well?" Jane noted the bemused, pained expression on her sister's face and rushed to her aid.

"I hardly know." Elizabeth shook her head slowly. *How could she have been so blind? And so judgmental of faults when hers were the very ones she disdained in others?* It was humbling to realise she was not just the product of her father but her mother as well.

"They are here, Lizzy." Mrs. Bennet felt the light coming in from the south window was complimentary to her eldest daughter's complexion and seated Jane there each time there was a possibility of visitors. It gave her a perfect view of the driveway. "Oh, Lizzy, it appears that all of the Netherfield party have arrived."

This was most unexpected. The Bennets had not been in company with Miss Bingley and the Hursts since church the Sunday prior. Something quite extraordinary must have stirred the women from their nests. When Mr. Darcy and Colonel Fitzwilliam reached back to assist a young lady from the carriage, the reason was clear. Miss Georgiana Darcy had arrived.

Once the group was inside and introductions had been performed, Miss Bingley moved close to Miss Darcy and bent her head to whisper her opinions of the room's occupants.

"Do not be distressed, dear Georgiana. We shall bear this company for a short while." Caroline's eyes were riveted on Elizabeth as she spoke. To no one in particular, she said, "It appears not all the Bennet girls are here. They tend to add a certain liveliness to the occasion."

"Caroline?" Bingley gazed directly at his sister and lifted one cautioning brow. He immediately turned to Jane to see whether she was affected by his sister's arrogance. Jane's head was bowed, and her face flushed.

Darcy was appalled. It had been his purpose in inviting Georgiana to expose her to Elizabeth's liveliness and warmth. He wanted to rip off his cravat and stuff it in Caroline Bingley's mouth. Discomfort radiated from his sister as Darcy pondered his move. He glanced at his cousin in time to see him reach for a sword that was not there.

Elizabeth stood and walked to Georgiana.

"Pardon me, Miss Darcy." She smiled as Georgiana finally raised her head. She was a lovely girl. "I was hoping to request a favour of you."

"Me?" There was no other word that came to Elizabeth's mind when looking at the young girl's eyes but limpid. A clear blue, framed with long black lashes, they were stunning in a face with much softer angles than her brother's. Georgiana's hand moved to her chest —uncertain.

Elizabeth laughed softly. "Yes, Miss Darcy, you." She offered her hand to Georgiana. "I have an interest in geography, in particular the northern portion of England. I have never been, though I have longed to visit the Lake District and the Peaks. Have you been?"

"Well, of course, she has been, Miss Elizabeth." Caroline Bingley's voice was filled with exasperation. "Pemberley is in Derbyshire, after all."

Ignoring Miss Bingley, Elizabeth continued, her tone steady and inviting. "Miss Darcy, would you be willing to show me the area of your home on my father's map? I believe it would give me a better sense of where you are from."

Georgiana almost bounced from the settee, taking Elizabeth's hand as she stood. At nearly sixteen years, she was alert to the attentions unmarried ladies paid her, like Miss Bingley. It was rare to have someone give her notice without also seeking that of her brother's. As far as Georgiana could tell, Elizabeth had not looked at her brother once.

Elizabeth tucked her hand in Georgiana's arm and walked her to the far wall where a framed map of the British Isles hung. It was cartographer Louis Brion de la Tour's 1783 version which was a particular favourite of Mr. Bennet's. The contention between him and his wife at his desire for its presence in the drawing room had been fierce. However, his will had won out. There simply was no more room available on the library walls for more. Elizabeth appreciated its presence on this occasion.

Once London and then Hertfordshire were found, Elizabeth slowly moved her finger towards the north of the country. Turning to face the younger girl she kept her finger heading up the glass-covered parchment. She watched as Georgiana became more excited the higher her hand rose. Deciding to have a bit of fun, Elizabeth moved the direction slightly to the west. Then she moved it slightly more. When her finger hit the northeast shore of Ireland, Elizabeth was pleased to see a slight lift to the corner of Miss Darcy's mouth.

Mr. Darcy walked up behind them. "Hmmm." Feigning a serious mien, he said, "As many times as we have travelled between Pemberley and London, I do not recall crossing the sea. Do you, Georgiana?"

Both ladies giggled, putting their hands over their mouths to fruitlessly hold in their mirth.

Darcy leaned forward between the two and placed his finger directly at the point in Derbyshire where his estate was located. "It is there, Miss Elizabeth. Sister."

Georgiana's radiant smile delighted him. Though she was naturally quiet, she had been a happy child. Until Ramsgate. Until Wickham. Darcy forced any thought of that despicable man from his mind. Today was a day for pleasure, not bad memories.

The Darcys closely observed Elizabeth as she studied the map.

"Pardon me. Are you looking for somewhere particular?" Darcy assumed, from its location, that she would be familiar with the map.

"Miss Darcy, here is a name I am familiar with which appears to be quite close to your home."

Georgiana moved closer to the map. "Which name, Miss Elizabeth?"

"Lambton. Do you know it?"

Yes, the small town was only five miles from Pemberley! Many of the staff had family who lived in Lambton. Because it held no attractions for visitors, it seemed odd that the village was the one Elizabeth mentioned.

"I do."

Darcy looked at his sister in anticipation of her adding more, however, her natural timidity kept her from doing so. When the silence continued, his curiosity got the better of him. "How do you know of Lambton, Miss Elizabeth?"

"It is where my aunt grew up. She has fond memories of traipsing through the woods and visiting the streams and rivers in the summer." Elizabeth put her finger to her chin, recalling past conversations with Madeline Gardiner. "In fact, she mentioned a great house in the area. I am wondering whether she was referring to Pemberley."

The Darcys looked at one another with a smile. There were few estates in England as large and well-positioned as Pemberley. It was the grandest in the county.

"I would imagine so." Pride laced Darcy's voice. "Do you know your aunt's name prior to her marriage?"

"Clark. Are you familiar with Miss Madeline Clark?" Elizabeth knew they ran in completely different spheres. Her aunt had been the daughter of a bookseller before marrying Mr. Edward Gardiner, her mother's younger brother. The Darcys were landed gentry with ties to the peerage.

Elizabeth was surprised to see Darcy check his cousin before replying. Still the colonel moved closer to the threesome.

Darcy cleared his throat before answering. "Yes, Miss Elizabeth. Miss Clark is known to me."

"Miss Clark? Miss Madeline Clark?" The colonel was intrigued.

"Who is Miss Clark, Brother?" The reactions of both men raised the curiosity in both ladies. "How did you come to know her?"

"Yes, Cousin, I would deeply appreciate being reminded of how you came to know her." The colonel rocked back on his heels, grinning from ear to ear.

Before he could stop himself, Darcy ran his hands through his hair. He wanted to ring his cousin's neck—a feeling he suffered quite regularly of late. Darcy noted the anticipation on Georgiana's face and closed his eyes, sighing.

Seeing he had the attention of the whole room, he released his breath and began his tale. Richard would pay later.

"It was summer, twenty years past, when Richard and his older brother were visiting Pemberley. Derbyshire summers are normally not as warm as they are in Hertfordshire. That August the sun was blistering hot. Whilst our parents relaxed in the coolness of the pavilion in the shade of the trees on the south lawn, the three of us boys, along with a childhood companion, decided to swim in the river to cool off."

"Of the four of us, I was the youngest and the smallest. I was desperate to prove I was as strong as the others. In addition, I longed to be as honourable as my father." He paused. "We came upon your aunt, a young woman of eight and ten in some distress." Darcy considered how much to mention in mixed company. Miss Clark's clothes had been torn, and it was his first sight of a woman's bare feet. "Apparently, she had tripped over an obstacle on the trail and twisted her ankle. All of us young boys thought Miss Clark the most beautiful woman and felt incumbent on being of service."

Elizabeth smiled in delight. "It was you? You were the boy who offered to carry her home?"

Darcy blushed. "I was."

"But, Brother, it is five miles from Pemberley Woods to Lambton, and you were but eight years old!"

"Yes, Georgiana, I am aware." Everyone laughed. The tops of his ears turned bright red. "I had hoped your aunt would keep the tale to herself."

Elizabeth was touched by the thought of this chivalrous little boy. "Rest assured, Mr. Darcy, that my aunt took your offer most seriously. She told us that story as one of her most cherished memories."

Even Mrs. Bennet had been impressed with the story when she first heard it from Madeline.

"Mr. Darcy, is it true you brought a white horse to carry her home?" Mrs. Bennet may have been the fiercest of matchmakers for her daughters in her own interest, but she was also a romantic at heart. "Imagine that!"

Elizabeth continued. "My aunt called you her knight, sir."

The colonel added, "We called Darcy 'Sir Knight' until he grew into his height. Now, we only call him that out of his hearing."

"Thank you for that, Richard." Darcy could not recall when his chagrin was so acute. He wished the tale unshared, until he looked at the faces of the women. Even Miss Bingley had a bemused expression on her face.

Elizabeth's eyes were wistful and bright. Had he known the story would have had this effect, he would have told her the first night they had met. *If only he had instead of the insult.*

Surprisingly Georgiana spoke to the attention of all in the room. "Mr. Clark keeps a tin of sweet peppermint candies under the counter, Miss Elizabeth. When I was young... I mean, when I was *younger*, I would beg my father or William to take me to the bookshop. Mr. Clark always managed to secretly give me one piece of candy which I would tuck in my mouth to suck on slowly." At her brother's chuckle, she admitted, "I imagine it was not really a secret, was it? The candy was fairly large, and I would have a lump in my cheek, would I not?"

They all laughed with Miss Darcy.

"Miss Darcy," Caroline chirped from her position on the settee. Had she realised her voice was as shrill as Mrs. Bennet's, she would have been horrified. Unaware, she continued, "I am certain you would not do the same now that you have grown into an accomplished young woman. It would be beyond you to ever do anything improper to call attention to yourself." Caroline looked directly at Elizabeth. "That would be left for those who were not raised and instructed as you were."

The cut was meant for the second Bennet daughter. However,

Caroline's words reminded Georgiana Darcy that she was not above reproach. Georgiana's guilt over her misjudgment with George Wickham was yet a fresh wound. In a moment, her joy of the afternoon diminished. Should a hint of the Ramsgate incident become public, it would ruin Georgiana's prospects and bring shame on the Darcy name. The Darcys and the colonel felt they were always walking a narrow ledge to potential disaster.

The change in their mood felt as if a brisk wind had snuck into the room. Elizabeth, though curious to its cause, rushed to bring Miss Darcy relief, for the men were reacting to her changed mood.

"Miss Darcy, do you enjoy riding?"

Georgiana did not raise her head and mumbled to the floor. "I have in the past loved to race over the fields at Pemberley. I rarely ride in London."

Mrs. Bennet and Jane were curious. They knew Elizabeth's fear of horses well. Even Mr. Darcy had witnessed Elizabeth's hesitation around his mare, though he realised any intelligent being would treat Katherina the same.

"To tell the truth, Miss Darcy, I am afraid of the beasts. I prefer walking on my two legs rather than riding on the four of theirs." Elizabeth spied a small smile beginning to appear at Georgiana's mouth. "Nonetheless, during the past few days I have been attempting to compose an ode to an unseated rider. I am unfamiliar with equestrian terms and thought you may be able to assist me."

Colonel Fitzwilliam saw the flame in Darcy's face and knew his conjecture as to the mud-covered clothing was proven true. Miss Elizabeth *had* witnessed the rare event of his falling off that miserable mare. Richard could not contain his laughter. *Oh, this was too good!* He could not wait to reveal all to Miss Lucas.

* * *

NETHERFIELD PARK

Later that night, Darcy had anticipated that his sister needed a break from the fawning attentions of Miss Bingley and Mrs. Hurst and invited Georgiana into the library for some privacy. Richard was still visiting the Lucas family, so they were alone.

"Georgiana, what do you think of Hertfordshire?" What he wanted to ask was how she viewed Elizabeth. *Did she find her as appealing as he did?*

"I have already found much pleasure here, William." The cushions of the oversized chair invited relaxation, and Georgiana sighed as she kicked off her slippers, tucking her feet under her. "The Miss Bennets are very different, are they not? Miss Bennet is quiet and reticent—a bit like me, I believe."

Darcy nodded his head in agreement. When she did not continue, he pressed. "And Miss Elizabeth? What is your opinion of that particular Bennet lady?"

"Oh, William." Georgiana smiled at him. "I like her very much. She is kind. And her laughter comes easily." The Bennets were not of the first circles and the expectations of the Fitzwilliams, her mother's family, was that her brother would seek a wife from the highest level of society, thus, the interest her brother was showing such a woman surprised her. Longbourn was a small estate and the family was unheard of in their sphere. However, Elizabeth had made her brother laugh, and Georgiana could not recall the last time he had done so in company.

"She does not seem intimidated by you, Brother."

Darcy snorted, scoffing at her remark. "Intimidated? Not hardly." Then he smiled. "Sister, dear, my position, my wealth, and my property mean nothing to her. From the first moment I noticed Miss Elizabeth, I knew she would not be a woman easily won." He bowed his head in shame, looking away from his sister into the flames of the fireplace. "I behaved abominably, Georgiana. Without thinking, I said horrid things which offended her greatly and made me look mean-spirited."

She started to defend him as he had only ever shown her kindness. "No, Sister, I speak the truth." He walked back and sat in the chair facing her. "I am only now beginning to repair the damage my words caused."

"I find that hard to believe of you."

He looked up at his sister and sighed. "Thank you for that, dearest."

"Then we will work together, Brother. She shall see the good man you truly are, and by the time we are gone from Hertfordshire, I may have a new friend. A true friend."

They were both surprised when the door to the library burst open. In strode the colonel, his face and countenance cloaked in anger. His words brought trepidation to them all.

"Wickham is here."

CHAPTER 12

Saturday, 12 October 1811
Meryton

Elizabeth sat on the wooden bench outside the bookshop waiting for Mr. Hill, Longbourn's longtime jack-of-all-trades, to return with the wagon containing the kitchen supplies. Typically, spending time in Meryton's variety of shops was a pleasant occupation, satisfying her curiosity of what might be new since the last time she strolled through the village. When her father had requested that she pick up his latest order of books, Elizabeth was pleased to make the one-mile journey with Mr. Hill. However, she knew Mr. Hill would be impatient should she make him wait—he knew her propensity to lose track of time in the bookshop. Hence, the bench.

The small town was quiet for a Saturday morning. It was early yet, so few people were on the footpaths bordering the main thoroughfare. The militia had arrived, and she would see small groups of officers walking in and out of the shops. As a whole, the men seemed to avoid the bookshop. Elizabeth chuckled to herself as she endeavoured not to be judgmental. A slight breeze had picked up in the minutes she had been seated outside, and bits and pieces of conversation floated her way.

She had a choice. Propriety demanded she not eavesdrop on the two men standing just around the corner from her. However, the mention of a particular young lady of gentle birth by an unrecognisable male voice caught her attention. Chills moved up her arms as one word added to the next. She leaned closer to the conversation.

"I never should have listened to you, Denny. The militia is not for me. We have been here a day and night, and I have yet to have a pretty face giving me the welcome I deserve. Had her brother not intervened, I would have been set for life as the husband of Georgiana Darcy. I had thirty thousand reasons for making her my wife." The man's frustration could be heard in his tone. "Meryton is not Ramsgate or Pemberley. I regret enlisting already."

"Wickham, you have been a lieutenant for less than one se'nnight. The life is not so bad," replied the second man. "Besides, what makes you think the sister of a gentleman would welcome your attentions?"

"Because Denny, I was raised as the godson of Mr. Darcy. I was good as family. I deserve the life of a gentleman because I was raised to be one. This life" —his voice became laced with derision— "is not for me. Make my excuses to Colonel Forster. I am off to find Georgiana to claim her for my own—her and her dowry."

Their footsteps could be heard clearly as they tromped through the fallen leaves on the pathway to the back of the bookshop. Before she could decide what to do, she heard the creaking of leather harnesses and wagon wheels as Mr. Hill guided the horses to a stop in front of Elizabeth.

She peered down the alley as she walked to the edge of the footpath and saw the backs of two officers dressed in red. The one was a tall man with a blond queue. The other was short and stocky with brown hair. Elizabeth watched them until she could see them no more, determined to impress any information she could into her memory. Climbing up into the wagon, she wished Mr. Hill to move faster to no avail. By the time she arrived at Longbourn, though, she knew her course of action.

Mr. Thomas Bennet was already regretting his decision to restrict Kitty and Lydia to the house. They showed no interest in any occupation he recommended. Neither did his wife. Yet, for the first time in their four and twenty years of marriage, the couple appeared to be working together towards a common goal.

Thus, when Elizabeth related the details of the overheard conversation and slander against Miss Darcy, he took it more seriously than he might have before. He knew how such speech could affect the good name of his daughters should it be bandied about. He shuddered to realise how uncontrolled Lydia was and how Kitty followed the lead of his youngest child.

"Write it down, Lizzy, all of it." Mr. Bennet moved from the back of the desk and invited his daughter to sit. He paced the small confines of his study while she wrote. As she finished the page, he sanded and folded it. When the missive was complete, he dripped hot wax to seal the document and impressed the Bennet family crest on the back of the letter.

She had carefully crafted the missive. It was not her opinion of the conversation which mattered, only the actual words spoken and as succinct a description of the men as she could recall. *Poor Miss Darcy!* If this information was made public, it would destroy the young girl. What a brutal reminder of how fragile a young lady's reputation truly was in society.

Her father had called for his horse. He walked out and left her in the study without a word. There needed to be no warning; no caution to keep the shocking tale to themselves. Elizabeth's report of the conversation between two officers added weight to his decision to protect his youngest from themselves by keeping them home.

Elizabeth prayed her father would not be too late, and Mr. Darcy and Colonel Fitzwilliam would be able to protect Miss Darcy.

* * *

NETHERFIELD PARK

"Mr. Darcy, if you please." Mr. Bennet handed his hat, coat, and gloves to Bingley's butler. He was directed to the front drawing room to wait. It was not long before the man returned indicating he should follow him down the great hallway.

Darcy and the colonel had met Mr. Bennet on one of their visits to Longbourn, however neither knew the gentleman beyond the intro-duction. Like Darcy, Mr. Bennet isolated himself during social gather-ings. Thus, it was a surprise when they received him in Bingley's study. Since Colonel Fitzwilliam had spotted Wickham the night before, the men had been closeted in the room, reviewing the plan of action to protect their ward. Georgiana was confined to Netherfield until they left in the morning. The cousins had spent the morning debating whether to send Georgiana to London or Pemberley. They both had strong opinions about what it would take to protect her and who had the priority in seeing to Wickham's immediate future.

Darcy got straight to the point when Mr. Bennet politely refused an offer of refreshment or a seat. "Mr. Bennet, how may we help you?"

Without a word, Thomas Bennet took the letter from his pocket and handed it to Darcy.

Fitzwilliam Darcy recognised that a woman's hand had written the letter. *Elizabeth?* His imagination took flight. Had they been seen together at the folly? If her father was delivering the missive by hand, it could only be bad news.

He read quickly and passed the letter to the colonel. "Dear lord." His heart was pounding so hard he was surprised the other men could not hear it. Turning from both gentlemen, he walked to the fireplace and roughly kicked the burning log to the back of the brick enclosure. *He hated Wickham!* Sparks flew to the hearth. "Blast and damnation!"

Richard looked up at Mr. Bennet. "You are aware of the contents, sir?"

"I am." Mr. Bennet could see the anger simmering in both men. "Pray be aware, gentlemen, that no one in my household other than Lizzy was witness to this. You can depend on her silence."

"Of that, we have no doubt." The colonel's voice was calm, and he seemed unaffected. Yet, it took only a glance at his face to see the fierce determination in his eyes.

"Darcy?" The colonel was not surprised when his cousin spun to face him. There was no resignation, no sorrow. His eyes were equally as determined.

"Do what you must, Richard. I will not interfere this time."

Without taking his leave, the colonel moved quickly out of the room and called for his horse to be saddled as he ran up the stairs. He gave no consideration to Miss Bingley as she tried to garner his attention as he rushed by her. He spent no time in worrying about his young cousin as he was confident Darcy would take care of her. For him, his attentions were all for Wickham. Only when he had the necessities crammed into his leather saddlebag, did he spare a thought for all he wanted to share with Miss Lucas. He exhaled quickly through his teeth. The whistle bounced off each wall in his bedchamber.

* * *

MR. DARCY HAD NOT the words to express his appreciation for Miss Elizabeth's actions. Her quick thinking allowed them to take necessary action to stanch the gossip. He knew Richard would ride to Colonel Forster and confront Denny before he chased after Wickham. Richard had the freedom to draw on all of Darcy's resources to isolate the two men so they would never be able to blacken the Darcy name. Ever.

"Mr. Bennet, please do be seated." Darcy's voice was firm, though cloaked in kindness. He looked carefully at the man in front of him and recognised the resemblance there was to his daughter. The older man dark eye's refused to look away—like his second child. He was not to be intimidated by Darcy's wealth or position—also very much like her. "I am indebted to you. Due to your quick action and the wisdom of Miss Elizabeth, we can protect my sister as best as we can. You have my sincerest thanks."

"What shall you do, sir?" Thomas Bennet was flabbergasted to see a calmness in the younger man. He had no doubt of the turmoil which would rule his household if one of his daughters was threatened. Mrs. Bennet would have a case of nerves. His silly daughters would fret and grumble and gossip. Jane would try to minimize any wrongdoing, and Lizzy would have lightning bolts shooting from her eyes.

"Mr. Bennet, in the week past, I had opportunity to speak with Miss Elizabeth about the propensity for gossip to have some foundation in truth, even if it was only a small morsel."

"I can only imagine how that conversation might have taken place," Mr. Bennet murmured.

"Sir, you have young daughters. You must feel the danger here." Darcy took the seat across from him. "Georgiana has been more of a daughter to me than a sister these past five years. Like you, I would do anything to protect her. This past summer, Mr. Wickham endeavoured to encroach upon my sister, whose heart had retained pleasant memories of him from when she was a child. After I was made aware of his attempt to coerce her into an elopement for the sole purpose of gaining control of her fortune, I confronted him with the consequences of his actions. Wickham has a long history of benefiting from my desire to protect my good father from finding out that his godson was a reprobate." Darcy sighed. "Therefore, Wickham did not fear me. He does, however, fear the colonel."

Darcy stood to pour them both a brandy. "When I first informed Richard of the events at Ramsgate, my cousin and I developed a strategy should he ever try to impose upon Georgiana again. It is this plan which will be put into action."

Mr. Bennet's curiosity could not be tamped down. He suspected his two youngest may yet cause him difficulty. They had had years to practice their little rebellions and soon would have it down to a fine art if he did not curtail them. "What, pray, is this plan, sir?"

Darcy drank from his glass. "The colonel will hunt down Wickham, whereupon he will be sequestered until passage can be obtained for Australia. I have purchased his mountain of debts which will guarantee Wickham's cooperation. If he does not choose to travel willingly, his only other option is debtors' prison—where he will reside for the rest of his pathetic life."

"And if he does not cooperate?" Mr. Bennet was skeptical of Darcy's confidence.

"I should think he will. George Wickham's greatest consideration has always been his own comfort and advantage."

"If not, he will die?" Thomas Bennet was appalled. He knew little of the man in front of him and even less of the colonel. Certainly, he had heard how Darcy had abominably insulted his favourite daughter. It had set Thomas Bennet against him. He owed Darcy only the general consideration from one gentleman to another. It was his Lizzy who had stirred him from Longbourn's library. She, the victim of this man's hateful words, had insisted they act with rapidity. This spoke more of his daughter's kind heart than the man's in front of him.

"Come, Mr. Bennet, does my cousin look like a cold-blooded killer?" Darcy lifted his brow in a manner Thomas Bennet was very familiar with from his Lizzy.

Mr. Bennet recalled the look of fierceness in the colonel's eyes upon reading the letter. "I do not know."

Darcy chose to ignore the older man's concerns and continue his description of the strategy. "Should it become necessary, I will immediately have a warning posted in the newspapers telling the good people of England that Mr. George Wickham, also known as Lieutenant Wickham, has not only deserted his post in the militia during times of war, but also, in an effort to protect himself from collectors of debts of honour and funds owed to many businesses, attempted to extort money from several gentlemen by attempting to damage the innocent female members of their family by starting false, scandalous rumours. He is not to be trusted or believed, but rather, turned over to the authorities for immediate transport to Marshalsea."

"Ah, a good plan, sir." Mr. Bennet considered Darcy's plan from all angles. In stating the information in such a way, no fingers would be pointed at any one particular young woman or family, no matter what Wickham said. "If he should then disparage Miss Darcy, she would have the sympathy of the people, rather than disdain."

"This is our hope, sir."

"And your sister? How does she fare?" Mr. Bennet recalled Miss Darcy was the same age as his youngest. Had this happened to Lydia, which was entirely possible if she had been left free to roam in society, their whole family's future would have been destroyed. His heart was affected by this young girl he barely knew. With five daughters, he comprehended how impressionable they could be at that age.

"As soon as she heard Wickham was in Hertfordshire, she locked herself in her room and will not answer anyone. Both Richard and I have tried to no avail." Darcy emptied his glass and set it down on the small table between them. His disappointment and hurt that his sister would not allow him to provide succor was heart-breaking. "As confident as I am about our plan, I am unsure how to help her."

"Might my Lizzy be of some assistance, or possibly Jane?" The words were out before Thomas Bennet could draw them back. The burden of Miss Darcy's needs weighed heavier in his heart than the cold, calculating attitude of her brother. Kitty and Lydia, and possibly even Mary, may not have known how to act when under test, but his eldest daughters knew how to properly take care of themselves and others. He had every confidence that either one would draw Georgiana from her own tender reflections.

Darcy pondered the suggestion. Miss Bennet's serenity might be the balm Georgiana needed. Miss Bennet's quiet attention to her family was to be admired. Yet, the memories of Elizabeth reaching out to draw his sister into conversation, taking an interest in her, and acting to direct her away from Miss Bingley's acerbic tongue, appealed to him. When they had left Longbourn, Georgiana had commented that she had felt safe with Elizabeth. In any challenging situation, it was Elizabeth he wanted on his side. *By his side.*

Darcy shook his head to dispel the thought. Miss Elizabeth was a friend and no more. She would be a friend to his sister as well.

"Sir, your offer is quite generous. I believe you to be correct that Miss Bennet and Miss Elizabeth would show Georgiana both kindness and a gentle hand to guide her past her current despair." Darcy looked the gentleman in the eye. He had nothing to hide. Had he and Elizabeth not progressed past their earlier misunderstanding, what he was considering would not have been possible. To his relief, he was grateful he had stepped outside his inclinations and talked to her—

actually talked. "I believe the best course of action would be to take my sister back to London. There she can be protected. My staff knows Wickham. He would never be allowed close to her."

"Good." Mr. Darcy's concern for his sister was a blatant contrast to his callousness towards Lizzy. Mr. Bennet could not help but wonder if it was because he believed those in Meryton to be so far beneath him. And yet, Darcy was staying in the home of a man with roots in trade. He was mystified by this young man's character.

"With your suggestion in mind, I would like Miss Elizabeth to travel with my sister." When Mr. Bennet started to protest, Darcy held up his hand to stop him. "Not as a paid companion, sir, but as a friend."

This was not what Thomas Bennet had in mind. He had hoped that an afternoon spent together would be enough. And the thought of his Lizzy travelling with both Darcys was unpalatable. Before he could express his concerns, Darcy continued. "Sir, at the risk of importuning you, I would ask that you travel with us to Town. In this way your daughter is protected, and you can become familiar with our household environment." Darcy appreciated that the man in front of him seemed to be giving consideration to the request. "You could spend as much time in my townhouse's library as you would like, staying as long as you would prefer, whereupon I would return you and Miss Elizabeth in one of my carriages at your pleasure."

Thomas Bennet was flummoxed. While the offer of the library was titillating, it was the inclusion of himself in the travelling party that had him confused. If a man as spiteful as Lizzy proclaimed Mr. Darcy to be would give such consideration to the concerns of a father and his own sister, how—or rather—why had he spoken of Elizabeth in such a shabby manner? In every other respect, Darcy had acted the honourable gentleman. It made no sense. But the opportunity to be of assistance to young Miss Darcy, whom Lizzy seemed to be fond of, moved him. And yet, his daughters must come first.

"My apologies but I think not." Thomas Bennet stood to leave. "Jane and Elizabeth shall be on their way soon to offer their assistance for your sister. My carriage shall remain here until their afternoon visit is concluded, whereupon they will return to my house." He raised his brow and waited for Darcy to acknowledge his decision. When Darcy stood as well, Mr. Bennet added, "Sir, there is no need to show me out. I know my way."

Gathering the reins of his mount, he pondered his second daughter's reaction, realising that he had absolutely no idea how Lizzy would respond to Mr. Darcy's officious request. He sighed again.

CHAPTER 13

itzwilliam Darcy knocked softly on his sister's bedchamber door. He was again met with silence. It had been the same each time he had attempted to comfort her since she heard of Wickham's slander. The weight of his failure pressed his shoulders down. He had failed Georgiana at Ramsgate. He was failing her now.

"Do not be discouraged, Mr. Darcy," Elizabeth whispered as she stood in the hallway alongside him and Jane. "Both my sister and I have much experience with younger girls." While it was certainly true, each sibling was different. You could not deal with stoic, righteous Mary, who only needed a word of correction to make an adjustment, in the same manner as the two youngest, Kitty and Lydia. Only harsh punishment seemed to do the trick, not that it was offered, as evidenced by their behaviour.

Stepping forward, Elizabeth knocked briskly on the door frame before he could respond. "Miss Darcy, it is Miss Elizabeth. Might I have a word with you, please? It seems I am again in need of your assistance."

At first, they were met with silence. Nevertheless, only a few moments passed before they heard soft footsteps approaching the other side of the door. When Georgiana peeked through the narrow opening, Elizabeth easily noted the evidence of tears.

"Yes, Miss Elizabeth?" Georgiana's voice quivered and her eyes remained firmly fixed on a spot in front of her shoes. "How might I be of assistance?"

Elizabeth reached her right hand forward, in the manner she had done at Longbourn, and waited. She kept her tone soft. "I am in desperate need of a remedy in offering my newest friend comfort. I hope to be of service to her, so she realises she is not alone; that she is loved and cherished by her family and those who are just now becoming acquainted with her. I have found this particular young lady to be quiet and mild in a manner, much like my most favourite person in the world, my beloved Jane. This very young woman is a regal beauty for one not yet out in society, and my heart aches that hers is troubled. Might you be able to offer at least one suggestion that might lift her up?"

Within a breath, Georgiana's hand clasped hers. Elizabeth stepped forward only to have the door shut firmly behind her, leaving Darcy and Jane in the hallway.

Jane noticed the shock registered on his face. She could not help the small smile on her own. "I pray you are not concerned. Lizzy will have things set to rights in no time."

"I cannot help but hope you are correct, Miss Bennet." He recalled how Elizabeth had described Miss Bennet and recognised how well-matched she and Bingley seemed—cheerfully blind to all that was unpleasant in the world. He sighed. "We may as well join the others."

Offering his arm, he escorted Miss Bennet to the drawing room where Bingley was poised to relieve him of his duty. Caroline rushed to Darcy's side, attaching herself as soon as Jane was seated. "Have you misplaced Miss Elizabeth, Mr. Darcy?"

Darcy could not help but compare the Bingley siblings. Even though the events of the morning had moved Darcy to commandeer the Netherfield study, Charles had not inquired into his business. Caroline, on the other hand, had tried every possible maneuver to find out what had driven Georgiana to her room and what had caused

Darcy so much tumult. Her efforts met with no success. *How frustrating for her!* He wanted to snicker at the thought, though he refrained.

"Come, Mr. Darcy. We have a lovely tea set out for your pleasure." Sure enough, his preferences seemed displayed to perfection. "I have brought many of your favourites in from London."

She turned her attention to Jane. "Come, Miss Bennet. I am certain you have not had the opportunity to try such delicacies. This is your opportunity to be adventurous and expand your palette."

Again Mr. Hurst loaded his plate while the other two men abstained, their hearts and stomachs engorged with the emotions of the moment. With Bingley not partaking, Jane had no desire to eat, however she indulged her hostess by asking Miss Bingley to select a few savory offerings.

Upstairs, Georgiana collapsed onto her bed, failing to look at Elizabeth.

"Miss Darcy, I have no desire to intrude. It is your business, not mine." Elizabeth kept her voice firm. "I would like to know how I might assist you— to give you present relief."

With no response from Georgiana, Elizabeth could only wait. Finally, Georgiana spoke.

"You will no longer wish to be my friend if you knew what I have done, Miss Elizabeth. My brother is everything kind and good. He has assured me that I am innocent, yet the weight of guilt I feel in my heart tells me differently." Georgiana took a deep breath and expelled it in a rush. "I cannot help but feel my brother's disappointment, that under these circumstances, he would wish me gone."

"Miss Darcy, I know about Mr. Wickham." Elizabeth laid her hand over those fisted together on Georgiana's lap. "Your brother made the circumstances known to my father and he shared them with me briefly before I departed Longbourn for here."

"Oh, how can you possibly stand to be in my company?" Georgiana continued to keep her eyes averted, her surprise at Elizabeth having knowledge of Ramsgate rapidly changed to dread and humiliation.

"Yet, here I am, am I not?" Elizabeth squeezed Georgiana's hand lightly. "I am wondering, Miss Darcy, whether the exact circumstances were available right at this moment, would you still be willing to elope with Mr. Wickham?"

Georgiana's eyes flew to Elizabeth's face. "Of course not!"

"Why ever not? What has changed since Ramsgate?"

"Because now I am aware he is not a gentleman. It was not me he was after—rather, my dowry was the attraction."

"Is that all?"

"No." Her voice was firm. "I clearly understand how my decision, even though I did not follow through, had consequences. Had I left with Mr. Wickham, those consequences would have been even more dire. I would never contemplate such a decision again."

"And I am glad of that, Miss Darcy." Again, she gave her hands a squeeze. "Do you believe this will be the only lesson you will have to learn in your lifetime?"

"No?" She pondered the question a moment longer. Her voice was more resolved when she spoke again. "I am certain it will not be the only lesson."

"You are right. It will not be. However, tell me, I pray you, what lesson has your brother learned by observing your growing maturity in developing discernment and understanding?"

"I had not thought of it in this manner, Miss Elizabeth." Finally, she looked at Elizabeth. "It would be my greatest desire to have him think well of me."

"Have you ever read or heard of the process of smelting?"

Georgiana shook her head, confused.

"It is where fiery heat is applied to metal ore to separate the pure gold from what is called dross. Only after it has been put under this fire, does the real gold shine through." Elizabeth leaned her shoulder into Georgiana's. "Would you describe your lesson from Ramsgate as a fiery test? Did it not produce in you something valuable? Something you can use to protect yourself and the Darcy name for the rest of your years?"

She nodded.

"The treasure is when we do not have to experience trouble to learn from it. No doubt, we should learn from our own mistakes. However, would it not be better to be observant and learn from the mistakes of others?"

Georgiana was deeply appreciative of the means Elizabeth used to help her set her mind at ease. "Is this what you do?" She was surprised when a chuckle erupted from Elizabeth.

"It is what I strive to do, Miss Darcy. Nonetheless, I fail with shocking regularity." She leaned into Georgiana again, laughing at her own comment. "I will share something I learned from my grandmother Bennet. When she pondered a decision that someone made, she would say, 'I could write a book.'"

"She was an authoress?" *What a curious thing for a grandmother.*

"Oh, no! She could not read or write." Elizabeth smiled at her. "What she meant was that she could tell the exact story of where that series of choices would lead right down to whether or not there would be a happy ending. For example, let us consider Mr. Wickham's preferences as you know them. Is he a pleasant man?"

She was hesitant to admit the truth due to the nature of the questions, however her inherent honesty bade her do so. "He is."

"Would you consider him a charming, handsome man?"

"That he is, Miss Elizabeth." His charm coupled with his good looks had appealed to her young heart.

"Would you consider him an honourable man?"

"No!"

"Is he a good man?"

"He is not!"

"Is he a responsible man?"

"Not at all!"

"Well done, Miss Darcy." Elizabeth had noted how each time Georgiana responded, her voice became more insistent. "Now, let us write the book. Should Mr. Wickham continue down this path, what will his story be?"

Georgiana thought for a moment. "In truth, I could see how other young women would be in danger. If he has chosen to find an heiress to wed rather than use the resources he has at hand, he will try the same thing again."

"Very good. We have an endangered, wealthy, *young*, lady and a villain." Elizabeth was relieved to see the small smile grace Georgiana's face. "What else, Miss Darcy?"

"Even though he was raised to good advantage, he has failed to use his education and the opportunities he had available to him to provide for his own future."

"I am sure you are correct." Elizabeth tapped her finger on Georgiana's hand. "What sort of husband would he be then? How would he treat his wife when the funds are gone? Would he work hard to provide support for her and their children?"

"I cannot imagine that he would. I now know it would be a miserable life to be the wife of George Wickham. Most likely she would be abandoned when he found another innocent to prey on."

"Would that not be a harrowing end of story for any young lady? A bit of a gothic novel, I am thinking."

"I believe so."

"Are you pleased you are *not* that young woman?"

"Indeed."

"Then, why were you downcast?" Elizabeth knew this to be the turning point in the discussion. If Georgiana was to truly absorb the lesson and find strength from it, she needed to fully comprehend and imagine the circumstances she had almost placed herself in. *I am, indeed, a hypocrite! How often have I had to learn the hard way?* Elizabeth sighed. It was not the time to consider her own failures.

Georgiana's embrace surprised Elizabeth. "I had not fully considered what I learned from Ramsgate and how this information would benefit me in the future. Surely, I wish I had never given Mr. Wickham any notice. My lack of experience with the stronger sex left me unprepared to make the proper choices. Now, I am not so ill-informed. Thank you, Miss Elizabeth. If you see my error and adjustment in this manner, I believe my brother would see it as well."

"After all, Miss Darcy, do not we all make mistakes? Are any of us perfect? Even Mr. Darcy, is he without flaws?" Unwanted memories of his insults at the assembly crossed her mind. *No, he was not a man without fault.*

"He feels things deeply."

"Like his sister, I believe." Elizabeth returned the embrace. "Dry your eyes, dear friend. We have a brother of yours to reassure."

* * *

DOWNSTAIRS, Darcy stood with his back to the group, worried about his sister and wishing he was privy to the conversation. He was appalled he no longer seemed to be a man under good regulation. *Richard was correct—he was a mother hen!* Wickham was soon to be travelling to Australia which would forever remove him from their lives. Miss Elizabeth had shown her perception and kindness so he knew she would be sensible in her approach to his sister. Surely, he had no cause to repine.

Darcy was well aware of the cause of his despair. Whilst Richard gave chase to the scoundrel, Elizabeth was comforting his sister, and *he* was in a drawing room trying to avoid the notice of Miss Bingley. He longed for the chase, a sword in his hand; or to have Georgiana turn to him for consolation. When she had done so in years past, he felt taller, stronger, and needed. It galled him that under these circumstances, he, Fitzwilliam Darcy, was not necessary.

Darcy heard them before he saw them. Soft giggles. *Surely that was not the sister who would, in her sorrow, not allow her beloved brother into her presence?* It was.

Again, Miss Bingley jumped to attention as soon as the two ladies walked into the room. Elizabeth was completely ignored as Caroline led Georgiana to a seat next to where she had been sitting. Within moments, she had a plate of sweets filled and tea poured for the younger girl. Nothing had been offered to Miss Elizabeth.

"Brother"—Georgiana's welcome voice travelled the distance to the window—"are these not the shellfish you enjoy so much?"

Darcy surveyed the raw oysters on the half shell as he walked closer. "They are, Georgiana."

"Indeed, Mr. Darcy. We are always happy to offer such hospitality to our esteemed guests. We had them brought from London this week."

"When did they arrive, Miss Bingley?" When he saw his sister start to daintily remove the meat from the opened shell, he put his hand out to stop her. He waited for Caroline's reply.

"I would have to check with Cook, Mr. Darcy. I believe them to have arrived on Wednesday with the rest of the items we were not able to procure in Hertfordshire."

"Do not eat them, Georgiana." He leaned over and took the plate away from her, placing it back on the tray. "I never eat oysters unless freshly harvested during certain tidal periods. The autumn has been unseasonably warm." His nose was in the air, as if the food was pungent, and disdain dripped from his voice. "It is unsafe."

Alarmed, Caroline's right hand went to her chest. Serving tainted food would be a blow to her reputation as an accomplished chatelaine. She despised shellfish so she never ate any herself. Glancing at the plates on the tray, she saw that her brother-in-law had a pile of empty shells before him while Miss Bennet had only two. *If only Miss Elizabeth had helped herself!* Caroline wanted to snort at the thought. She did not. "No harm done."

Darcy's frustrations with his own inactivity bled over into the tone of his words on this subject. "I beg to differ, Miss Bingley. It is highly dangerous to serve shellfish not fresh from the sea."

The words were hardly out of Darcy's mouth when two things happened at once. Gilbert Hurst ran for the Chinese vase on the sideboard as he emptied his stomach into the only available vessel in the room, and Colonel Fitzwilliam strolled into the chaos, his face thunderous.

CHAPTER 14

*P*anic ensued. Louisa Hurst paled at her husband's display, while two footmen were summoned to assist him to his room. The volume of his gagging rose as he ascended the stairs. Jane Bennet flung her arms around her waist as her face vacillated between shades of yellow-green and pasty white. She had never tried oysters before. They had looked unappetizing on the plate, rather like blobs of gelatinous, grey phlegm, but she had not wanted to insult her hostess and had imitated Mr. Hurst in swallowing them quickly.

"My hands and legs are tingling, Lizzy."

Elizabeth pulled her sister to her feet as Bingley rapidly approached them.

"Pray, accept my assistance." Bingley lifted Miss Bennet in his arms, calling orders as he bounded up the stairs. Elizabeth and Georgiana followed.

"She may use my room." Georgiana offered.

Caroline Bingley demanded the maids remove the revolting service. Windows were opened, and the tables were cleared. It was not until the maids were finished that she realised she was left alone in the room with her sister. The men were gone, and her reputation as a hostess was in ruins.

* * *

"WHATEVER HAPPENED HERE? I have never seen Hurst move so fast." Richard was momentarily distracted.

"Miss Bingley served shellfish harvested from the estuary early this week." Darcy could hear the disgust in his own voice.

"Oh lord!" The cavalry had been stationed off the coast of Spain the summer prior. Stores and munitions had not been delivered, and the delay had left his men hungry and suffering in the torrid sun. An enterprising few had begged for some oysters from a merchant who was perfectly willing to part with the *berberechos*. The tidal flats were filled with a substance that turned the muddy waters red and unbeknownst to the soldiers, the local populace would not eat the shellfish. The merchant was overjoyed at the unexpected income and was unconcerned at the damage the little oysters might cause foreigners. The men who gorged themselves were miserable, which made the others who did not partake suffer as well. They lost fourteen of the soldiers within a day—strong, hearty, active men. He worried about the fair Miss Bennet. And Gilbert Hurst? His lifestyle of overindulgence would make it a challenge to recover. He wished them both well, but rather dreaded there would be bad news by the morrow.

Miss Bingley entered her brother's study. "Do you believe a doctor should be called?"

"Yes!" They watched her leave. Richard closed the door behind her.

* * *

"YOU HAVE NOT WRITTEN to post the notice about Wickham's desertion in the papers have you?" The colonel blurted to his cousin. The hours since he left Netherfield Park had been frustrating to the extreme, and he was barely holding on to his anger.

"I have not, Richard. And why have you returned so quickly? Has the miscreant been found?" A bad feeling roiled in the pit of Darcy's stomach which he knew was not from Miss Bingley's fare.

"Wickham chose not to desert."

"What?" Darcy was stunned. "How is this possible?" The strength left his legs, and he collapsed into one of the leather chairs in Bingley's study. He *knew* Wickham. *How could he not have deserted the militia?*

The colonel ran his hand over his face. "When I arrived at the encampment, I reported my suspicions that Wickham had abandoned his post to Colonel Forster. Imagine my surprise when Wickham was quickly collected from his tent and sauntered into the office." The colonel's voice was rife with disgust. "When I challenged him with making unsavory comments about a young lady of quality, he admitted to doing so in a fit of disgruntlement against his present circumstances. Then he promised Colonel Forster never to do so again."

"What?" Darcy jumped from the chair and started pacing, putting his large hands to both sides of his head. "Richard, please tell me this is a sick joke. Tell me it is not true."

Brandy! They needed brandy. The colonel moved to the crystal decanter and poured two glasses to the brim. Darcy failed to acknowledge the glass his cousin held out to him.

"Yes, imagine my surprise, Darcy. I wanted to take my sword and carve the smirk right off his face. He knew what he was about." Richard downed the glass, drank Darcy's, and refilled them to the brim. He set Darcy's on the table and watched him pace. Leaning back against the desk, he knew a flanking maneuver was warranted. If a frontal attack was ineffective, a change in tactics was needed. "We cannot continue to worry what he will do next. You must call in his debts, Darcy. Now."

"If I do, Richard, he will talk to all and sundry about the Darcys. He still could besmirch Georgiana's name… However, if we offered transport along with a sizable monetary inducement to somewhere other than Australia, he may be willing to leave England."

"I do not fear he would be a threat to you once he was in debtors' prison but… What do you have in mind, Darcy?"

"Either Boston, New York, or Baltimore. Tensions between the governments are high and the probability of war between the former colonies and England is equally as high." Darcy stopped and pondered a moment. "If I pay for passage and give him enough money for a good start, he could travel to the western frontier away from the fighting, or he could stay in the city as long as he was welcomed. I cannot imagine any monies I provided lasting him any length of time. Then he would need to fend for himself."

"But why do you care if he can fend for himself? Lord, Darcy!" The colonel continued, his voice rich with sarcasm, "Might I suggest India, Cousin. Fortunes are still being made for an intelligent man. Wickham is without morals or conscience, yet he has been like a cat with nine lives. You could drop him from a tower and he would still land on his feet. His self-preservation skills are unparalleled." Richard had spent many of his summers growing up in Wickham's company. He had never understood why his uncle Darcy allowed the steward's son such close contact with the heir to Pemberley. Whatever the reason, no good had come from it. And why would Darcy fund a fresh start for the man when he held all his vowels was a puzzle?

"With the war moving from France to spread across the continent, are ships even getting to the coast of Africa and beyond? And what about pirates? And slave ships? They both exist even though they have long been outlawed." A thought niggled at Darcy. "I do not want him to die as I could never wish that for any man." He was surprised at the thought and pleased he did not wish his nemesis dead. "Do I want him to pay for the wrong he has done the Darcy family? Yes. But the simple truth—" Darcy sighed heavily "—I just want him gone—out of my sight and out of any influence over Georgiana's future."

"Then you care not where he ends up?"

"I do not."

Richard stood and placed his empty glass on the table. He turned to the door, knowing his cousin would follow. "You have your ledger and the receipts of his debts?" Darcy nodded. "Then let us go."

* * *

MR. JONES, Meryton's apothecary, had arrived and examined both patients. They were seriously ill. Both had purged the offending food but now a level of paralysis had set in. Neither were able retain drink or the apothecary's draughts to calm their stomachs. Elizabeth was fearful as Jane had never been so ill.

The response from her mother was terse and incredulous.

Lizzy,

How clever of Jane to be ill at Netherfield Park. Mr. Bingley will certainly offer for her. Do not hurry home.

Mama

SEATED NEXT TO THE BED, Elizabeth watched her sister's chest rise and fall in an irregular rhythm. The apothecary had given little hope. It was his experience that relief or death would take place before the next day was over. Elizabeth begged him to stop at Longbourn on his way into the village to inform her father. She doubted her mother had told him, and she did not wish to be on her own should the worst befall Jane.

"Miss Elizabeth, my maid has finished moving my things to the room next door. Can I provide anything for yourself or Miss Bennet?" Georgiana had remained unruffled during the throes of Jane's illness.

"I thank you, no." Elizabeth would not take her eyes off her sister. It was as if she feared that to do so would invite more harm. "I would be pleased if you would keep me company, Miss Darcy. I am not comfortable with all that is going through my mind."

"I imagine so, Elizabeth. You do not mind if I call you Elizabeth? You must call me Georgiana. It seems fitting under the circumstances." Elizabeth squeezed Georgiana's hand in acquiescence.

"Tell me of your home, your family, your greatest desires, your most morbid fears, Georgiana, I pray you." Elizabeth giggled as Georgiana's eyebrows rose with each request. Smiling, Georgiana understood Elizabeth was frightened and needed a distraction—and a small measure of humour.

They spoke softly and watched over Jane. Always watched.

* * *

Dinner had come and gone with most taking a tray in their rooms. Mrs. Hurst now sat with her sister and brother in the drawing room, awaiting news of her husband's health. Georgiana and Elizabeth had not left Jane, and the male cousins were again in Bingley's study.

"Mr. Denny was a welcome surprise," said Richard, recalling the events of the afternoon.

"Yes. At Wickham's comments, his determination to shun all contact with the blackguard was to our benefit. Having a younger sister of his own caused him to reflect on the harm a misplaced word could have to a girl's good name." Darcy was relieved.

Wickham had chosen the Americas as his future home, and he bargained for five hundred pounds for a new start. It was quickly promised—though not a farthing would be paid him until he climbed aboard the ship. Neither man trusted Wickham. In fact, they did not trust his word at this new arrangement. As a matter of honour, Mr. Denny had volunteered to keep his eye on his former companion until Richard could collect the rake the following morning. It promised to be a long night.

"You are pensive, Cousin." Darcy understood Richard's anger. He was a man of strong feelings who tended to see matters in black and white. Yet, his position in the military was earned, not purchased. He was the commander of a large regiment of men. Darcy knew his thoughts and worries ran deep. "Are you thinking of Wickham?"

The colonel was not. His mind was filled with a charming woman who lived less than four miles away at Lucas Lodge. He wondered as to the activities of her day, knowing she would have been a calm port in the storm of events that had blown into Netherfield Park. In his heart, he felt strongly that she would hear him out without judgment, understanding his need to cut Wickham down to size to protect his ward. She would have soothed his brow...

"Richard." Darcy had rarely seen such exhaustion on his cousin's face. *No, that was the wrong emotion. Weariness.* "Do not feel the need to stay with me. We have done all we can for the day."

In truth, Darcy was weary as well. From the moment Mr. Bennet had arrived with Elizabeth's note to the arrival of the apothecary, all had become a tempest. He could not help but reflect on his earlier desire to remove Georgiana and the Bennets to London. How much better it would have been for all. He ran his fingers through his hair and dropped his head to the back of the chair. *If only!*

* * *

IT WAS NOT until Georgiana had returned to her new bedchambers and Jane fell into a less troubled sleep that Elizabeth felt she could leave the room. Mr. Bingley had offered the full use of his home, so she crept downstairs to find the kitchen. The house was quiet. She knew a servant could be found to help her, but she did not want to be a bother or to wake someone. It was not until she reached the bottom of the staircase that she saw Mr. Darcy, his hands filled with a plate of food and a mug of cider. They had been alike in their thinking.

"Might I inquire as to the health of Miss Bennet?" Darcy's baritone whispered into the emptiness. His pleasure at being in Elizabeth's company filled him with satisfaction. For the past few hours, he had hoped to see his friend, to be in her presence. Again, he wished they were safely tucked away at Darcy House in London.

"Mr. Jones has explained his concerns with this type of poisoning, sir. I still fear for my sister." Relief that she finally had small progress to share coloured her comments. "I should not be long away from her, though she is finally sleeping soundly. My stomach was complaining so loudly I was afraid it would wake her."

Darcy snickered, the sound a rumble bursting from his chest. "Take mine, Miss Elizabeth. My diligent search of the kitchen has already been completed. I know where the treasures are. You would have to start anew." He moved the plate closer to her. When she did not readily raise her hands to grasp the edge, he added, "It will return you to your sister much quicker if you take advantage of my offer, would it not?"

Elizabeth dipped into a quick curtsey and clasped the plate and mug. With her hands full, she stepped back from him. A feeling of reluctance to be away from his company caused her to hesitate. He must have felt the same as he stood in place.

"Are you satisfied with your day, Mr. Darcy?" Georgiana had merely reported that the men were returned from their task, not knowing what the task might have been. Elizabeth had not spoken to him about her earlier conversation with his sister and did not know whether Georgiana had spoken with him either. She was surprised at how much she wanted to reassure him how well Georgiana had fared. The candlelight showed furrows in his brow. *This man was not at peace.* Elizabeth realised he had not been since the first night she noticed him at the Meryton assembly. He had weighty troubles, she suspected.

"I wish your father had allowed us to travel to London... We would have escaped many of the troubles of this day had he done so."

Exhaustion and worry over her sister coupled with the stressful conversation with Georgiana, added up to a flashfire of confusion and resentment. "My father shared your request, sir. You cannot be at a loss to understand why he refused."

On this day he had reaped one trouble upon another. Sighing, he said, "For the safety of my sister and even yours, it would have served us well to have gone."

Elizabeth felt her ire rising. "Sir! What good does this do? Why are you saying any of this now?" Without thought Elizabeth shoved his food back into his hands. Her voice rose with her temper. "Your invitation solely reflected a concern for your family and not mine. I have four unmarried sisters. Four, Mr. Darcy. The militia is camping less than one mile from our home. They come with their own dangers as their welcome in any community typically wears off quickly. My father's cousin, the heir to Longbourn, will be arriving in but a few days. My father is needed at home, sir."

She pushed his plate at him a little harder, stepping closer as she did. Both of them now had their hands on the plate and mug.

"As I understand matters, you, on this day alone, have striven to make decisions for Mr. Wickham, your sister, my father, and me." Elizabeth hissed. "You have no authority over me, sir. You have no authority over anyone in this household other than those named Darcy. It was the height of presumptuousness for you to assume we would pick up and travel miles away from our own responsibilities. Yes, I was pleased to speak with your sister. She is an intelligent girl with a kind heart. Nevertheless, Mr. Darcy, while you are looking out for the best interests of *your* sister, I am doing the same for my own."

"I see, Miss Elizabeth." Surely, he had no idea how condescending he sounded. He had stopped listening at the mention of the militia. He knew how young maidens liked to flirt and tease military men. His cousin's stories had left him with disdain for these girls who were attracted by a red coat and some fancy buttons. He had thought Elizabeth Bennet was above that. "You would rather spend your time with the officers than people of elevated rank. I had surmised you were more like your father but find I have chosen the wrong parent." They were harsh words stemming from bitterness and frustration which proved to be as painful as a direct slap to the face.

Gasping, Elizabeth released her grip on the dinnerware and stepped back. Never could she recall feeling this much animosity towards another human. "I was wrong, Mr. Darcy. For days I have castigated myself for allowing my poor, first impressions of you to rule my belief in your character. Your affability both in the field and at the folly fooled me. You are, indeed, arrogant and selfish. You act above your present company because you truly believe you are above us. You were raised as a gentleman and I am a gentleman's daughter. In this we are equal. Should you remember how to act the gentleman, there may..." She did not finish her thought. "Until then, I can only regret your sweet sister Georgiana having a brother such as you."

"You have said enough, madam." Her eyes shot fire. She had never looked so beautiful to him, magnificent in her anger, though her words cut him to the bone. How dare she call into question his conduct? Ungentlemanly? *Hardly!* His first inclination was to show her, to prove he could do as he liked. Inside he knew he was not that kind of man. *Or was he?*

Darcy slowly took a breath. *He was a gentleman!* Before he turned away from her, he offered her the plate. His voice softened as he said, "You were hungry."

Pushing the plate and mug again, her fingers instinctively clasping them, he turned and walked into the study. It would be a long night.

CHAPTER 15

Sunday, 13 October 1811
Lucas Lodge

Every morning, including Sundays, Lady Lucas complained when Charlotte returned from gathering the eggs from the hen house. It was a task deemed by her to be far beneath the daughter of a knight. Nevertheless, it was an undertaking Charlotte had enjoyed since her youth which she was unwilling to give up—her own subtle rebellion.

She first heard the sounds of a horse when she dropped the latch on the coop. Though the hens were still complaining of her daily thievery, the noise of the bridle bit moving against the equine's large teeth, the creak of well-used leather, and the shuffle of hooves moving through the loamy earth drew Charlotte's attention. It was a sound out-of-place in the early hours at Lucas Lodge.

"Colonel Fitzwilliam, you are about early this October morn. And you have caught me tending the chickens!" She was surprised to see no teasing smile on his comely face. Placing the egg basket on a bench, Charlotte approached him.

He dismounted immediately. She was even more disconcerted when he quickly moved so close to her that she could feel his breath on her forehead. His arms reached up as if they instinctively sought comfort in her embrace, though they halted their movement before he touched her.

"Colonel, what has happened?" Charlotte struggled for calm. She took his hand and led him to the bench. "Tell me, sir." Then she waited for him to gather his thoughts.

Richard knew she would be the voice of reason away from a chaotic household. He had to come. He had to see her. Removing his hat, he dropped his clasped hands between his knees. He had no sense of how defeated he appeared.

"Hurst has died." Richard heard the intake of her breath, though she said nothing. He appreciated her steadiness. "Tainted seafood was served yesterday at tea. Miss Bennet remains seriously ill. Needless to say, the household is in an uproar." He finally glanced at his friend, taking in the flush to her cheeks from the crisp morning air and the escaped locks from her straw bonnet. His urge to pull her to him was strong—stronger than he had ever felt for a woman. He did not feel weak for wanting her. That thought made him reflect on the relationships at Netherfield Park.

"Though I never observed affection between Mrs. Hurst and her husband, her wails of sorrow throughout the night filled the upstairs hallways. But..." he added with a sigh, "I suspect she will find much more contentment being a widow than she did as a wife." He scoffed at the thought. It was not the type of marriage he wanted. *He wanted marriage?* He tucked the thought away for a later perusal.

"Miss Bingley has closeted herself in her rooms as her misguided and ignorant mistakes resulted in grave consequences. You see, Miss Lucas, she knew Darcy to enjoy the oysters when he was in London, so she had them brought in for his pleasure. Most everyone knows it is not safe to eat shellfish that are not fresh from the sea! Only Mr. Hurst and Miss Bennet ate them—but have suffered tragically for Caroline's ignorance." His voice was heavily laced with bitterness. "Had Darcy not asked her about the oysters, the whole household might have been poisoned."

After a pensive moment, he continued. "It is fortunate for Bingley that Darcy is in residence, though my cousins will be removing to

London tomorrow. Darcy's help to his friend will be invaluable. Hurst's family has a crypt outside of Town. The burial will be done as soon as they arrive. My cousin has far too much experience with funerals and arrangements."

"And you do not?" It was the first time Charlotte had spoken since they sat. She had imagined the life he led in the military many times since the Meryton assembly. Yes, she had heard reports of war. The loss of life of those who served shoulder to shoulder with the man who sat alongside her would have been far too common an occurrence.

His chin dropped almost to his chest. "I do."

"And Eliza? How does she fare?" The relationship between the two eldest Bennets was strong. Charlotte worried for both women.

"She was comforted by the arrival of her father soon after the apothecary left Netherfield. Mr. Bennet was not able to stay so she sat with Miss Bennet the whole of last night. Georgiana spent some time in her company, but eventually Miss Elizabeth encouraged her to find her own sleep. I have not yet seen my young cousin this morning."

"And Mr. Darcy?"

"Gratefully my cousin has taken control of arrangements. In spite of Miss Bennet's illness, Miss Elizabeth desires to have her removed to Longbourn, which I comprehend. There is nothing like being home for a faster recovery." He reflected on the times he had suffered in military encampments and how he had longed for a warm bed—his warm bed—and the gentle hands of his mother. Yes, he understood.

"But should she be moved? I cannot imagine Mr. Jones recommending such a course."

"You are correct. Nevertheless, with the uncertainty of the arrangements for Mr. Hurst and Miss Bingley's removal to her quarters, Miss Elizabeth agreed that their departure from Netherfield would be better for all concerned, including Miss Bennet."

"Then matters are finally at peace between Mr. Darcy and Eliza?"

"I know my cousin, Miss Lucas, I know him well. I watched him and Miss Elizabeth as they spoke of what needed to be done. Neither would look at the other, and their speech was stilted." Richard's mood finally lightened. "Of course, that is not untypical of Darcy when in company. Miss Elizabeth though? Rarely have I seen her as restrained. Her worry weighs on her."

Charlotte nodded her agreement. "And you, Colonel Fitzwilliam?" Charlotte reached over and rested her hand on his forearm. "What are your plans?' She held her breath in fear of his reply. With his cousins removing themselves from Hertfordshire, there was no reason for the colonel to stay. If the Bingleys also left for London, she might spend the rest of her lifetime without seeing this man again. The pain that filled her chest was excruciating, drawing her shoulders together to shield herself from the agony. She wanted to weep.

"I will be escorting one of the officers to Portsmouth this morning." He had no desire to share the history of Wickham with this woman. "Indeed, I should have already left. Colonel Forster is expecting me."

He stood and reached out a hand to help her stand as well, engulfing her delicate fingers in his own. He could not have stopped himself had General Wellesley given him a direct order. Colonel Richard Fitzwilliam, a man who had promised himself the day he entered the military that he would never give his heart to a woman, drew her hand to his mouth and kissed it. His lips lingered as he closed his eyes to record this moment in his memory.

Before he could change his mind and remain in her company for the rest of his life, he stepped back as he released her fingers and walked to untie his horse. Mounting quickly, he turned to face her.

"Goodbye, my friend."

Charlotte was only able to manage a hint of a smile. She raised the hand he had held so tenderly in farewell. As she watched him ride away, she whispered, "Goodbye, my friend." Then she wept.

NETHERFIELD PARK

Gloom moved through the rooms of Netherfield. A glimpse from the drawing room window revealed the landscape outside the manor to be shrouded in low clouds and the ground covered in dampness. The days past had begun the same only to lose the murky shadows to a vibrant sun-filled sky. This day the melancholy would reach to the heavens, and the heaviness of the mood inside Netherfield would migrate to the outside world.

Darcy sat alone before the fireplace, listening to the snap and crackle of the burning logs. His only visitors that morning had been his cousin, Bingley, and Elizabeth. *Miss Elizabeth!* His sigh was ponderous.

Why had he spoken to her in such a way? He was frustrated with himself and the events of the past four and twenty hours. First Wickham, and then Georgiana, and the fawning of Miss Bingley had placed him on unsteady ground. *Who was he trying to fool?* It was Elizabeth— always Elizabeth who caused him such turmoil. In his memory, he could never recall speaking to another woman in such a manner. *What was it about her that brought out such strong feelings and sharp words?* From the beginning—from the first time he had laid eyes on her—his behaviour had been abominable.

When she had sought him out earlier, he noticed how truly weary she was. Deep shadows rested under her beautiful eyes, which were rimmed in red, a silent testimony of tears spent on behalf of others. Yes, it would be like her to mourn the passing of a man she barely knew.

He had been uneasy in her company, though she did not remain long. He deserved her scorn. He deserved her derision. He expected her censure. He received only consideration.

"Mr. Darcy, Colonel Fitzwilliam, I am hesitant to approach Mr. Bingley as I imagine he is with Mrs. Hurst during her mourning." She barely raised her eyes to the men in front of her. "Because of the loss of Mr. Hurst, I believe it best to return with Jane to Longbourn. There she can receive care without interfering with the Bingley family. Thus, I beg your assistance in loaning us your carriage." The last was said as a whisper.

Darcy had easily agreed to her request and called the footman outside the door to have his personal carriage readied. He would have done so much more for her if she only knew the power she held.

Elizabeth then left the room to return to ready her sister for the three-mile trip to Longbourn. It would be a slow, miserable journey for Jane Bennet. The colonel left immediately after for the encampment.

The long night before had been one of reflection for Darcy. As the rest of the household battled illness and sleep, he struggled with his emotions and his view of himself—the man he had allowed himself to become. *How had he let his own concerns overrule politeness?* Though he believed much of what spewed from his mouth the night before, a gentleman never would have said those words to a lady. *Elizabeth would have castigated him for that exact thought. He deserved it. He was justifying his actions—again.* Not only should he not have said them, but he never should have cultivated such arrogant impressions of her family. It was not like him to make excuses for himself—*or was it?*

Yet, how dare she call him out for his conduct? Who was she but a farmer's daughter? Of course, though he was the grandson of an earl, he was the son of a farmer. He sighed. *Lord, he wished it had been him who had partaken of the shellfish.* Surely, they tasted better than the leather from the bottom of his Hessians he had so craftily crammed into his own mouth.

When the carriage was outside the front door, Bingley had yet to return downstairs. Rather than have an unknown footman attend to the task, Darcy carried Miss Bennet from her bed to her transport. After stepping inside the conveyance and laying her carefully on the squabs, he pulled heavy rugs from under the bench to cover her. He backed out of the carriage and assisted Elizabeth up the step.

It had to be instinct which moved him back into the carriage as he had given no consideration to making the trip with them to Longbourn. He doubted Elizabeth welcomed his company.

Elizabeth looked up in surprise when she felt the carriage move with his weight. With a slight shrug, which he did not fail to notice, she wrapped her sister securely in the blankets. Then, they were off.

Darcy could not take his eyes from her while she could not take hers from Jane.

* * *

LONGBOURN

Mrs. Bennet was frantic. Her assumption that her eldest two children had finally taken her wise counsel and connived to remain at Netherfield Park was ever so wrong. The thought of harm coming to her firstborn was devastating. She loved her children enough to do whatever was needed to see them happily settled. Worry for Jane stubbornly warred with her inclination to match her eldest with the young man leasing the neighbouring property. She did not know what to do.

Prior to receiving an explanation of Jane's illness from the apothecary, Mr. Bennet's cousin, Mr. William Collins, had arrived. He was a tall, heavy-looking young man of five and twenty. His air was grave and stately, and his manners were formal. At first sight, Mrs. Bennet had no desire to have him in her household. She worried he was taking stock of the furnishings and cataloging whether they would be useful or not when he inherited them.

After the apothecary left and her husband raced to Netherfield Park, she finally understood the gravity of the situation. She wished Mr. Collins gone.

Mr. Collins failed to perceive his presence during this crisis as an inconvenience to the household. Moreover, he was incensed by the lack of welcome and slighted that attention for a sick daughter was greater than a distinguished guest.

"Mr. Collins, you must understand why we are in such an uproar. My Jane, my beautiful Jane, is deathly ill." Mrs. Bennet wrung the lacy handkerchief between her hands. She had not the desire to place his comfort ahead of her own child. "Mightn't you shorten your stay and return at a less difficult time, sir?"

"Indeed not, madam!" The parson grabbed each jacket lapel and moved his weight onto his toes, increasing his height exponentially.

Looking down his nose at her, his nasally voice intoned, "On the contrary, Mrs. Bennet, my spiritual guidance can serve to bring solace to the household should Miss Bennet not survive."

Mrs. Bennet's outburst was not unexpected. He was used to the wailing of women in grief. "My patroness, Lady Catherine de Bourgh, has long assigned me to oversee the transition after the loss of a family member. I could not possibly remove myself now." He continued, unaware the woman in front of him was stunned by his ill-manners. "She has determined, in her wisdom, that I should seek one of your daughters as the wife of my future life. Acting on a nature most humble, I resolved at once to do so. When Lady Catherine explained how my Christian duty would be glorified by lightening the burden to the Bennet family of the entail made by my esteemed grandfather, there was no other choice but to travel forthwith to complete the task."

Mrs. Bennet was rarely without words. Within a few sentences of conversation, his intention to help place one daughter in the grave while seeking a wife from amongst her remaining children appalled her. Then realisation of what he said lightened her mood. *Elizabeth, married to the heir of Longbourn? A most convenient alternative.* Mrs. Bennet was not a complicated woman. She had long calculated that having one of her daughters settled in marriage to a man who would help the rest of the family should Mr. Bennet die, would guarantee the future of the rest. Therefore, her welcome became much more gracious.

* * *

WHEN THE CARRIAGE arrived at Longbourn, Mr. Bennet ran to open the door and climbed inside almost before it stopped. Oblivious to the other occupants, he gathered his eldest child in his arms, along with the assortment of blankets, and carried her into the house.

Elizabeth finally looked at Mr. Darcy. Propriety demanded she leave the intimacy of the closed carriage immediately. However, she could not go without giving thanks for his efforts to see them to Longbourn.

"Please know, Miss Elizabeth, I did it only for you," was his soft reply.

She looked at him questioningly. *What, in heavens name, had he meant by such a comment?* She shook her head and left the carriage. She would think about it later.

It was not until she was upstairs with her sister before she realised that he might have regretted the harsh words spoken between the two of them. Or perhaps he was merely stating the obvious? She had asked for transportation, and he provided it at her request. Whatever his meaning, she would probably never know. Filled with something like regret, she doubted she would see him again.

Before leaving Netherfield, Elizabeth had been able to offer condolences to Mr. Bingley. She also arranged a correspondence with Miss Darcy. It would be good to have another confidant, though she could never imagine being able to speak as freely with her as she did Charlotte or Jane. *Jane!* Elizabeth wanted to sob at the sight of her sister lying on her bed. The paralysis which had set in the first hours after ingesting the oysters had lessened into a tingling during the night as sensations moved from Jane's torso to her extremities. By this morning, Jane was able to keep the water and weak tea in her stomach.

Resolved, Elizabeth would think, pray, and hope for Jane's recovery. Any other thought, especially of the master of Pemberley, would be most unwelcomed.

* * *

Mrs. Bennet was surprised to see that it was Mr. Darcy who had accompanied her daughters back home. She had hoped for Mr. Bingley. The mistress of Longbourn did have to admit, though Darcy was an abominable man, he had elegant equipage.

CHAPTER 16

Netherfield Park

By the time Darcy returned to Netherfield Park, Charles was downstairs trying to empty the brandy decanter on his own. Even under these dire circumstances, it was not a fitting activity for a Sunday.

"The fault belongs to me." Bingley took another drink.

Darcy was relieved to see the amber liquid was still near the top of the crystal decanter and yet, he found a man undone. He was still in his clothing worn the night before with the exception of the cravat being askew and his waistcoat open. Strands of his auburn hair were sticking up like spiked heads of wheat in a scanty harvest. And his hands—they were shaking violently enough to slosh the contents of his glass onto the floor.

"What do you mean, Charles? What fault?" Darcy doubted he would ever see Elizabeth again, and he knew where to place blame—solely with himself.

"All of it, Darcy. The poisoning. Hurst's death. My sister becoming a widow. Miss Bennet being so dangerously ill." Disgust dripped from his tongue with each phrase. "If only I had not put my desires ahead of what was the proper course, none of this would have happened. Had I listened to you and the colonel and sent Caroline to London, she would not have brought in the shellfish to try to gain your favour. Hurst would still be alive, and Miss Bennet would be well." He inhaled deeply. "You see? It is all my fault. All mine."

Darcy shook his head. While there was a measure of truth to his friend's arguments, he was not to blame.

"I understand, Charles, and I sincerely regret the loss to your family. I enjoyed Hurst. He was a good man." Darcy comprehended the pangs of death: the powerful ache in the heart and the feeling of uselessness against such a foe. Death was an unyielding enemy. "However, you could never have foreseen what would happen with that one decision. Who would anticipate ordering delicacies from the London markets would have such repercussions? It was a mistake, nothing else."

"But, Darcy, one death and possibly another, should my dear Jane not recover." Bingley's face reflected anguish. He was unaware that he had spoken of the eldest Miss Bennet in such a familiar, affectionate manner. "I do not believe I could live with the loss of such a woman, Darcy."

"Again, my friend, I understand." Darcy sat in the chair across from him and removed the dangling glass from Bingley's hands. "When both my mother and my father died, I was convinced there was something I should have done to prevent it from happening. Something more. It took years to realise I had no power, no authority, and no wisdom to save them. Daily we face events outside of our control. Unfortunately, this is one of them."

"But how did you conquer this, Darcy?" Bingley sat back in the chair, his head resting on the back with his eyes to the ceiling. "How do I no longer harbour this feeling of hopeless, helpless loss, and blame?"

"Time, Bingley." Darcy paused in thought and then added, "And insight."

"I feel I have neither, I am afraid."

"Think ahead, Charles. At this point in time, this miniscule second in your life, how can you learn from this?"

Bingley stared him in the eye.

"Will you put your own desires ahead of doing what is proper?"

"I would hope not, though I fear I am a selfish creature."

"Then give consideration to this. Charles, as a property owner, you will face hardships brought on by others and even your own decisions. With this disruption to your home, your first home, there is an opportunity you may not be aware of." Darcy was firm. "It is reported that Julius Caesar stated almost two millennia ago that 'experience is the teacher of all things.' It is up to you to decide whether or not you will learn from this. We are all selfish creatures, my friend." He could not help but think of the way matters ended with Elizabeth. "Me more than most." He rested his elbows on his knees and hung his head.

He should not have been surprised when Bingley failed to correct his last comment. Nevertheless, he was. *Am I truly so dreadful?* First the colonel, then Elizabeth, and now Bingley. He sighed. He had failed to act the gentleman to all of them to one extent or another and they, all of them, each in their own way, brought it to his attention—especially Elizabeth. Her words still stung that inner man who foolishly bolstered him at inappropriate times.

Charles Bingley sat forward in his chair, a growing determination on his face.

"I will give consideration to your words, Darcy, and I appreciate you sharing them with me. I have final arrangements to make." He let out a shuddering breath. "And I need to see Miss Bennet."

As Bingley stood to walk out of the room, he extended his hand. Darcy stood as well, all the words which had been said still echoing around the room.

Minutes later, Georgiana tapped on the door seeking her brother. The few moments that morning she had spent with Elizabeth before the two Miss Bennets' departure had left her spirits improved, but she still had concerns which weighed heavily in her heart.

"Brother?" She stepped into his extended arms.

"Oh, Georgie." He had not used the shortened form of her name since before the death of their father. "Your own experience with loss cannot help but cause you sadness. I worry for you."

"I love you, Fitzwilliam." They sat next to each other on the only settee in the room. "And the truth is, dear brother, I spent much of the night worrying about what might have been. I worried about you."

"How is that, poppet?"

"Miss Bingley ordered the tea based on your preferences, Fitzwilliam." When he started to speak, she put her hand on his arm to stop him. "I have never appreciated the briny taste and texture, so they were not a threat to me. However, I know how you enjoy them. I am so relieved you were not inclined towards shellfish yesterday, but had you done so, Mrs. Hurst and Miss Bingley might not have been the only sisters who lost a loved one."

Darcy put his arm behind her shoulders and pulled her to him, brushing a tear from her cheek. "Do not fret so, Georgie. It did not happen."

"No, Brother, it did not." She made sure she had his full attention. Her tears had ceased. "I could not fail to notice you never seem to eat much when the Miss Bennets are here for tea. Is Richard correct?"

"What did Richard say?" It was a challenge born of discomfort.

Georgiana blushed. "The first time Elizabeth was here, he said love could affect a man's appetite adversely. Is it true? Are you in love with Elizabeth?"

Darcy sucked in his breath. "Georgiana Catherine Darcy! That you should ask such a question is bold and improper." His lack of ease was evident in his tone. "What you are wanting to know is my concern and my concern only."

His sister grinned. "You do not frighten or intimidate me with your master of Pemberley growl, Fitzwilliam. I am growing immune. I merely pretended to feel threatened as you seemed to find such justification for your sternness in me doing so."

"Who are you and what have you done with my darling, dutiful, sweet sister?"

"I do love you, Brother—dearly." She patted his chest just below where her head rested on his shoulder. "Elizabeth kindly reminded me that no human is without flaws." When she felt his head move back at the mention of the lady, Georgiana continued. "Yes, she even included you."

"Well, I am not perfect as Miss Elizabeth is very well aware." Darcy sighed. "Georgie, I believe I am in trouble where she is concerned. Every negative aspect of my character seems to come to the fore in her presence. Thus, she has called me arrogant, proud, and disdainful of the feelings of others." He could not fathom sharing such information with his little sister, but it seemed his jaw was unhinged, and he was unable to stop. He also noted she did not jump to correct his statement. His frustration with himself was thriving. "I am no fool, though I seem to act the part when Miss Elizabeth and I are in the same room.

"My words to her on occasion have been unkind. Her response is dissonant. At other times, we speak as freely as I have never before with a woman. We have already tried to start over as friends." He shook his head. "It did not last."

"Were those severe words said under duress? Consider, I pray you, the circumstances behind the words. Brother, you implied that the turning point was with your portion of the conversation. Why was this, do you think? What allowed you to feel you could say such things to a woman you consider a friend?"

Darcy thought about her questions and was at a loss how to answer.

"Fitzwilliam, when I spoke with Elizabeth about Ramsgate, she prodded me to consider what lessons I had learned from the event. I have learned several things. I learned people were not always what they appeared to be. I learned to not put faith in my own judgment alone, to seek counsel for matters I do not clearly understand. I learned that ignorance of the ways of the world is a dangerous thing for an innocent. And I also learned it was best to make decisions which would protect my future and the Darcy name. So, while I wished my conduct undone with Mr. Wickham, at the same time, I am grateful for these powerful lessons which will serve me well when I am out in society. You cannot always be there to protect me, Brother.

"So I ask you now, what lessons have you learned from your conflicts with Elizabeth? What prompted your conversations to fall apart, and why did you respond so vehemently? How can you prevent it from happening again?" At this, she sat back and looked directly at him. She felt like she had learned to be like her new friend and that Elizabeth would be proud of her for being so bold. "Are you in love with Elizabeth Bennet?"

Every single one of his wise words of counsel to Bingley were coming back to bite him. That his young sister would offer those same principles was humbling. He dropped his head back to rest on the settee in the manner Charles had done earlier. He wished for the presence of his mother. She would soothe his wounds. Georgiana's counsel was not offered from spitefulness but from the strongest love which was willing to cause pain so there could be a healing.

Finally, he spoke. "I will give serious reflection to all you have said, Georgiana." He noted her slight smile. "Do I love Elizabeth Bennet?" He was shaking his head slowly back and forth. His voice softened. "I regret the chasm between us. I regret the loss of a friend, but I do not think the emotion I feel is love."

His eyes closed with his last comment, so he completely missed his sister's eyes roll in disbelief. She wanted to give an unladylike snort.

Behind his lids, Darcy clearly saw the events of last night play out again—how her eyes sparkled like diamonds in the candlelight and how a becoming blush born of ire had cloaked her cheeks. Yes, she was magnificent. And, because of his own deeds and words, she was lost to him.

The pain was excruciating and almost robbed him of breath. He damned himself for being such an arrogant fool. He knew what to do.

"Mrs. Hurst and Miss Bingley will be returning to London, and I have offered to share our carriage. Charles will be transporting Hurst to be buried at the Hurst family's crypt. I will attend him there. He plans to return to Hertfordshire and remain until Miss Bennet recovers, offering whatever assistance he can."

"But what of you and me? Will we return to Hertfordshire? Will we be in company with Miss Elizabeth again?"

The breath escaped him. "I think not." Darcy needed to remove himself to come to terms with all he had learned about himself. He had been in error and knowing this shamed him deeply. He would forget Miss Elizabeth in time and so would Georgiana. With her coming out in two years, Georgiana would be too busy to recall the events at Netherfield Park. Her next words put an end to his plans.

"Elizabeth and I promised to start a correspondence, Brother."

He wanted to sigh.

* * *

LONGBOURN

Longbourn had been robbed of peace, pilfered by a man so offensive that it threatened never to return.

Mary, Kitty, Lydia, and Mrs. Bennet hovered silently next to Elizabeth around Jane's bed. Words were whispered and prayers were said. Their worry united them in a way never before. Mary moralized, "Whether one member suffer, all the members suffer." None wanted to be anywhere other than at Jane's bedside. After less than a day since his arrival, despite her plans for her second daughter, not even Mrs. Bennet wanted to spend another minute in Mr. Collin's presence.

The day prior, Mr. William Filbert Collins had seated himself in the largest chair in the drawing room waiting for the eldest daughters to enter Longbourn and greet him when they returned from Netherfield. It was his due. The odious man had not deigned to rise until Mr. Darcy assisted Elizabeth from the carriage and walked to the entrance hall. The parson's ire was raised as both Jane, carried by her father, and Elizabeth immediately—without giving him any notice—retired upstairs. Mr. Darcy heard his offended snort. Curious, he entered the parlour.

"You are aware that travel is not done on the Sabbath?" Mr. Collins postured himself in the same manner he had with Mrs. Bennet the day before, though standing on his toes did not quite put him at eye level with Mr. Darcy.

The insolence of the man did not thwart Darcy. "Who might you be?"

"I am the heir to this estate, Mr. William Collins, parson of Hunsford in Kent whose patroness is Lady Catherine de Bourgh. You have heard of the great lady, I imagine?" Recognising a man of Quality in Mr. Darcy's fine clothes and demeanor, Mr. Collins simpered, "And who might you be?"

"No one who would possibly be of interest to you." He stepped back away from the cleric, turned, and left Longbourn. *Of all people to run into—his aunt's new rector!* Knowing his aunt, he was unsurprised at the man's ignorance. Still, Mr. Collins' conceit angered him. *Just who was he? Heir? There was an entail? That man, that bumptious twit, would inherit Longbourn?* An entail would mean the Bennet daughters would lose their family home when their father died. Such disturbing news. Darcy made the three-mile trip back to Netherfield Park in deep thought.

* * *

THEY HAD BARELY SEATED themselves for dinner when Mr. Collins began. "Mrs. Bennet, I have been here more than four and twenty hours and have yet to meet Miss Elizabeth. I am certain this is an oversight. Lady Catherine de Bourgh is quite attentive to propriety. Your neglect to introduce me to all members of the family is a slight upon that great lady herself."

Mr. Bennet looked down the table to his nephew. "How so, Mr. Collins? How could I possibly offend any human with a modicum of intelligence?"

As Elizabeth was still attending Jane, Mary vowed to report it all to Lizzy. How she would laugh at the ridiculousness of the man.

Mr. Collins had not expected the challenge and was left quite speechless.

"You have not responded, Mr. Collins, so I do wonder whether you did not understand my questions." Sarcasm dripped from Mr. Bennet's tongue. Both Lydia and Kitty started to giggle, but one look from their father stopped them immediately. "Allow me to make myself understood." He cleared his throat into the room filled with silence. "You will not disturb my daughters. And you will not concern yourself with their conduct." Mr. Bennet sat back in his chair and lifted his wine glass, twirling it slowly to watch the light refracted from the vintage. "I believe a se'nnight should be long enough for you to become familiar with our small portion of Hertfordshire and the neighbourhood. I suggest you walk out tomorrow and every day henceforth. By Saturday next, you will return to Kent to report your findings to Lady Catherine de Bourgh. I am sure she would find solace in having you at her convenience."

The dissatisfaction emitted from the victim of Mr. Bennet's instructions was all that was heard from his section of the table.

Mrs. Bennet looked to the man she had been married to for over two decades. Never could she recall him offering such protection for their daughters—nor for her. A warmth bloomed throughout her chest, and she could not contain the smile directed at her husband. She was not aware that her husband saw the twinkle in her eyes and could not know his chest swelled as a result.

Hours later, Mary told Elizabeth what had happened at the dinner table. Lizzy almost cried in relief.

CHAPTER 17

Friday, 18 October 1811
By the end of the week, there was cause for celebration in the Bennet family. Jane's health was improving daily, albeit slowly, and after his return to Netherfield Park from London, Mr. Bingley had not failed to visit once and sometimes twice each day. Unfortunately, Mr. Collins's propensity to capture Elizabeth's attention as the object of his affections could not be hindered. A woman so devoted to the care of a loved one would be an asset to his home.

"Mama, does Mr. Collins wake early?" Elizabeth had avoided her odious and condescending cousin by dutifully remaining at her sister's bedside. He spoke of his own humility in such a way that an educated person could easily discern he was anything but lowly-minded. He reminded Elizabeth of the old rooster who ruffled his feathers every time a hen was in his sight.

Mrs. Bennet, though her mind still hoped for one of her daughters to marry the heir to Longbourn, accepted that her own heart balked at the idea. Over the past days, she conceded there were fates worse than the hedgerows.

"The man does not rise until the noon hour. You are safe to walk out if you would like." She gave her daughter a knowing look. "I will stay with Jane."

That was all the invitation Elizabeth needed as the day beckoned her to enjoy its rich blessings. She kissed her sister's cheek, padded softly down the stairs, and donned her outdoor coat and boots.

While she strolled briskly through the countryside, she thought of her last confrontation with the presumptuous Mr. Collins the night prior. The household had long since quieted for the night and Elizabeth had left Jane's room to fill a pitcher of water. She had not expected anyone to be in the hallway. Therefore, when Mr. Collins whispered out of the darkness, she almost dropped the pottery in her hands.

"Mr. Collins!" He had startled her and continued to do so when he approached far too closely. "May I be of assistance?

"My dear Elizabeth. How fortuitous to meet you here. Alone." He wiped his brow with his meaty hand. "At the request of my patroness, Lady Catherine de Bourgh, I have come to Longbourn to seek a wife. Your patience and fortitude in dispensing care to your sister is admirable. I have heard the eldest Miss Bennet is the beauty of the family. Though I have been in the household for nearly a se'nnight, I have yet to determine whether this is so. However, Mr. Bingley continues to call on her, so I feel it incumbent upon me to seek the next best daughter. I would at this time approach your father for his permission to court you. I can imagine no impediments to his agreement."

"Mr. Collins! You presume too much, sir." Elizabeth could not recall ever being this angry, not even with Mr. Darcy. She also had never felt as uncomfortable as at that moment in her own home. Feeling her courage rise, she continued in hushed tones. "I have not given you permission to address me so familiarly. I am *Miss* Elizabeth to you. Furthermore, you have yet to ask my permission for a courtship. Therefore, there is no basis for you to approach my father with such a request." She was livid and could feel her whole body tremble. A picture formed in her mind of taking the heavy water jug and smashing it on the side of his head. She was momentarily stunned at the intensity of her desire to commit violence against another human and realised how long it had been since she had slept a full night through. "Now pardon me, sir, I shall not be detained."

She brushed by him and crossed the hall to her father's bedchamber. Pounding on the door with the side of her fisted hand, she stepped back when the door swung open.

"Lizzy!" Mr. Bennet had been in his chair reading. He noticed the man hovering behind his daughter. "Mr. Collins, why are you up at this time of night, and what are you doing with Elizabeth?"

Elizabeth had never heard such a tone from her parent. It was threatening and demanding. When her father stepped out of his room and in front of Elizabeth, Mr. Collins retreated down the hall to his own room, whimpering a muddled excuse, though no apology.

"Lizzy?" Even in the barest of candlelight, Elizabeth could see the hitch in his brow. "Did he frighten you, child?"

"I will admit he makes me ill at ease, Papa. I thank you for your rapid response."

"Ah, my girl." Mr. Bennet gently tugged the ribbon at the end of her thick braid, which had swung forward and draped over her chest to land at her waist. It was something he had done to each of his daughters since childhood. It made the girls giggle to have the bows undone and made his wife furious. He stepped back into his bed chamber and motioned her inside. "Is Jane asleep?"

"She is. That is why I thought to fill the pitcher." She breathed in deeply to calm herself. "I did not expect to find *that man* in the hallway."

"No, I do not suppose you did." He took the pitcher from her hands and placed it on the bedside table and patted his own bed. "Come."

Elizabeth had not crawled into her father's bed in years. Yet the childhood memories were welcome reminders of when she and Jane would beg him for a tale of knights and princesses. Though he was a scholarly man, he was imaginative enough to entertain little girls with fairy tales.

"I have not had the opportunity to speak with you, dearest daughter, since your return home. How did you find Mr. and Miss Darcy while you were at Netherfield Park?"

It was the opening Elizabeth had longed for. She knew the impression her father had of Darcy.

"Papa, I confess to some confusion where Mr. Darcy is concerned." She paused to place her thoughts in order, pulling the blankets up to her chin as she piled the pillows behind her back. "The man has been both high-handed and considerate. He is an excellent brother and a good friend to the amiable Mr. Bingley yet has been shockingly rude to me. Further, he expresses such strong opinions about matters which are entirely wrong." Elizabeth was not one to cover her own errors. "Our last conversation surely resembled two gladiators fighting over a cherished prize." She sighed. "I said some terrible things in defence to his unkind words, Papa. I am not proud of my conduct. And I do not believe I can ever forgive his."

Mr. Bennet easily recalled how Darcy had publicly embarrassed his favourite child. If he had done so again, unlike the last time, he would have an interview with him for his ungentleman-like behaviour. Darcy wore his pride of position like a fashionable outer garment and Mr. Bennet anticipated the satisfaction of stripping it off him.

"Has the man left Hertfordshire?"

"He has." Elizabeth confessed. "Miss Darcy and I have agreed to a correspondence. They are now residing at their London home." She saw the anger radiating off her father. "Papa, before you ride off to confront him, you should know that Mr. Darcy and I had the opportunity to speak in private—twice. Father, he let down the mask he hides behind, and I found him to be a surprisingly pleasing man. He is intelligent and has a sharp sense of humour which greatly resembles your own. If you could see, as I did, the tenderness he has towards his sister. You would know with confidence that he cherishes her and would take any steps to protect her. He has hundreds of people he is responsible for. He is a complex man."

Mr. Bennet held up his hand. "Yes, yes, I know the bounds of his loyalty for his sister." Still, Mr. Bennet was perplexed by her speech. "Lizzy, do you like the man?"

"Oh, Papa. I do, and I do not." Elizabeth was just as confounded. "His apology for his words at the assembly was clumsy but heartfelt. It raised him in my estimation. Then his assumption that he could direct my life and the life of my family by expecting you and me to forget our own concerns to attend Miss Darcy—in London—was the height of presumptuousness." She felt her words were making little sense. "How could one man behave in such extremes? I do not understand?"

"Lizzy, dear. Men are simple creatures." Mr. Bennet chuckled at the thought. Though he would like to think himself outstandingly different from the masses, he knew he was not. "We are not unlike two stallions that ignore each other until a new mare is introduced. When a pretty miss is involved, men become antagonistic and aggressive—entirely out of character. Whether someone threatens our authority or our position, the same result is achieved—antagonism and aggression, or in Mr. Darcy's case, arrogance and excessive pride." He sat next to his daughter. "By chance, did Mr. Darcy explain why he acted in such a manner?"

Elizabeth reflected back to the apology after she found him on the ground in the field. "Yes, Papa. However, he did not offer a reason why he was so…officious…when we argued at Netherfield."

"Think of what you know about the day the man had. If he is the sort of brother that you claim him to be, how challenging would it have been to keep calm with the threat of serious harm to his sister? How could he have helped but have his senses heightened by the danger?"

Elizabeth bent her head, meditating on the questions. She had felt the tension at Netherfield Park. Before the food poisoning, Elizabeth had looked forward to reassuring him of the ease with which she had been able to speak with his sister. All had changed by the time she had met him on her way to the kitchen.

"Papa," she whispered. "At the end of our heated discussion, when the harsh words were still echoing in the hallway, he handed me the food he had gathered for himself, knowing I was hungry. I do not understand the man at all."

"Do you want to?" Mr. Bennet's heart felt the first twinge of break. Suddenly he felt his years. "My Lizzy, is all this your frustration at not having had the opportunity to find a way to make peace with the man? Are you concerned for him?"

"It is of no consequence, Papa. Mr. Bingley reported that he does not expect a return of his guests. I will write to Miss Darcy, but I do not believe I will ever see Mr. Darcy again."

Mr. Bennet wondered whether she knew how despondent she sounded. *Perhaps he would not call on the man after all.*

* * *

Lucas Lodge

Lady Lucas welcomed Mr. Collins with open arms. Her hopes for a match between Colonel Fitzwilliam and Charlotte were crushed when he departed Hertfordshire with no promise to return. Though she secretly hoped to crow about her daughter marrying the son of an earl, even a second son, she was not willing to overlook any possible candidate for a son-in-law—particularly the heir to Longbourn.

Mr. Collins was impressed with Miss Lucas's countenance. She was a calm woman who appeared well-qualified to run a home. As his cousin Elizabeth was strong-willed, Miss Lucas appeared amenable, thus, he accepted the invitation to remove himself from Longbourn to Lucas Lodge with little misgiving.

However, Miss Charlotte Lucas was seriously displeased.

* * *

LONGBOURN

Elizabeth's walk was as restorative as she had hoped it would be. She returned in time to meet Mr. Bingley as he handed off his horse to Longbourn's groom. His smile seemed a hazy outline of what it had been prior to the loss of Mr. Hurst.

"Miss Elizabeth, I was longing for a chance to speak with you."

Elizabeth walked closer and saw the lines furrowing his brow.

"Please, tell me how it goes at Netherfield Park?" She led him to a bench below the drawing room window, where they could be observed but not heard.

"My home is filled from the bottom to the top with silence." He grimaced. "I am met with it when I enter each room. It is my most constant companion."

Elizabeth's heart ached for Bingley. She wished to make it return to the days before the tea.

He grimaced.

"How *are* Mrs. Hurst and Miss Bingley? Have you had news of them?"

"I have had letters from them both. Louisa complains about Caroline, and Caroline does the same about Louisa." Bingley snorted. "It seems the death of my brother-in-law shifted the power from my single sister to the new widow. Caroline writes that Louisa has let it slip several times how Caroline was responsible for the poisoned food." He was not surprised to see Elizabeth's eyes widen. "In addition, the fact that Caroline is required to be in mourning along with Louisa, has seriously affected Caroline's spirits." He shook his head. "I do not believe my youngest sister is at all pleased with the situation and finds London not as pleasant as she thought it would be."

Elizabeth noted the sly smile on his face. "And you? Are your spirits improved?"

"I will admit that they are." Bingley's mood lightened. "I have heard from Darcy that Caroline called on Miss Darcy the day after they returned to Town and was quite put out when she was told she was not receiving anyone." Bingley nodded his head. "If I may, I will share this next intelligence with you for two reasons. The first is that I hold you and your sister in the greatest of confidence, and the second is because you were often the victim of Caroline's barbs as she endeavoured to attach herself to Darcy."

Elizabeth's curiosity was at its peak. Her joy was just as high. That he would speak of Jane as an intimate brought such pleasure to her heart. It was a struggle to keep her countenance.

"Darcy informed me that he had let it go too long… He wrote that he told Caroline in clear terms that she would never be mistress of Pemberley…though he considered her the sister of one of his closest friends, they would never be more." Bingley let out a breath on a huff. "I can only imagine how she has excused his decision as being the result of the tainted oysters and is undoubtedly calculating how long until he realises that she was not at fault." He shook his head. "My sister is a fool."

Elizabeth agreed, though she did not say it aloud.

"Mr. Bingley, I am not owed the information you shared. Nevertheless, might I repeat this to my sister?"

He blushed. "Pray, do."

She believed it incumbent to offer him relief by telling him what he most wanted to know as he had just done the same service for her. "I hope you are aware that each day you sit in our parlour, Jane is told. My mother reports to her exactly what is said, even what you wear." She saw his face take on a crimson hue.

Charles Bingley was the most precious of men. His inexperience with being a landowner was not a degradation to a knowledgeable woman, and Jane Bennet was knowledgeable. His coming to Longbourn showed a devotion that any woman dreamed of. "She speaks of me then?"

"Quite often." Elizabeth was keenly aware how embarrassed her sister would be if Jane knew she was speaking of such to this particular young man.

"Might I, if you would not think me too bold, leave a message for your sister?"

"For a certainty."

"I overheard you and Darcy speak about poetry's impact on the heart, so I will not attempt a verse. But I would appreciate it if Miss Bennet knew that the sun pales, the sky is less blue, and the grey clouds hover over Netherfield Park each day she remains unwell." After pausing to compose his thoughts, he continued. "My heartbeat is not as strong and my breath is but a whisper. It will take her full recovery, Miss Elizabeth, before I am able to enjoy life again."

Elizabeth's eyes filled with unshed tears at the beauty of his words.

"Will you tell her?"

"I will." She closed her eyes to indelibly inscribe each syllable in her mind. She would not forget one word.

"Then I will take my leave."

As they approached the front of the house, they observed Charlotte Lucas hurrying towards them, her face beet red with anger. "My mother, the very woman who gave me life and who should do what is in my best interest, has demanded I accept Mr. Collins as a husband." Her vehemence turned to panic. "What am I to do, Eliza? I cannot marry that man."

CHAPTER 18

Saturday, 28 March 1812
Rosings Park, Kent

The *man was an imbecile!* Darcy was shocked at how few seconds it took in the company of his aunt's parson to remember the man was idiotic. He could tell from the expression on his face that the colonel felt the same. Their annual sojourn to Kent had been a relief to Darcy, an opportunity to distance himself further from his lingering feelings for Elizabeth Bennet. In prior years, the trip to Rosings had been an obligation. Now, it was a farce.

Georgiana's correspondence with Miss Elizabeth had provided him with months of self-imposed disparagement followed by flashes of justification for his actions, which were usually only temporary. He was not proud of how he treated Miss Elizabeth and from the regular intimations, Georgiana was not either. He wished he had not shared with his little sister his initial opinions of the Bennet family as it did nothing to decrease Elizabeth's appeal in Georgiana's eyes—it served to influence her opinion of him.

* * *

DARCY HOUSE, **London**
The winter months

Before he left for Kent, she made a last-ditch effort to move him to act. "Brother, why can we not return to Hertfordshire? Mr. Bingley is alone and has written several times to offer an invitation. Miss Bingley is no longer there to distract you. Besides, Miss Elizabeth reports on her sister's improvement and her joy at having Mr. Bingley call each day. In her last letter, she said he had been a faithful attendant—not missing even one day since we departed Netherfield Park five months ago—in calling to check on Miss Bennet." Sighing she said, "Is it not the height of romance, Brother, when Mr. Bingley daily shows his constancy and devotion?"

Georgiana had no idea how he longed to pick her up, throw her in the carriage, jump in after her, and head twenty miles north to Meryton—as soon as he finished kicking himself. It was madness how often he mulled on the beauty of a fine pair of eyes and an intelligence most likely superior to his own. If he sighed one more time in his sister's presence, she was likely to send him to Bedlam. He was acting like one of the characters in Georgiana's romance novels that he told her he would *never* read.

* * *

FOR MONTHS, Georgiana had desired a relationship between her brother and Elizabeth. She was the only woman of Georgiana's knowledge who was capable of drawing her brother out from himself. She filled a room with life and vitality by her mere presence. Darcy House needed it and Pemberley desperately cried out for someone like Elizabeth. Georgiana longed for a sister and recognised how well Elizabeth fit the part.

It confused her, at first, how two such intelligent people who were so well-matched could not seem to get along peacefully. Then she thought of the little she did know of their interactions. They were both strong-willed, both confident of their own intelligence, and, most likely, both passionate by nature. A volatile mix.

When she and her brother first returned to London, she noticed his interest whenever Elizabeth's name was mentioned or when a letter from her arrived. At first, she satisfied him by imparting the information. When nothing was done, when her brother refused to even speak about returning to Hertfordshire, she stopped sharing the contents of the letters. *She chuckled to herself.* Her plan had worked. His desire to hear about Elizabeth grew exponentially. Over the months, Georgiana had learned when to speak and the value of when to keep quiet.

* * *

SHE HAD BEEN VERY secretive with the information from her correspondence from Longbourn. He had even been tempted to search her rooms for her stash of letters while she was at her lessons.

How do you explain to a younger sister why a normally reasonable brother acted contrary to his own inclinations? He sighed, then immediately determined he would not do so again. He was not some pitiful hero from a gothic story written by a woman whose idea of a valiant gentleman was a troubled soul with longish hair and sad eyes who could not control his fortune, his friends, or his enemies!

Darcy trusted Miss Elizabeth not to complain to Georgiana of his behaviour. It was not her way to sneak behind an issue when forthright confrontation was possible. However, they had been separated the whole of the winter, so she was not able to fully charge him with his crimes. Nor was she available to see his efforts to change.

Good heavens! I am as lovelorn as that...what was his name in the last book? The hero who actually cried at the temporary loss of his lady love? It had been a ridiculous story. Even he knew that within the remaining few pages they would have their happy-ever-after. He wanted to throw the book at the wall or in the fireplace instead of sneaking it back on Georgiana's shelf.

"Has she spoken of me?" Darcy asked before he left for Kent.

The left eyebrow on Georgiana's face shot up. Though she had cautiously mentioned Elizabeth during the past months, her brother had rarely said her name, nor had he responded with interest. His usual comment was to inquire whether there was any news and then shrugged his shoulders to indicate his lack of concern. She knew better. She saw the longing which filled his eyes when a new letter was resting on the silver salver waiting to be opened. She often caught him closely observing her own responses to what she read. *Oh, yes. He was interested.*

Fitzwilliam Darcy had been a large, dark, growling bear to live with since they returned to Town. Georgiana had observed his efforts to interact more with those not in his circle. She speculated it was due to Elizabeth's rejoinders to his actions in Hertfordshire. She also watched him try to be more pleasing to their aunt and uncle, Lord and Lady Matlock, in spite of their pressure to attach her brother to an heiress of their choice. The real challenge would be Lady Catherine. If only Georgiana did not have her lessons in Town, she might brave her fearsome aunt to enjoy such a spectacle—for she knew beyond a doubt that Lady Catherine's domineering ways would test her brother's goal of improving his character. Fortunately, Richard would be accompanying him in her stead.

PORTSMOUTH, **Hampshire**

Richard Fitzwilliam had turned Wickham over to the waiting ship's officers and stood on the Portsmouth dock as the boat sailed out of sight. It had not been a fond farewell for either man. Even as George Wickham stepped on the gangplank, the colonel wanted to push him in the water and hold his head under until he blew bubbles, one last effort to instill a fear of consequences into the man. The crowds surrounding him and the fact that he had no dry uniform to change into had stopped him.

NEWCASTLE, **Northumberland**

Upon his return to London, his commanding officer presented him with orders to take his regiment to Newcastle for training. The weather had been bitterly cold, and they were isolated from the rest of the country. He had long, lonely hours to reflect on his choices: his family, his career, and Miss Charlotte Lucas. Each time one of the recruits expressed heart-felt sadness when they mentioned a wife and children waiting in some other part of England, he was reminded why he had decided never to marry. How he envied those same men when they received correspondence from that same family. Heartache and heaven!

* * *

ROSINGS PARK

Darcy's eyes rolled to the ceiling as Mr. Collins praised his aunt's choice of grey thread for the housekeeper at Hunsford Parsonage to mend the wool socks he wore. Darcy shuddered at the thought of the poor woman touching the coverings for the clergyman's massive feet. If they were like the rest of his garments, it would seem they rarely left his person to be laundered. *Of all the asinine things his aunt chose to share her expertise on, this was the oddest!*

Darcy looked to his only female cousin to see that Anne had fallen asleep sitting slumped in her chair. Richard had a small smile on his face. Darcy wondered what might cause such mirth and then he noticed Anne's companion, Mrs. Jenkinson's, head bob—she too was ready to settle into the same fate as her charge. Darcy smirked at the ridiculous of it all.

"Mr. Collins, do you not depart in three days for your return to Hertfordshire?" Lady Catherine had a bad habit of waiting until the parson was starting to sit down before she asked him a question. He then popped back up to stand before her. Once he answered, he paused to await her caustic rejoinder or farcical advice. When it did not come or when he assumed she was finished, he sought again to sit. Darcy wondered whether it was a deliberate ploy on his aunt's part to have the man dance like a marionette as she pulled the strings.

Mr. Collins looked Darcy's way. He had been surprised to learn the man who escorted the Miss Bennets back to Longbourn was none other than his esteemed patroness's nephew, Mr. Darcy. In the ten months he had held the living at Hunsford, he had often listened to Lady Catherine expound on the importance of the great name of Darcy. He wondered what Darcy had been doing at Longbourn but had not the boldness to ask.

"You failed in your mission last time you travelled to survey your inheritance to bring home a wife. I anticipate you will not fail this time." Though it was not stated as an order, it was intended to be one.

"Yes, Lady Catherine. I am pleased to inform you of two particular ladies who are vying for the position of mistress of Hunsford Parsonage." He stiffened his spine and raised his nose in self-importance. "My cousin, Miss Elizabeth Bennet, and the daughter of Sir William Lucas, Miss Charlotte Lucas, are well-qualified and long for the position. It is my intent to choose the one who would be most docile and appreciative of your kind attentions and guidance, Lady Catherine."

"What?" Darcy and the colonel exclaimed at once. They looked at each other in disbelief. That man had bandied about the women's names as if he had the right to do so. *Vying? For Mr. Collins? Absurd!*

Lady Catherine's head snapped to Darcy. "What is the meaning of this?"

At the eruption, both Anne and her companion startled awake. Darcy's mind was spinning. He recalled Mr. Collins arrogance at Longbourn and his claims of being the heir. He was an ignorant braggart! That the vile man thought Elizabeth as docile showed a tremendous lack of understanding of her character. That he would consider her as a potential mate was revolting. He could not allow it to happen. He would not allow it.

Darcy glanced at Anne, relieved she had not pressed a marriage with him. When he met with her earlier in the day, she clearly and without hesitation informed him it had never been her desire to wed Fitzwilliam Darcy; it was a figment of her mother's dreams—not hers.

As if facing his future, Darcy studied the parson. *A husband to Elizabeth Bennet? I think not!*

Why had it taken a comment from a sycophant to bring clarity to his own heart? He no longer wanted Elizabeth Bennet for a friend. He wanted her for his wife. If anyone was to marry Elizabeth Bennet, it would be him. She was the reason he had taken it upon himself to improve his character. She was the woman who nightly invaded his dreams, whom he wanted by his side for the rest of his years. She was a woman who deserved to be pleased, and he determined he was the only man to do so—not some puffed up toad.

"Well?" Lady Catherine insisted, as was her wont. "What have you to say for yourselves?"

Colonel Fitzwilliam spoke up. "Aunt Catherine."

Lady Catherine de Bourgh detested it when he spoke in such a familiar manner. He was the only one of her nephews who did it with what sounded like teasing disrespect. To her, he had never outgrown his childish foibles. She wanted to shake her finger at him and vowed to give him a tongue-lashing as soon as she found out what had stirred both men to their rude behavior.

"Aunt Catherine" —striving for an excuse to disguise their outburst, Richard thought of Georgiana—"I have only received a letter from Georgiana asking for our immediate return to London. I was attempting to gain Darcy's attention."

"That makes no sense, Richard. What would cause such an outburst? Where is this letter? She is my niece, and I am her closest living relative. Bring it to me?"

"No!" Her nephews erupted in tandem.

Lady Catherine had gone from confusion to anger. "I demand to know why you are allowing a young, foolish girl to dictate the lives of two adult men. Has she become so spoilt? I command you to give her over to my care unless…." Lady Catherine stood in front of Darcy. "I demand you honour your name by marrying Anne. Then, and only then, would you have a stable home to bring up Georgiana—to present her at court and see her entry in society."

Anne was unseen by her mother as she rolled her eyes behind Lady Catherine's back. She shook her head at Darcy, reminding him of her desires. They would not marry.

"Mr. Collins could read the first of the banns tomorrow. By the end of your stay at Rosings, you could be wed. It was your mother's fondest wish to unite the two estates and it was Anne's wish as well. She was formed to be your bride." Lady Catherine's voice grew louder as she spoke, and Mr. Collins nodded his head in agreement.

With each word, Anne shook her head more vigorously. Darcy did not need her signal to know Lady Catherine was demanding the impossible from Anne and himself. There was only one woman for him. Darcy was determined he must arrive in Hertfordshire before Collins and convince Elizabeth that he was the only man for her.

"That will not be necessary, Lady Catherine." Darcy's voice was firm. "I have no plans to make an offer to Anne, and she does not want to be mistress of Pemberley. There will be no marriage between us and no joining of two estates." Before she could interrupt, he continued. "As for my sister, it was my father's expressed wish that she remains under our care. I thank you for your solicitous advice, but I am decided." He bowed to his aunt and then looked to Richard. "With that, the two of us will leave for London as soon as our bags are packed. Georgiana is my priority and always will be."

Darcy bowed over Anne's hand, and whispered, "I wish you health and happiness. May God bless you." Then he turned to the clergyman.

"Mr. Collins." He would not wish him success on his travels. His purpose was in direct opposition to his own. "Safe journeys." It was the best he could do.

While Lady Catherine sputtered, Darcy walked out of the drawing room, closely followed by Richard. Within an hour they were in Darcy's carriage headed to London. A rider had been sent ahead with instructions for Georgiana to pack. An express would then find its way to Netherfield Park to inform Bingley that he should expect guests before nightfall.

* * *

"Richard…" They had been on the road for almost a quarter of an hour before Darcy asked the question uppermost in his mind. He had hoped his cousin would volunteer the information; however, Richard had remained silent. "What caused such chagrin when Collins spoke of Miss Elizabeth as his future wife? Are you attached to her?" Darcy rubbed at the ache in his chest.

"Miss Elizabeth? Why would you believe my interest lay in that direction?"

"It does not?" Darcy could not fathom an intelligent man *not* loving Elizabeth Bennet. "Then why did you react as you did?"

Darcy saw the tips of Richard's ears turn red. It was the clue he always looked for—his tell—that revealed he would soon be privy to Richard's innermost thoughts.

"It is Miss Lucas, Miss Charlotte Lucas, who captured my heart without even trying." Richard shook his head. "I have no right to offer for her. My prospects are better than most officers in the military, but it will be a hard life for a good woman. And Miss Lucas is an outstandingly good woman."

"Is it money that holds you back, Cousin?"

"You know it is." Embarrassment laced Richard's voice. "I work hard and give my all, and it will not be enough to see her settled with a husband who is present to care for her." He ran his hand over his face. "I want to offer her the world."

"Is it the world she wants, Richard, or is it you?" Darcy wanted the world for Elizabeth as well. "Until her father gained his knighthood, their family was in trade. Miss Lucas leads a simple life. She is a close friend to Elizabeth, Richard, which means she is both intelligent and generous. Had it been material wealth she wanted, would she not have tried to catch mine or Bingley's attention at the assembly? She did not. I believe you should offer for her. You cannot allow such a woman to marry a man like Collins."

The men rode in silence for miles, both staring out at the passing countryside. Then Richard wondered aloud, "You feel the same way about Miss Elizabeth? You called her by her Christian name. You love her."

Darcy pondered how much he wanted to share with Richard.

Looking across the carriage to his cousin, Darcy sighed. In the hours until they reached London, he confessed it all.

Just before they reached the coaching inn at Bromley, the axle broke on the carriage. They would not be able to travel further that day, nor would they be able to travel on Easter Sunday. It was small comfort that Mr. Collins was not able to travel on that day either.

Both men were frustrated. Instead of arriving in Hertfordshire three days ahead of Mr. Collins, putting into place the strategy they had developed over the last hour, they would have only one day's lead.

"Surely nothing else will go wrong." The colonel reassured himself.

"I hope so as well."

CHAPTER 19

*M*onday, 30 March 1812
Longbourn

Spring was Elizabeth's favourite season. The fields were dotted with a carpet of colourful wildflowers standing erect to soak up the light of the sun. For the past five months, whenever she received a letter from Georgiana—rain or shine—before breaking the seal—she would walk to the folly and seat herself on the same bench where she had sat next to Darcy. On this day, Elizabeth was torn. The joy of the day and the receipt of a missive from a friend was dampened by her father's announcement that morning that Mr. Collins would be returning to Hertfordshire the next day. His purpose? His letter had been specific: he was there to obtain a wife, and ostensibly Elizabeth was still an object of his desire. She scoffed at the idea.

The family had quietly celebrated the festive season at the Meryton chapel the day prior. The disaster at Netherfield Park in the autumn had cast a hushed calm over the Bennet household, a result of the length of Jane's recovery and Mr. Bingley's mourning. There had been no social gatherings. Even Elizabeth's favourite relatives, the Gardiners, had come and gone during the winter with little notice. The only shopping trips to Meryton had been solely for necessary items to run the household. All attention had for Jane's recovery.

Charles Bingley had become such a permanent fixture at Longbourn that his daily presence was no longer unexpected. He had recently informed Jane that he would continue to wear the black crepe armband for another month. After that time, he would seek a moment of privacy with her to ask an important question. Jane had fallen deeply and irrevocably in love with the man. Everyone agreed it would be a good match.

With an arrangement between Jane and Bingley imminent, Mr. Collins was no longer a matrimonial threat to Elizabeth. Whether the clergyman would realise the ladies no longer worried about their protection should the worst befall Mr. Bennet was yet unknown.

Charlotte, too, was a regular visitor to Longbourn. At first, Elizabeth was surprised how interested her long-time friend was in the correspondence from Georgiana. Once Charlotte confessed her pain from the loss of the colonel's company, Elizabeth shared any mention of Richard Fitzwilliam. Charlotte savored any news though always wished for more.

Elizabeth understood. The mention of Georgiana's brother was equally vague and rare in her friend's letters. Like Charlotte, Elizabeth memorised each line and pondered its meaning. Georgiana said Darcy spent much more time with her than he had before coming into Hertfordshire, even after her new companion, a Mrs. Annesley, had been employed. While Elizabeth appreciated the expressions of brotherly affection that Georgiana shared, she wondered at Darcy's motives. Elizabeth sighed and hoped this latest missive would be filled with news which would ease both her and Charlotte's minds. It was not.

Charlotte had whispered to Elizabeth after services that her mother still anticipated her daughter becoming the future mistress of Longbourn. Apparently, Lady Lucas was the sole occupant of Hertfordshire who desired her cousin's arrival.

Elizabeth contemplated the view from the folly, easily recalling Mr. Darcy as he dismounted his horse and stood before her. It was as if it happened yesterday, rather than five months prior. They had sought understanding of each other, had shared introspection, and discussed the emotions which could no longer be contained. She closed her eyes and wondered what her future held. *Would the Darcys and Colonel Fitzwilliam ever find their way into Hertfordshire again?* She could only hope.

* * *

WHEN ELIZABETH MEANDERED BACK to Longbourn, she intercepted Charlotte on the way. It was rare for Charlotte to walk further than the house. Something weighty must have been on her mind to move her to tread outside her normal limits. As Elizabeth moved closer, she saw that Charlotte's face and neck were blotchy from crying, and her eyes were damp and red-rimmed.

"My dear friend, what has happened?"

Charlotte took a deep breath. Taking a well-used handkerchief from her sleeve, she wiped her tear-stained eyes. "My father informed me"—Charlotte gulped and dropped her head in misery— "my father informed me that either I marry Mr. Collins, the only man likely to offer for me, or I must leave my home."

"Oh, no." It was in every way wrong. Charlotte Lucas had quietly managed the running of Lucas Lodge while her parents relished their new positions in society with a languor of inflated self-importance. Elizabeth's heart ached. Though Charlotte did not deserve such a fate, it was often the lot of many ill-dowered women. "What will you do? Where will you go?"

"I can..."

Her comment was stopped by the sound of harnesses jangling and horse hooves dancing in tandem. The young women were standing just beyond the garden of Longbourn so were able to observe the approaching carriage. Was it Collins who was arriving a day earlier than planned? Elizabeth knew no other was expected. As it came to a halt, she realised the matched greys and the crest on the door identified the carriage as belonging to Mr. Darcy.

Her heart pounded fiercely, and her breath quickened. When the door opened and he stepped out, she hesitantly stepped closer. They had parted company under troublesome circumstances, so she was confused at his presence. When he turned back to the carriage to hand down his sister, she understood: Miss Georgiana Darcy came to call at Longbourn.

Though she knew she should cherish the compliment that her friend travelled so far to visit, she could not help but feel the loss of disappointed hopes. She looked at the ground, searching for a calm she could not find within herself. *How could this be?* The strength of emotions took her by surprise. Truly, she was grateful to see her young friend. *But Mr. Darcy...*

Though she had kept a clear image of him carefully tucked away in her heart, his stature and handsome looks drew her eyes as if she was seeing him for the first time. He had yet to notice her so only his profile was in view. *What would his expression reveal? Would he return to the stoic man with a mask of iron? Would he be the teasing man from the field or the bruised and battered man from the folly?* Her anticipation churned in her stomach.

As the man in uniform exited the carriage behind Georgiana, Charlotte walked towards him, no hesitation in her step.

Colonel Richard Fitzwilliam heard his name whispered on the breeze. He looked to see Miss Lucas steadily approaching. His steps towards her were far more confident than he was feeling inside. *Lord, how he had missed her!*

He could not know her brilliant smile belied the evidence of distress in her heart. He thought her the most attractive woman in all of Christendom. As he finally stepped in front of her, an arms-length away, he could not help but whisper, "Is your heart in agreement with mine?"

Charlotte looked into the world-weary eyes of the man standing before her and comprehended in full all he asked.

"It is." The words were barely out of her mouth when the colonel closed the distance between them, wrapped his strong arms around her, gathering her to him, and kissed Charlotte with a passion of a man starved, hungering for the touch and taste of the woman he had dreamed about since he had left Meryton in October. Georgiana gasped in shock, and Darcy uttered his cousin's name. Colonel Richard Fitzwilliam wanted to shout to the world the worth of this wonderful lady and smile until his cheeks hurt. He did neither. He kissed her until the giggles of his young cousin reached his ears. He loved Georgiana to distraction, yet he wished her anywhere but there.

When Richard finally broke the kiss, he brought his hand up to stroke her tears away—his roughened, calloused fingers scraping against the softness of Charlotte's skin. *Would she be willing to live the life of a soldier's wife? Would she be willing to follow him wherever his career would lead? Would she be willing to remain behind should he be assigned somewhere unsafe? Would she wait for him?* Her eyes said "yes" to all his concerns.

"I will speak to your father."

"Yes."

Richard paused before stepping back and taking her hand. He finally looked at the others.

Beaming with joy for her dearest friend and her own unease nearly forgotten, Elizabeth had joined the group and exclaimed, "You are all welcome to Longbourn."

"Ah, the lovely Miss Elizabeth." The colonel bowed to her curtsey, pleased to see her affectionately embrace his betrothed.

Richard knew he had broken every rule of propriety in his manner of greeting the woman he loved. But he cared not. "Darcy, I will escort Miss Lucas back to Lucas Lodge and find my own way to Nether-field." As he walked away with Charlotte at his side, the colonel was confident Darcy and Elizabeth would have the situation under control in no time. It was their way.

He wanted to hum but remembered his musical abilities were on par with Darcy's. His heart was full of all the pithy sayings of love and hearts that he used to tease his married comrades about. They were now his realities. And yet, he cared not whether he had earned their teasing when they learned the least matrimonially minded soldier of their acquaintance was intending to hurry his bride-to-be to the altar.

* * *

DARCY WANTED to rush to Elizabeth and embrace her as his cousin had done Miss Lucas though he doubted he would have the same reception. She did not know him; the man he had worked hard to become. Surely, in her eyes he was as abominable as she had thought him last autumn. He had much to repair and prove to the woman he was a man worthy of her.

"Brother, what has happened here?" Georgiana interrupted his thoughts. Though she saw the evidence with her own eyes of her cousin's attachment to a woman she knew little about, it unsettled her to see such intense emotions displayed so blatantly before her.

Darcy turned to his sister and realised her question was rhetorical. She knew. He watched as she shook her head as if trying to dislodge a stubborn thought.

"Lizzy?"

"Georgiana, welcome to Longbourn," she said laughing and tucking her arm in her young friend's as they turned to walk through the garden paths to the house. She looked over her shoulder and tilted her head to Mr. Darcy, summoning him along too.

Darcy was pleased as both young ladies found delight in the reunion. Their embrace was warm and welcoming. How he longed to be part of it. He watched them both try to politely allow the other to speak first. When they both chuckled, it moved his heart to beat in a happier rhythm.

"You quite caught me unawares, my friend." Elizabeth quickly hugged Georgiana again. "Your letter arrived by this morning's post, and it mentioned nothing about you coming our way."

The muscles in his upper arms twitched and his hands unknowingly flexed. Instead of reaching out for Elizabeth as his body seemed to desire, he tucked his sister's other hand in his arm. "We spent very little time at the midway point of our trip this morning as someone"— he tipped his head to his sister— "was overly excited to surprise her friend. Might we accompany you on your walk?"

The garden path was lined with sunny daffodils, vibrant primrose,

175

and swaying bluebells which seemed to open their faces and smile at the threesome, inviting Georgiana to collect her fill.

"May I gather a bouquet for your mother?"

"She would enjoy that very thing, Georgiana."

As his sister moved towards the blue flowers, Darcy extended the arm Georgiana had abandoned to her friend.

When Elizabeth accepted his offer, Darcy felt contentment melt into the cracks and crevices of his worn and beaten heart, soothing him and filling him with peace.

"Oh, Lizzy. I am happy to be returned to Hertfordshire. Yet, to be truly pleased, I must know, is your sister truly recovered?" Georgiana, turning back towards the couple with a handful of fragrant posies, had been thrilled when her brother's express had arrived Saturday evening. However, she was beside herself with worry when he did not appear until early this morning. His frustration by the delay was evident as he hastened her into the carriage to continue on to Longbourn.

"She is, Georgiana. The doctor recommended months of bed rest, which I am pleased to report Jane obeyed far more calmly than had it been me. It has been only two months since she has been allowed downstairs. Mr. Bingley was ever so grateful."

Georgiana sighed. "He loves her, does he not?"

"Georgiana!" Darcy was surprised to hear his sister speak of something so personal.

"Oh, Brother, do not worry so." Georgiana patted his arm with her right hand. "Lizzy and I are the best of friends, almost like sisters. Really, it is no different from you and Richard, except we most likely shall have fewer periods of ponderous silence."

She had no idea the impact her words would have on him. He stopped in his tracks and looked at each lady to determine their expression. On his sister's face he saw freedom and joy, and his heart lit up to see her so recovered from Ramsgate.

Elizabeth's smile was more restrained. He could not blame her. Again, Darcy recalled his words and actions at Netherfield Park with self-disdain. *How could she not be wary?* Oh, but to have her stand next to him. If he indulged in fancy, he could pretend she was his... well, he refused to indulge. It was not manly.

"Do Bingley and Miss Bennet have an understanding?" His friend had not been at home when they arrived at Netherfield Park. Bingley's housekeeper indicated she did not expect him to return until dinner.

Elizabeth looked up at him. The sun was at his back, so his face was in shadow. *Was he upset that Bingley might be attached to a Bennet?* Elizabeth realised that was the crux of the problem between herself and Mr. Fitzwilliam Darcy, master of Pemberley. She saw no distinction of rank where he did. Thus, she was cautious in her reply.

"They do not as of yet, sir. As you know, Mr. Bingley has remained in mourning these last five months."

"It will be a good match for Bingley."

The simple statement had much impact, and Elizabeth caught her breath, realising she waited for the insult to follow. When it did not come, she slowly exhaled. *Did he mean what he said?* She knew Mr. Darcy chose his words carefully. He was a precise man. *Was he in support of the match then?*

She gently pulled on his arm until he faced her. Elizabeth's eyes had not left his face. What she saw there filled her with warmth. There was no censure, no arrogance. His eyes were clear, and the corners of his mouth relaxed.

"We believe so, as well." Elizabeth refused to blink as his eyes stared intently into hers.

The desire to bend his head and capture her lips was fierce. He could not. He would not. Darcy smiled at the reaction such a deed would have had on his sister. Georgiana had never observed him acting outside of the rules of propriety, and he hoped to keep it that way. Nor would it do to encourage rebellion, not when so much progress had been made.

At that moment, Elizabeth thought him more handsome than she had ever thought him before. She found the shadow of his whiskers a curiosity, evidence of the early hour he had risen. *Would they be sharp or soft?* Her free hand, on its own, rose to touch his face. A bird chirped, and Elizabeth regained control of her senses, returning her hand to her side.

She quickly turned towards her young friend. "Miss Georgiana Darcy, I do believe you have grown taller than me in the past months." Her cheeks flushed and eyes sparkled. "You appear the same height as Kitty, who is nearly eighteen."

Georgiana's smile was luminous. "You really think so, Lizzy? I do not believe sweeter words have ever been uttered about me."

"Did you not write that you are now sixteen years of age?"

"I am." To be thought two years older was... She loved her friend even more for saying it in front of her brother. "I thank you, Lizzy." Georgiana wanted to skip, then remembered she ought to act the age she looked.

"You are most welcome."

"It seems love is in the air. First Mr. Bingley and your sister and now Richard and Miss Lucas. I wonder who will be next."

Darcy narrowed his eyes. *The minx.*

Elizabeth's hand left Darcy's arm and went to her throat.

"Lizzy, what is wrong?"

"Pray, pardon me." Elizabeth looked from brother to sister and back. "It has occurred to me how matters are changed now that the colonel has attached himself to Charlotte. My father's cousin, Mr. Collins will be here on the morrow. He is returning to Hertfordshire to claim a wife. Sir William and Lady Lucas had intended their daughter to be his bride. Now that she is no longer available..."

"He will want you." Darcy spoke up before she could voice the thought. The parson had been clear in his intentions. Miss Elizabeth Bennet would now be the object of his desire.

Darcy snorted. *Not if I can help it!*

CHAPTER 20

*I*t was a grand reunion when Elizabeth and the Darcys entered the Longbourn drawing room. Bingley had been a notoriously poor correspondent with his friend, so the pleasure of the two men being in each other's company was evident.

"Mr. Darcy, how good of you to return to Longbourn." Mrs. Bennet was notably less frenzied than the last time they were in company. "And you brought your sister. How lovely. Did I not see the dear colonel step out of the carriage as well? Where could he possibly be?"

"Mrs. Bennet, as unexpected guests, I thank you for your kind hospitality to both my sister and myself. We have only just arrived from London. And my cousin...was in need to stretch his legs...and offered to escort Miss Lucas back to Lucas Lodge."

He sipped his tea which the mistress of the home had perfectly prepared. *Why had he not noticed before how diligent she was in seeing to his preferences?* "I can see for myself, how Miss Bennet has been restored to her fair bloom. Is the rest of your family in good health?"

"Of course. We are always hale. Mr. Bennet is ensconced in his bookroom and, as you see, all of my girls are here." Mrs. Bennet studied Mr. Darcy. His whole countenance seemed changed from the stern, critical man they met at the Meryton assembly—he seemed fairly relaxed in company! Yet, she knew Darcy had disapproved of Bingley's interest in Jane when he was a guest at Netherfield in the autumn. And the looks of disdain and the boorish comments about her second daughter had not endeared him. She wondered at the change. *Possibly he has found a love of his own? A woman of intelligence and wit— who held herself above the common crowd. Someone skilled in navigating the ton who would leave him to his business.* Mrs. Bennet looked at his handsome mien and intelligent eyes...and discovered they were fixed on Elizabeth. *Lizzy? How interesting!* She could not check the small smile that appeared at the corners of her mouth.

Georgiana noted the difference in her brother's friend almost immediately. Whether it was from the loss of Mr. Hurst, or not being constantly belittled by his overbearing sister, Charles Bingley bore a reserve she had never before seen in the man. She watched Mr. Bingley with Miss Bennet. He carefully assisted her with her tea. He sought her comfort. As he spoke to her brother, he would, from time to time, reach over and touch Miss Bennet's hand. Georgiana wanted to sigh at Bingley's tender concern. Mr. Bingley was such an attentive lover...much like the heroes in her novels.

And Miss Bennet? She appeared delicate, but glowed with the attentions of the man she was so obviously in love with. Georgiana could not help but recognise the beauty resulting from these emotions and fathomed that what she thought was love for George Wickham paled against the reality.

While the others exchanged greetings and had small conversations, Georgiana scrutinised the couple's interactions. When her brother and the colonel had arrived in London early that morning, they had given her the briefest greeting before hustling her into the coach so they could continue on their journey. Their impatience had piqued her curiosity, and she hoped that Darcy was hastening a reunion with Elizabeth.

Georgiana had been entirely unaware of Richard's attachment to a woman. As long as she had known him, he had been resolved never to marry. She had no reason to know he had changed his mind. Richard had returned from Newcastle in time to depart with Darcy for Kent. For a certainty, he never shared matters of the heart with her, especially because of the difference in age. She knew Richard struggled to accept she was no longer a little girl. Georgiana was deliriously happy for her cousin. Next to her brother, he was the best of men. Obviously, he was a man of action. Georgiana blushed at the kiss she had witnessed.

Darcy had to look at the older woman twice to verify it was truly her. They had been inside Longbourn for several minutes, and he had yet to hear of Bingley's or his income or the need for her many daughters to marry well. He was all astonishment with the calm and decorum in the Bennet parlour and surmised that the illness of Mrs. Bennet's eldest—combined with the faithful attentions of a wealthy suitor—had reassured Elizabeth's mother of matters more important than her own future prospects. It shamed him how he had used her conduct against Elizabeth the last time they had met. Though his words may have even been the truth then, he shuddered to think of his ungentlemanly comments. He dropped his head to his chest and breathed in slowly. This was his opportunity to make a start in setting things straight. If he ever hoped to gain Elizabeth's favour, he needed to begin immediately and make amends with her family. Darcy took another deep breath. *Begin, fool!*

Darcy noticed the two youngest Bennet sisters whispering quietly as they attended to their needlework on the settee. They had stood and curtseyed at their entrance but had not spoken since. The middle sister—Darcy could not remember her name—was in the only pose he had ever found her, immersed in a book. *Was she hiding behind it as he often did or enjoying the text?* Darcy was determined to find out.

Walking to the middle Bennet child, he glanced across the room and noticed his sister was still in conversation with Elizabeth.

Mary looked up at his presence. "Sir?" She was wary. Never had she been approached by such a man.

"Miss, might I enquire as to the subject of your reading material? You appear to find it of immense interest."

Mary snapped the book closed showing him the cover, and her face flushed violently.

He read the title aloud. *"Sermons to Young Women* by James Fordyce, *Volume One".* It was not a book he had read, though there was a copy of both volumes in his library at Pemberley. Certainly, it was appropriate reading material for a lady who was as serious-minded as the third daughter appeared. *He wondered at her discomfort.* Darcy looked closer at the book. *Odd!* The spine was bent and slightly off-kelter, causing the front cover to extend over the back. He suspected its cause and chose not to further her embarrassment. Her mother had other ideas.

"Mary, show Mr. Darcy your book." Befuddled, if Mr. Darcy showed an interest in her most uninteresting daughter, Mrs. Bennet would do everything within her power to promote a match. The passage of months had made Mr. Collins far more tolerable than she remembered and with his anticipated arrival... Lizzy would be his bride. *Three daughters engaged!* She sighed.

Darcy was unsurprised when tears pooled in Mary's eyes. "Mrs. Bennet, that is not necessary."

"Nonsense! Show Mr. Darcy the book, child." Mrs. Bennet recalled Mr. Darcy seemed the bookish sort.

Mary had no choice. She lifted the book from her lap and handed it to Mr. Darcy, immediately balling her fists together and dropping her head. Darcy could see her shoulders tremble. He opened the cover and glanced inside. It was the same novel he had surreptitiously read of Georgiana's. He breathed in deeply, wondering how best to handle the precarious situation. He did not want to increase her distress, nor did he wish to disappoint Mrs. Bennet.

"I see, Miss Mary." Misery filled her eyes when she peeked up at his comment. "Though this is not the subject matter I typically read, I have read this very volume from cover to cover."

"You have?"

"Indeed, I have." He handed her back the book and smiled. "I believe this current book is one my sister has in her room as well. She finds pleasure in the subject and has many other books of like quality. Perhaps the two of you could discuss the matter?"

Mary's relief was obvious. Elizabeth observed the entire scene and wondered what Mr. Darcy was playing. Mrs. Bennet glowed at promoting common ground between Mr. Darcy and Mary. Georgiana was confused. She had no copy of *Fordyce's Sermons* in her bedchamber or her sitting room, nor did she plan to. *What was her brother about?*

"Georgiana, might you join us?" Darcy's eyes pleaded for his sister's obedience. She acquiesced.

Seating herself next to Mary, Georgiana easily recognised the title of the story inside the loose cover. It was one of her favourites. She looked at her brother, her eyebrow raised in question. *He hated disguise of any sort.* She was all astonishment!

Leaning closer to Mary, Georgiana whispered so Mrs. Bennet could not hear, "I, too, have a book with the same cover."

When Mary looked at her with shock, the two girls burst out in giggles.

At that moment, Mary's opinion of both Darcys underwent a dramatic change. That Mr. Darcy would admit to reading a woman's novel was surprising. That Miss Darcy had done the same soothed Mary. They were kindred souls and if Miss Darcy was willing, she would have a friend.

Elizabeth had watched the drama play out. She had been worried as she encouraged Mary to conceal her novel with *Fordyce's Sermons.* Mrs. Bennet was single-minded in her matrimonial pursuits for her daughters. She despaired of both Elizabeth and Mary's constant companionship with a book as few men found it an attractive occupation for a wife.

Elizabeth appreciated Darcy's kind efforts to put Mary at ease and keep Mary from being embarrassed by their mother while in company. Their mother had made considerable progress in restraint over the past months but could still be volatile when the occasion least warranted it. Because of the concern Darcy expressed for Mary, Elizabeth smiled at him, and he viewed her smile as an invitation.

Thus, he was soon seated next to her, slightly closer to her than was his custom.

"Mrs. Bennet, I must tell you how I appreciate this apple cake. If your cook would share the receipt, I would have them served in my homes."

At this, Fanny Bennet sat higher in her chair. Darcy was the nephew of an earl. To think of a peer of the realm eating her apple cake made her giddy. It was worthy news to share with the ladies in the community. "Consider it done, Mr. Darcy."

He looked back to Elizabeth to see a soft glimmer in her dark eyes. His heart glowed knowing he had made her happy.

* * *

COLONEL RICHARD FITZWILLIAM had faced Napoleon's troops and stared death in the face several times. He would not be intimidated by approaching Sir William Lucas. Since Charlotte was past her majority, asking permission to wed was out of respect for her parents. They did not need Sir William's approval. They would marry.

"Come in. Come in." Sir William's welcome was hearty. "I did not know you had returned to Hertfordshire, Colonel." He turned to his daughter, who had followed Richard into her father's study. "You may go now. Tell Mrs. Burt I will have my tea with the colonel in here." With that, he summarily dismissed his eldest child.

"I prefer Miss Lucas to remain."

Sir William was puzzled, though his general amiability moved him to agree. "To what do I have the pleasure of your company, Colonel?"

"I am come to request the honour of your daughter's hand in marriage, sir."

Sir William dropped into his chair. "Charlotte? You want to marry my Charlotte?"

It irritated Richard that Charlotte's father had no expectations of him making an offer for his daughter. Thus, his words were more abrupt than he had planned. Richard reached over and clasped his beloved's hand in his. "I have offered my hand to your daughter, and she has accepted me. Out of respect, I now ask your permission to marry Charlotte."

"Charlotte? You want to marry Charlotte?"

"I do."

Once Sir William comprehended the seriousness of the colonel, he remembered Richard Fitzwilliam was the son of an earl. His Charlotte might one day be a countess. The thought lifted his heart until his dreams of glory almost robbed him of speech.

"Such a marriage. Such possibilities." Sir William smiled at the prospects running through his mind. "Capital, capital. We can even meet at St. James." Charlotte's father could not contain his excitement.

"Sir, I am a humble soldier. Though I am a second son of an earl, my brother is hale and quite happy with his role of viscount." Richard watched as the man's chest deflated. "Our life together will be simple. I have a small property in Derbyshire which is close to my cousin Darcy's estate. It will be there where my wife will await my return each time I am called away. When I am in London, we will not have the resources or the desire to participate in the activities of the *ton*."

Sir William was not one to be easily dissuaded from his desires. "But, Colonel, imagine how this will elevate my Charlotte? The daughter of an earl!"

Charlotte squeezed his hand. She knew her father was not doing well and any respect Richard had had for him was quickly reducing.

"Our plans are set, sir. We will not participate in the season in London now or later. Your desires are not our own." Richard was adamant.

"Are you saying my daughter will not be spending time with the earl?" Sir William did not even look at his daughter. He was disappointed and angry that he was to be denied. "Maybe the better situation for you, Charlotte, would be to continue with our plans for you to marry Mr. Collins. After all, he will be in constant attendance to Lady Catherine de Bourgh. Yes, Daughter, I believe that when Mr. Collins arrives on the morrow, we go ahead with the banns. You will be wed and in Lady Catherine's company within a month."

"She will not!" Richard Fitzwilliam felt his blood boiling. "It will be *our* banns which will be read, Sir William. Your daughter is too fine a woman to be attached to a sycophant like William Collins."

Sir William was livid. How dare this man override his authority! This was his daughter. He had plans and they were what his pressing the marriage to Mr. Collins was about.

"Colonel, if you would promise me access to the higher circles…"

Charlotte gasped.

Richard interrupted him before he could continue.

"I am not prepared to negotiate with a man who failed to recognise the intrinsic value of his own daughter." Richard leaned forward towards the man, his position threatening, though his words were not. He had Sir William's full attention. "I give you notice here and now that banns will be read this Sunday and the two following Sundays at the chapel in Meryton for Charlotte and myself. We will wed as soon as this is done. She will marry no other."

Sir William backed down. This was not a man who would give in easily, so he did. The higher echelons of St. James were lost to him and his wife. It was a bitter disappointment.

Charlotte felt humiliation at the crassness of her parent, but her heart sang with the words of her betrothed. They had discussed their plans and desires as they walked from Longbourn to Lucas Lodge. In three weeks, she would become Mrs. Richard Fitzwilliam. She smiled at the lovely ring to such a magnificent name. Mrs. Charlotte Fitzwilliam. Charlotte Fitzwilliam. Yes, it was a name she could bear for a lifetime.

CHAPTER 21

*L*ongbourn
Since Jane's recovery, it had become the custom each evening for all five Bennet daughters to gather in Jane's room for a conference before retiring to bed. On this night, those reclining on the bed and draped over the chairs included one more than usual, Miss Georgiana Darcy. The subject under discussion was the engagement of Charlotte to Colonel Fitzwilliam instead of Mr. Collins.

"I never would have thought it of Charlotte Lucas." Kitty's estimation of their neighbour had greatly improved after hearing about the kissing business. "And she kissed the colonel back?"

Georgiana chuckled as Elizabeth confirmed the truth of the matter. Six female sighs filled the room.

Both Kitty and Lydia had dreamed of the handsome colonel since they met him at the assembly in the autumn. His red coat and easy smile had caught their eyes. Nonetheless, the seriousness of Jane's illness had pacified the girls' wild disposition. While Lydia had learned a measure of restraint, she was still bold. "Has Mr. Bingley kissed you yet, Jane?"

At that five of the ladies burst into giggles. Jane's face flamed.

"Lydia!"

"While he is not as brazen as the colonel, we see the way Mr. Bingley looks at you, Sister." At almost sixteen years of age, Lydia was in love with being in love. Having a mother who—from birth—constantly impressed on each daughter the importance of matrimony had not helped Lydia to have a mature outlook on the subject.

Kitty added, "And we see the way you look at him too, Jane Bennet."

"Do you love him, Jane?" Mary Bennet had romance on her mind. She had finished the novel Mr. Darcy had caught her reading and knew beyond a doubt that she longed for the happily-ever-after that came on the final page. Like Jane and Lizzy though, it was not her way to put herself forward.

All the girls quieted at the question. Though Jane had admitted her feelings to Elizabeth, she had not made them known to anyone else, including Bingley. She looked at the anticipation and expectation on each of the younger girl's faces. How could she not share her joy?

"I do, Mary. I love him dearly."

More sighs swirled around the bed as each girl was delighted for Jane and hoped for her own handsome prince at the same time.

Lydia, being Lydia, was not yet done.

"What about your brother, Georgiana? Will he marry?"

"I believe so, Lydia." Georgiana had no sisters and was unused to the intimate camaraderie.

"Well, I had not imagined it." Lydia bluntly added. "La, I could not think anyone would have wanted to be his wife, even with ten thousand a year and a great estate in Derbyshire. He always looked like he ate something sour when in company."

Georgiana gasped. So did the rest of the females.

"Lydia!" exclaimed both Elizabeth and Jane. "Hush!"

"However, he has changed so. He spoke to Mary today and Mama —where he would not have done before." Lydia continued, not aware of the distress she was causing by her words. "He even smiled at Lizzy. Is that not a joke?"

Georgiana was upset. "My brother, Miss Lydia, is the best of men.

He is not one to be teased or made fun of. He bears much responsibility and is highly respected by his peers and those he has under his care, including myself." Georgiana fought hard to contain her tears. She had found no hilarity in the youngest girl's words. Gone was the easy discourse of moments earlier. She wished she had returned to Netherfield Park with her brother. "Further, over the past five months, Fitzwilliam has made extraordinary efforts to change, to become a better person. Therefore, it is incumbent upon me to ask you, Miss Lydia, what have you done to improve yourself during that same period?"

"Girls!" Jane's soft voice begged for peace.

Lydia was quiet—for the moment.

Elizabeth sat back in her chair and observed, her mind spinning. Jane would see to the two youngest. *Was that the difference in his character?* Oh, yes, she had noticed there had been changes. Darcy had shown fine manners with her family, and the pleasure at his cousin's betrothal to a woman of inferior birth had been genuine. He had graciously thanked her mother for Richard and Charlotte's spontaneous engagement dinner, complimenting her on each course and the number of sauces. *What had been his motive?* Elizabeth understood that whatever had been the impetus, she was grateful. Possibly there was hope for a friendship after all.

"It is time we all were in bed." Elizabeth stood and held her hand out to Georgiana, in a gesture which was now familiar. She turned to her youngest sister, her voice firm. "Apologise now, Lydia."

Truculent, Lydia sat with her arms fisted at her hips, her eyes narrowing and her lips firmly compressed. Elizabeth could see her struggle with the old personal attitudes and the new. Evidently, Mr. Darcy was not the only one who had changed. Eventually, she succumbed. Her apology, when finally offered, was well done.

"I pray you accept my sincerest apologies, Georgiana. I was not thinking properly. My motive was to lighten the mood, and I chose to do it at the expense of your brother, without thinking how my words would hurt you." Lydia abandoned her defiant pose. "I am truly sorry."

Georgiana Darcy had a choice. She could overlook the slight, or she could hold a grudge. She sighed. It was not only her brother who was learning to get on with others. She accepted Lydia's apology and left to share Elizabeth's room. With her, Georgiana felt safe.

* * *

TUESDAY, 30 March 1812

The next morning, Mr. William Collins arrived at Lucas Lodge to find that Miss Charlotte Lucas was recently engaged to another. That it had been Lady Catherine's nephew who had stolen his potential wife from under his nose was as yet unknown to him. He was undaunted at the disruption to his plans. He had his instructions from Lady Catherine; therefore he had no doubt he would return to Hunsford with a wife. He immediately removed himself to where the only other prospect resided—Longbourn.

Collins speculated that leaving an unmarried woman alone for such a length of time without declaring himself had left his prospects vulnerable. *What lady would not want to be the mistress of his humble home under the guidance of his patroness?*

"Mr. Collins, were we expecting you?" Mr. Bennet had come to despise his heir. During the time since Collins had departed Longbourn, Thomas Bennet had researched every possible avenue for breaking the entail. He found none. Unless, miraculously, he produced a son, Mr. William Collins was the heir presumptive. It galled him to think the most ridiculous man in England as master of his estate.

"Sir, I sent a letter by post more than a fortnight ago with directions for preparation for my arrival. I cannot imagine the post has been delayed to an extent that would not have given you enough notice to prepare for me." Mr. Collins elevated his nose into the air as if he had come across an unpleasant odor.

Mr. Bennet had met Mr. Collins in the entrance hall rather than receiving him in the drawing room. He felt no need to welcome a man he did not want residing—even for a short time—in his home.

"Yes, Mr. Collins, I received your missive." The master of Longbourn took a page from Darcy's book of social etiquette, he stared without blinking, standing erect and unbending. "Nevertheless, you clearly stated your intent of boarding at Lucas Lodge. Have you decamped already?"

It was easy to imagine what had happened. Turmoil must have met Mr. Collins at Lucas Lodge's door, so he sought refuge in an alternate home. Mr. Bennet knew he would have to offer hospitality, though he did not have to make it so comfortable that the rector stayed for an extended period of time.

Collins cleared his throat. Charlotte Lucas had been his preference for many reasons. First and foremost was her meekness. Her plainness and maturity guaranteed him a spouse who would see to his needs and desires out of gratitude for having a man of worth offer for her. That she was no longer available was a blow to his tenuous confidence.

"Mr. Bennet, I believe your closest neighbour, Sir William Lucas, has failed to comprehend my close association with the elevated ranks of society. My patroness will be displeased that I have had to alter my plans. For a certainty, sir, a lady of such keen understanding would…"

Thomas Bennet quit listening. As the voice babbled on about the superiority of Lady Catherine de Bourgh, the elder man weighed the timing of the announcement of Charlotte's betrothed so it would have the most affect. In mulling it over, he realised there was no time like the present.

"Mr. Collins." He interrupted the younger man. "Are you aware that Miss Charlotte Lucas was offered marriage only yesterday to the nephew of your patroness?"

Mr. Collins sputtered to a stop. *How was this possible?* Sir William had reported an engagement. Nothing had been said as to who had made the offer. Mr. Fitzwilliam Darcy was betrothed to the fairest gem in the nation, Miss Anne de Bourgh. *What to do?* If he sent the news to Lady Catherine—which she would expect him to do—the grand lady would most likely demand his withdrawal before he procured a wife. Should he give precedence to obedience to her original demands—returning to Hunsford with a wife—he would not have time to involve himself with the business of her nephew.

"I was unaware." *A dreadful situation, indeed!* "Sir, I find myself with a dilemma which necessitates privacy and a length of time to meditate on the potential influences of both choices. Might I enter your book-room to do so?"

"You may not!" Mr. Bennet could not fail to notice the disquietude his announcement had caused. *Was the man's heart attached to Charlotte?* The poor man, as he had no chance of regaining her favour whether he had ever had it at all. The elder man sighed and ran both hands over his eyes. He resigned himself to the inevitable. "Very well, I will have a room prepared for you. In the meantime, you could use the small sitting room at the back of the house. Most of my daughters are in other rooms in the house, and Lizzy is out of doors. You shall be undisturbed."

Mr. Collins was grateful to have privacy. He had much to think upon.

How had his life become difficult? His instructions from Lady Catherine were clear. He was to take a wife. *Why did not the families of those involved understand the seriousness of this charge? Did they have no respect for Lady Catherine?* The mere idea was untenable.

The noise of a lady humming a melodious tune came through the opened window. Looking out into the far reaches of the garden, he spied the second Bennet daughter, Miss Elizabeth. With her face turned to the sun and a smile on her lips, she was pretty. It was an easy step for him to lose focus and picture her seated next to him in Lady Catherine's drawing room at Rosings. Lady Catherine was a musical proficient. Elizabeth Bennet would benefit from the great lady's instruction. At that, his mind was fixed. No longer did he feel the loss of Charlotte Lucas. Miss Elizabeth Bennet was the companion of his future life.

If he could conclude an engagement quickly, he could still contact Lady Catherine in a timely manner. How pleased she would be to know he had followed her commands to the letter. William Collins smiled to himself. Walking back to the entry, he obtained his black hat, coat, and gloves and strolled outside.

* * *

"Cousin Elizabeth!" Mr. Collin's voice easily rose over the noise of the birds calling out their locations in the trees surrounding the garden.

She turned to him, surprised. She had been unaware that her father's cousin had arrived at Longbourn.

"Have you only arrived from Kent?" He still wore his travelling clothes. His skin was pasty white, evidence that he spent little time out of doors. He had a feral look to him, and she suddenly felt like prey.

"Indeed, I have. Cousin Elizabeth, it is my mission, both to please Lady Catherine and to assure my own felicity that I offer you my hand in marriage. Almost as soon as I entered the house, I singled you out as the companion of my future life. But before I am run away with my feelings on this subject, perhaps it will be advisable for me to state my reasons for marrying—and moreover for coming into Hertford-shire with the design of selecting a wife."

The idea of the solemn Mr. Collins being run away with his feelings, especially as she knew he had already corresponded with Sir William about marriage to Charlotte, made Elizabeth choke on her laughter.

He continued. "My reasons for marrying are, first, that I think it a right thing for every clergyman in easy circumstances (like me) to set the example of matrimony in his parish. Secondly, that I am convinced it will add very greatly to my happiness; and thirdly—which perhaps I ought to have mentioned earlier, that it is the particular advice and recommenda-tion of the very noble lady whom I have the honour of calling patroness. You will find her manners beyond anything I can describe; and your wit and vivacity I think must be acceptable to her, especially when tempered with the silence and respect which her rank will inevitably excite. But the fact is, that being, as I am, to inherit this estate after the death of your honoured father (who, however, may live many years longer), I could not satisfy myself without resolving to choose a wife from among his daughters, that the loss to them might be as little as possible, when the melancholy event takes place—which, however, as I have already said, may not be for several years. This has been my motive, my fair cousin, and I flatter myself it will not sink me in your esteem. And now nothing remains for me but to assure you in the most animated language of the violence of my affection. To fortune I am perfectly indifferent and shall make no demand of that nature on your father, since I am well aware that it could not be complied with; and that one thousand pounds in the four percents, which will not be yours till after your mother's decease, is all that you may ever be entitled to. On that head, therefore, I shall be uniformly silent; and you may assure yourself that no ungenerous reproach shall ever pass my lips when we are married."

It was absolutely necessary to interrupt him now.

"Upon my word, sir," cried Elizabeth, "you could not make me happy, and I am convinced that I am the last woman in the world who would make you so, nay, were your friend Lady Catherine to know me, I am persuaded she would find me in every respect ill-qualified for the situation."

"You must give me leave to flatter myself, my dear cousin, that your refusal of my addresses is merely words of course. My reasons for believing it are briefly these: it does not appear to me that my hand is unworthy of your acceptance, or that the establishment I can offer would be any other than highly desirable. My situation in life, my connections with the family of de Bourgh, and my relationship to your own, are circumstances highly in its favour; and you should take it into consideration that in spite of your manifold attractions, it is by no means certain that another offer of marriage may ever be made you. Your portion is unhappily so small that it will in all likelihood undo the effects of your loveliness and amiable qualifications."

Elizabeth seethed with anger. For the sake of her own conscience, she vowed to be as kind as possible under the circumstances.

"I thank you for the honour you have done me in your proposals…" Before she could finish, she was interrupted by her sister Jane.

"Lizzy." Jane noticed a man she correctly assumed to be Mr. Collins standing next to her sister. They both looked upset. Not knowing what to do, she continued. "Mr. Bingley and Mr. Darcy sent a note that they will be riding to Longbourn. Since we expect their arrival at any time, Mama has asked that you come inside."

"Thank you, Jane." She turned to look at Mr. Collins who had remained silent. *Did the man have any limits to his rudeness? He had not even acknowledged Jane.*

Mr. Collins was stunned. He had never in his five and twenty years seen a woman as beautiful as Miss Jane Bennet. He instantly regretted his offer to her younger sister. Jane's calm, serene beauty would be the perfect accessory for his arm each time he attended Lady Catherine at Rosings.

"You are Miss Jane Bennet?" In a hurry to establish his own happiness, he failed to await a proper introduction. "My dear cousin, might I assist you back inside?" He walked to the eldest sister, completely ignoring the woman whose hand he had just applied for.

Elizabeth Bennet felt the ire rise until it threatened to choke her. The man was detestable how he transferred his affections one to another in a moment. *What a revolting prospect for his future wife!* Picking up a sizable stone which fit perfectly in her hand, she threw it as hard as she could. Hearing a thud, then a groan, she pushed through the hedgerow and found the unanticipated sight of Fitzwilliam Darcy, once more on the ground next to his recalcitrant horse. From the way he was holding onto the left side of his face, Elizabeth judged her aim had been true.

She ran to him as Bingley dismounted from his horse.

"Mr. Darcy! Mr. Darcy!"

Darcy's eyes flickered open to a sight more beautiful than any other he had ever seen. Without thought, he raised his hand and cupped her cheek, whispering, "My darling, Elizabeth." Then his eyes rolled back in his head, and—in a move which would embarrass him when he came to—he fainted.

CHAPTER 22

*L*ongbourn

She killed him. The tears pooling in her eyes blurred her vision so she could not see Darcy's torso rise and fall with each breath he continued to take. The agony filling Elizabeth's heart threatened to crush it to pieces. *How could she go on knowing she had ended a good man's life? How would she tell Georgiana that she lost the last remaining member of her immediate family?* Dropping her head on Darcy's chest, she sobbed.

Bingley quickly mounted and rode the short distance to Longbourn, calling for assistance as he approached the front of the house.

Darcy, his mind in a daze, thought he was in paradise. He cared not for the reason Elizabeth was holding him, only that she was. He wrapped his arms around her and held her tightly.

"My Elizabeth, do not cry, I pray you." He whispered into her hair; grateful she had walked outside without her bonnet. He ran his hand up her back, entangling his fingers in the dark curls at her neck. When he felt her stiffening, he opened his eyes.

"You are alive!" Elizabeth's head shot up to see his face. The area above his left eyebrow was swollen and inflamed, evidence of her poor aim. Guilt flooded her, followed by immense embarrassment. Pulling away from the intimacy of his embrace, she jumped to her feet and stepped back, carefully avoiding his beast of a horse. She could feel the warmth from her face and knew she was a brilliant scarlet hue. She looked at the sky, the ground, and the trees—anywhere but him.

Wringing her hands, she sought to reassure Darcy. "Mr. Bingley has gone for help, sir."

Darcy started to sit up and quickly fell back to the ground. His temple was pounding, and his head started to swim. Closing his eyes was his only relief.

"What happened, Miss Elizabeth?"

She had been afraid he was going to ask. *How much should I reveal?*

Inhaling deeply, Elizabeth decided to confess all. "I was walking in the garden enjoying the beauty of the spring day when Mr. Collins approached with an offer of marriage." She paused in memory. "When Jane came to inform me of your impending arrival, the man took one look at her and abandoned me. I had no desire to be Mr. Collin's bride, Mr. Darcy, however, to be summarily disregarded in addition to having my wants and opinions entirely ignored infuriated me. I, unfortunately, chose to vent my anger with a rock from the garden, sir."

"How could that be possible?"

Mistaking his meaning, Elizabeth's ire started to rise, feeling a bit bruised from his assertion. "Indeed, Mr. Darcy, he did ask for my hand."

Darcy groaned. *Why were they always misunderstanding each other?*

Elizabeth assumed he was in pain. She dropped back down to her knees beside where he lay. "Mr. Darcy, is there anything I can provide for your comfort?"

Darcy drew in a breath and concluded he had had enough. Clasping her hand in his, he clarified his meaning. "Miss Elizabeth, it was not my intent to doubt that the rector proposed marriage to you. Rather, it was that he turned his attention away from you to your sister. *That* was what I considered an impossibility." He gave her a moment to take in this information. "Furthermore, while we have this opportunity, you need to be aware that, while Miss Bennet has an elegant sort of prettiness, it is you who sets the standard for true beauty, Miss Elizabeth Bennet. It is your eyes which sparkle with vitality, your hair that glows with vibrant health, and it is your face and form I see in my dreams. That Mr. Collins was unaware of such proves he does not have a discerning eye and that he has a decided lack of character." Fitzwilliam Darcy had no regrets at laying his heart bare.

In the five months since they had been in each other's company, he had compared every woman he met against Elizabeth, and they all fell short. Yes, she was quick-tempered and capricious. Yes, she boldly reached intellectually where most women did not. And she was principled and kind, all attributes which complemented his own personality. She would be an accomplished mistress of his estate and his heart if he could only convince her.

"Oh!" She was bereft of speech, and her thoughts slowed. His words were like a lullaby, soft and soothing, giving her peace. Then their meaning filtered through her brain.

Elizabeth looked into his eyes, seeing the sincerity. She gasped, holding her free hand to her chest. *Can he love me?*

"Would you have regretted it had I accepted him then?" She held her breath.

"Had you done so, Elizabeth, I would have stormed the church, tossed you over my shoulder, put you atop my white steed, and carried you off to Gretna Green like the knight I wanted to be in my youth. Does that answer your question? Do you have any confusion as to my meaning?"

She was unable to move her eyes away from his. Elizabeth knew Darcy well enough to know he would never elope to Gretna Green. He was an honourable man. However, the picture he painted with his words made her heart rejoice.

"No, Mr. Darcy. I comprehend you quite clearly."

"Then..." Darcy started to speak. He had a question which begged an answer from the only woman who held his heart in her small hands.

Darcy was interrupted by a flurry of activity which suddenly surrounded him. Georgiana, tears streaming down her face, dropped to her knees beside Elizabeth.

Mr. Bennet, Colonel Fitzwilliam, and the rest of the Bennet family surrounded him, all inquiring as to his well-being. The cacophony of noise again faded as he lost consciousness.

* * *

ONCE DARCY WAS SETTLED in an upstairs bedchamber, Bingley was quick to return to the drawing room where the rest were gathered. He had yet to greet Jane and looked forward to mending his poor manners. As he entered the doorway, he was stunned to see her cousin standing close to his beloved. As Jane stepped back, Mr. Collins moved closer. It was a dance the lady was not wanting to participate in.

"Miss Bennet." Bingley moved to her side and took her hand. He raised it to his lips and placed a soft kiss to the back of it. "You are well after the excitement of the morning?"

Jane appreciated his attention as she sought to evade the same from Mr. Collins.

"I am, sir." She looked into the bluest eyes—kind eyes that drew her to him. "And Mr. Darcy, how does he fare?"

"That you put the concerns of others ahead of your own is admirable." He continued to hold her hand. "Darcy is being attended to by the apothecary, Miss Darcy, Miss Elizabeth, Miss Lucas, and Mrs. Bennet. I believe him to be in good hands."

Bingley wrapped Jane's hand around the crook of his arm and settled her on the settee furthest from the parson. Then he sat close to her to hint that Jane was likely to be very soon engaged. Bingley kept his eyes on the man, not realising how much challenge was in his gaze.

Mr. Collins understood the message clearly—as did the others in the room. Mr. Bennet chuckled to himself. Bingley still had one month to go before his self-imposed mourning period ended before he could offer for Jane. Bingley waited until Mr. Collins left the room, then he made eye contact with Jane's father. *It was time.*

* * *

WILLIAM COLLINS now realised where his duty lie. He needed to write to Lady Catherine. Putting pen to paper, he wrote:

30 March 1812

Longbourn, Hertfordshire

My esteemed patroness, Lady Catherine de Bourgh,

It is with regret and concern that I write to inform you of the events that have occurred since my arrival in this humble county. I only wish I could be with you at the arrival of this missive to provide the solace you have come to expect from your humblest servant for I fear your reaction, and I regret the need to cause undue pain and suffering.

IT GRIEVES me to inform you that, though my intentions were to follow your most excellent counsel to offer marriage to either Miss Lucas or Miss Elizabeth Bennet, I found that your nephew, Mr. Fitzwilliam Darcy, as a result of being one step ahead of me, had become betrothed to Miss Lucas only yesterday. When I then applied to Miss Elizabeth for her hand in the holy state of matrimony, I—who have learned from your magnificent benevolence—found her to be lacking in character in a manner which would cause unrest in my home as she—who has an elevated opinion of her position in society—was resistant to my influence. I fear she would not know her place in comparison to the exalted rank at Rosings.

My lady, it is my duty to further inform you that Miss Elizabeth Bennet has—by her own hand—caused terrible harm to your nephew. He—as I pen this letter—is lying unconscious here at Longbourn. I fear for Mr. Darcy and can only wish for your guidance.

I can only guess what has happened to cause a great man, your nephew, to forget the obligations to your lovely daughter, Miss Anne de Bourgh. With the looseness of oversight on the young ladies of this county, it is my humble opinion that he was pressed by compromise to offer for someone so far beneath him.

It saddens me to know the heartache you will endure as you read this, Lady Catherine. Your elevated knowledge of acceptable conduct in young ladies is needed in a county overrun with savage activity and opinions.

I shall be following this letter as soon as I verify that your nephew is on the mend. As he is important to you, Lady Catherine, he is important to me.

Yours most humbly,

Mr. William Collins

* * *

"CAN you ever forgive me for causing your brother harm, Georgiana?" Elizabeth held the young girl in her arms as they waited with Charlotte and Mrs. Bennet in the hallway for the apothecary to finish his examination. "I had no idea he was behind the hedgerow." She could not seem to stem her fears. What if her unladylike actions caused him permanent harm? "My wicked, wicked temper!"

Georgiana squeezed her even tighter but made no reply.

"I am curious, Eliza." Charlotte asked, "Were you aiming at him?"

"Certainly not!" Elizabeth answered. "If I was to aim at anyone, it would be my father's cousin, Mr. Collins."

"Lizzy, a lady does not throw stones." Mrs. Bennet added her own instruction though an hour too late. "And why would you want to hurt Mr. Collins? Certainly, he has much to overcome as a man, but with a bold and intelligent woman as a wife, improvement could be made. He would provide a secure home, and one day you would be mistress of Longbourn. That in itself is reason to accept an offer from him."

The three girls looked at her in confusion.

"I thought you were against Mr. Collins, Mama." After his arrival in the autumn and his subsequent departure, Mrs. Bennet had railed on and on about what a miserable man he was. "You *wanted* me to accept his offer?"

"He *did* ask you to marry him?" Mrs. Bennet was beside herself with joy. "When Mr. Bingley marries Jane, I will have two daughters well settled. My future is secure."

"Mama!" Elizabeth released Georgiana and moved in front of her mother. "I refused Mr. Collins, and he immediately turned his attention to Jane. I will not marry such a man—no matter that he will inherit Longbourn! I will not sacrifice my future to secure yours."

"What! He now longs for Jane?" Mrs. Bennet heard as much of the conversation as she wanted to hear. "Never! She is destined to be Mrs. Bingley, mistress of the greatest estate in Hertfordshire, Netherfield Park."

With that, Mrs. Bennet left to return downstairs to make sure at least one of her desires would come to fruition.

"I am deeply sorry you were witness to that, Georgiana."

"Think nothing of it, Lizzy." Georgiana was timid, but she had a plan for her brother and Elizabeth; the refusal of Mr. Collins worked well for her. If only she could lock Elizabeth inside her brother's bedchamber until they learned to appreciate how perfectly they fit each other.

* * *

IT WAS another hour before the apothecary left. Darcy had regained consciousness, and it appeared he would stay awake. Both Elizabeth and Georgiana sat at his bedside while a maid took care of a basket of mending in the corner.

Mr. Collins returned to the drawing room after arranging with Mr. Bennet to have his letter sent express. Once the missive was dispatched, his pleasure at knowing he had served Lady Catherine well faded into a bitterness born of frustration. He could not seem to find favour with anyone at Longbourn, thus he would continue to see to the concerns of his patroness.

"Miss Lucas, I have written to Lady Catherine de Bourgh about your betrothal to her nephew. Do you not think you have reached rather high for a husband?"

Even Mrs. Bennet sucked in air at the insult. The colonel, who had been standing next to Charlotte, stepped forward.

"Who are you to question what Miss Lucas does or does not do? Who are you to report to my aunt events of which are none of your concern?" He walked forward until he stood toe-to-toe with the man. "Who are you to insult a woman whose shoes you are not fit to polish?"

Colonel Fitzwilliam was every inch a soldier who was much affronted. *How dare the insufferable toad!*

"Sir, you know not who you are defending." Mr. Collins had no idea his counsel would stir the colonel's ire. The man was dangerous, but Collins believed he stood on secure ground. His patroness had expounded extensively on the importance of remaining in the sphere in which you were born. Seeking to increase status or rank was considered by her to be vulgar. "Any woman who would use arts and allurements to capture such a man is not worthy of the attention of my patroness and your aunt. Surely you must agree."

"If I did not think you would hurt someone else in the effort, I would call you out. You, Mr. Collins, are unworthy of being in the same room with Miss Lucas. You are allowing your rancor at being turned away from offering your suit to a woman of quality to colour your words. I issue you this warning, Mr. Collins. You may have the favour of my aunt, but you do not have mine. If you continue to disparage my betrothed, I will personally see to it that you will never be able to return to the living at Hunsford. Am I clear?"

"Your betrothed? How can this be?" Mr. Collins looked between the colonel and Charlotte; his confusion blatantly evident. "She is engaged to Mr. Darcy."

Richard Fitzwilliam laughed so hard he had tears pouring from his eyes. When he was finally able to stop long enough to talk, he turned back to the man standing in the center of the room. "The letter you just posted; you wrote to Aunt Catherine that Darcy was engaged?" At the parson's nod, he snorted. "You are a fool, and I am pleased she will be turning her disdain from me to you." The colonel slapped Collins on the back. "Yes, a large repercussion for a small man. I am delighted, Mr. Collins, that I am not you."

Leaving the man with his mouth wide open, he seated himself next to Charlotte.

"You are my hero, Richard," Charlotte whispered to her betrothed with a smile.

"I am. Always." *Oh, he could not wait until she was his bride.*

Lydia Bennet, witness to the entire confrontation, wanted to swoon at the colonel's actions. Laughing, Lydia exclaimed, "What a good joke!" If only a man would defend her in the same manner, it would be love, she was sure.

That a young girl would make sport of him was the last straw. Mr. Collins requested his trunks be brought back downstairs and arrangements were made to take them to Meryton where he would hire a carriage to transport him back to Kent. He had much to think on and much to repair when he got there.

* * *

DARCY DID NOT WANT to open his eyes. Not only did his head still hurt, but his pride was also bruised again.

"Do you think he will recover, Lizzy?"

"Mr. Jones has assured us that the effects of the blow are temporary." Elizabeth pulled Georgiana to her, draping her arm across her slim shoulders. "He *must*." She added almost to herself, "We have important matters to discuss."

"Do you love my brother, Lizzy?"

Darcy held his breath, and then breathed shallowly until she replied.

"When I first met him, as you are aware, his conduct was abhorrent. Nonetheless, I noticed a change in him yesterday when he visited here. And today?" Her breath rushed out at all he had shared before help had arrived. "Today, his words to me were…enchanting."

"Do you want to love him, Lizzy?"

Elizabeth chuckled and pulled her closer. "I believe you are rather persistent, Miss Darcy."

Darcy could not see them, but he could hear the smiles on the faces of both females he cherished above all others.

CHAPTER 23

ednesday 31 March 1812

The next day, Darcy was hardly enjoying the company sitting next to the bed in his temporary chambers. With little success, Colonel Fitzwilliam and Charles Bingley had taken it upon themselves to try to cheer him out of his frustration at not being able to leave his bed.

Neither visitor understood that sharing their future felicity with him was not encouraging to Darcy. Nor did they understand that they were not the particular individuals he longed to have at his bedside. However, Elizabeth and Georgiana were required downstairs for a serious consideration of Jane's upcoming wedding finery. Lace and ribbons! It was not a discussion Darcy wished to participate in. Only that reason, and that reason only, kept him from storming downstairs to join Elizabeth—well *that* and his constant state of dizziness.

Charles Bingley had been jolted into action the day before by Mr. Collin's attentions to his beloved. Before the parson had vacated Longbourn, Bingley sought a private moment with Jane and then with Mr. Bennet. On this morning, he had arrived to visit his friend as an engaged man. He was deliriously happy—far too jovial for Darcy.

"You have to admire my future sister for taking such prodigious care of her victim once he surrendered to her assault." Bingley snickered, enjoying Darcy's annoyance. Nevertheless, as soon as Darcy was out of danger, there was no reason not to derive a measure of entertainment from the experience.

"Major-General Wellesley could use a soldier with an aim like Miss Elizabeth's," Richard Fitzwilliam teased. "Was her throwing arm the same weapon that unseated you the last time?"

Bingley laughed. "Ho! What is this? Unseated twice? Darcy? How can this be possible?"

"I thank you for that, Bingley." Darcy blew out his breath. He was seated up in the bed. He intended to look fierce, though his lap covered with a lavender-coloured quilt which surely originated from Elizabeth's room, rendered the powerful look of his facial expression void.

"So, tell me, Darcy. Did she throw a stone the first time, or did Miss Elizabeth hit that miserable mare over the head with her reticule?" quipped the colonel.

"Nothing of the sort." Darcy continued, "Further, there is nothing wrong with Katherina. She is a spirited horse who needs a firm hand."

"Ah, an evasive tactic which my superior experience with military matters will easily overcome, my friend." Richard leaned back in his chair until it teetered on the two back legs. He could not keep the smugness from his face. "Now, tell us, Darce. What was in Miss Elizabeth's arsenal that first time you returned to Netherfield Park covered in mud?"

Conceding the truth to his obstinate cousin, he sighed.

"She smiled."

"What?"

"Yes, Richard. Miss Elizabeth smiled."

"You fell off your horse because she smiled?"

"I will say no more to either of you." At that point, Darcy realised that not satisfying their curiosity gave him the upper hand. Now it was him who smiled. Darcy chuckled at the memory. The confused expressions of his two friends also did much to lift his spirits.

* * *

NEVER WOULD Elizabeth have guessed that Jane was as fastidious as their mother when it came to the details of a wedding which would take place three months hence. Even Georgiana, who seemed to relish the lively exchange at first, was weary of the bickering.

Elizabeth tilted her head towards the garden, and they both quietly removed themselves from the drawing room.

Butterflies danced from flower to flower never seeming to land, always looking to the next bloom as they waltzed around the spring blossoms. Bees buzzed, and birds flew about, tending their young hatchlings. It was a glorious day which was made even better with the company.

"Did you ever want sisters, Georgiana?"

"I suppose I had longed for a sibling who was closer to my age to share my secrets."

Elizabeth laughed softly. "I notice your use of the past tense. The Bennet sisters are overwhelming as a whole, are we not?"

Georgiana had been surprised at the firm hand Jane was exercising with Mrs. Bennet, Kitty, and Lydia. They each had such strongly expressed opinions as to how the bride should look on her special day. Mary and Elizabeth had sat back and watched. It was not until Lydia became loud, in an effort to make her point, that Elizabeth entered into the fray.

Having a group of sisters was not what Georgiana had thought it would be. *Having just one sister, one like Elizabeth, would be perfect.*

"I apologise for Lydia's thoughtless comment about your brother to Mr. Collins yesterday."

The young girl's eyes flew to Elizabeth's. "Yes, your sisters are so boisterous, I confess to being astounded often." Elizabeth took her hand and put it on her arm as they continued a slow stroll down the path between well-tended rose bushes.

"I cannot comprehend how Lydia cannot admire my brother, Elizabeth. He is all that is good and generous." Georgiana's eyes filled with tears. "Why is it that negative opinions adhere to a mind while positive efforts to change are merely smiled at and forgotten? It is most unfair."

"Oh, dear friend, I believe you have stated a universal truth in your observation." Elizabeth led her to a bench where they sat, feeling the warmth of the sun. "I love each of my sisters dearly. Needless to say, I recognise others may not feel the same. However, I would ask that you consider something about Lydia before you judge her harshly.

"When Lydia loves, she loves deeply and unconditionally. She would be the first to defend if someone threatened someone she cares for, and she would be the first to praise any accomplishment." Lizzy patted the back of Georgiana's hand. "Also, Lydia is just now learning proper comportment in company." Elizabeth looked out of the corner of her eyes to see if she had Georgiana's attention. "Thus, we must forgive much. Needless to say, if a few years from now she still acts with a lack of restraint, we would be obliged to lock her up forever."

Georgiana sighed. "Like Fitzwilliam and Lydia, I long to improve my character."

Elizabeth laughed aloud. "Who would have imagined you using those two names together in one sentence?"

* * *

BINGLEY HAD RETURNED TO NETHERFIELD, and Richard rode to Lucas Lodge to visit his intended. The banns would be read the next three Sundays, and they would marry the next day. Twenty days until the wedding. Darcy realised it could not come soon enough for his cousin. Jealousy ate at his insides.

The musical notes of the ladies' laughter wafted up through Darcy's window and settled over the bed. He needed to see Elizabeth.

As if wishing for her would magically produce her presence, he was unsurprised when soon after she appeared in the doorway of his chambers. He smiled in welcome, completely missing that his sister accompanied her.

"Mr. Darcy, I must say it is good to see you sitting up."

"Both Bingley and Richard were here earlier. I am certain that even Mr. Jones would not find reason for complaint with their efforts to adequately fuss over me."

Elizabeth smiled as she noted the two men must have appropriated every spare pillow in Longbourn. "Then I must compliment them on a job well done." She could not help but chuckle at his delighted smile. This was a side of Mr. Darcy she had not seen before. Upon reflection, in the two days since his return to Hertfordshire, he had revealed himself to her as a man with a lighter countenance, yet, she knew he still bore the weight of responsibility for many.

"I heard your laughter from the garden. It made me smile to hear you and my sister together." He paused, before continuing. "You approve of her then?"

"I should certainly hope so, Brother." Georgiana stood with her hands fisted on her hips—a stance he had never witnessed from his little sister.

"My apologies, Georgiana." Sheepishly, he added, "I had not noticed you."

Georgiana Darcy had never in her lifetime laughed at her brother. However, under the circumstances, she could not help herself. As she wiped the tears from her face, she truly looked at her elder sibling. *The man needed her help!*

Over the years, she had observed him speak with peers of the realm, men of business, and men and women of their circle. Never had he been so befuddled or inept. If Fitzwilliam and Elizabeth were ever to get beyond his discomfort with expressing his feelings, it would require a miracle. While that was beyond her power, she did have the choice to assist him to better advantage. Thus, she told the couple that she wanted to retrieve a book from Elizabeth's chambers, and not waiting for an answer, left them alone in the room.

* * *

"Mr. Darcy, while we have this time of privacy, I must ask whether you recall your words yesterday while you were lying on the ground."

As Elizabeth wrung her hands and bit the lower corner of her lip,

Darcy thought back to the words. *Had he been articulate? Had she understood his meaning? Should he give a positive response and hope things had gone as well as he remembered them? Or should he answer in the negative in hopes he could do better this time?* He was an honest man. "I do."

"Twice you called me 'your Elizabeth,' sir," she said in hushed tones.

"I did." Darcy cleared his throat. "I may have only mentioned it two times, Elizabeth Bennet, however I have thought of you thus a million times over."

"Have you, then?" Elizabeth could not take her eyes away from his.

"Furthermore, Elizabeth"—Darcy reached out to take her hand —"what I left unsaid yesterday, was the hope that you would give me leave to use your name freely when in company."

He held his breath.

"A courtship, sir?" Elizabeth put her right hand to her chest.

"Do we need a courtship, Elizabeth? Do you doubt my heart?" He desperately wanted her answer to give him the peace he sought.

Surprise and pleasure warred within Elizabeth. Once Georgiana had finally fallen asleep the night before, Elizabeth had pondered at length what Darcy might have started to say before they had been interrupted. She wondered if he would ask for a courtship and how she would respond if he did. His implication was for so much more!

He waited for her answer.

"I do believe I know you well enough, Mr. Darcy."

"And, Elizabeth, what will you do with that knowledge?" He could not help but gently squeeze her hand and draw her a step closer until her knees touched the edge of his bed.

Those eyes! They reflected wisdom and knowledge, compassion and love.

"I will share it with my father when he asks me why I have accepted the hand of such an abominable man."

He bowed his head to kiss the back of her hand. Unheard was his sister's sigh from the hallway.

"I thank you for accepting my offer, Elizabeth. You have made me the happiest of men." He wanted to pull her into his arms and show her how heartfelt were his affections.

With a brilliant smile, Elizabeth said, "Pardon me, sir. You made an offer? I am afraid I failed to hear it, sir."

He chuckled. How he loved this teasing woman!

"My dearest, darling Elizabeth. It fills my heart that in spite of being unworthy and undeserving, in spite of my difficulty in speaking what is in my heart, you have come to comprehend me as the man, Fitzwilliam Darcy, and not the master. You have looked beyond my wealth and position to see *me*. You have accepted my sister and treated her no differently from your own siblings." He swallowed, his mouth suddenly dry. "From you, I have learned much, and I vow to you this day to continue to respect your opinions and strive to live up to your worth. I long to be your husband, Elizabeth. I long to take you home. I long to live with you each day of the rest of my life." He took a deep breath and let it out slowly. "Elizabeth Bennet, would you accept the hand of this abominable man? Would you ease my loneliness and my burdens? Will you marry me so that my heart finally beats in rhythm with yours? Will you be my wife?"

In her lifetime, Elizabeth never hoped to hear such beautiful words spoken to her. None were empty. None were meaningless. Each syllable was a gift—a treasure worth more than diamonds and pearls. Though he was a man of few words, the ones he chose to speak of his love filled her heart.

"Fitzwilliam Darcy, yes, I…"

Unbeknownst to them both, Georgiana stood outside the room listening for her reply as well, wanting to squeal for joy. In the midst of these happy tidings, neither Darcy, Elizabeth or Georgiana had heard the carriage arrive. A terrible furor sounded from the entrance hall, and an intensely angry woman's voice travelled up the stairs to the bedchambers.

"Where is my nephew? Step aside! I will see him now?"

Easily discerned was both Mrs. Bennet's and Jane's voices attempting to calm the older woman but to no avail. Footsteps stomped heavily up the staircase. It was Georgiana, standing in the hallway who first announced the newly arrived guest.

"Lady Catherine!" Georgiana wanted to faint. She longed to be invisible. She did neither. Lady Catherine de Bourgh had been the scary goblin in all her childish nightmares. That she had arrived at this particular moment was maddening! She had to stop her aunt.

Stepping into the center of the hallway, Georgiana shivered in fright. Yet, she would not be moved.

"That is far enough, Lady Catherine!" She used her cousin's commanding voice. Never had Georgiana spoken to her in such a manner.

"Georgiana Darcy." The voice dripped with rage and condescension. "I will see your brother immediately, and I will right this jumble he has entangled himself in." She pointed her bony finger at her niece, shaking it like a barren stick, whipping back and forth in a strong wind.

Before Georgiana could reply, a strong male voice was heard from the doorway.

Darcy roared from his bed. "Lady Catherine, you will not speak to my sister in such a manner."

Elizabeth did not fear him but knew his aunt should. Sparks were shooting from his eyes. She could tell the exact moment when Lady Catherine became aware that Darcy and Elizabeth were alone in a bedchamber together.

A growl started low in Lady Catherine's chest, growing in intensity and volume. Red flared up above the collar of her dress, her eyes opening so wide her lashes were no longer visible.

At the sight, Darcy, Georgiana, and Elizabeth were frozen in place. Fear filled them as Lady Catherine's hand clutched her chest and within seconds, the lady's eyes had rolled back in her head, and she collapsed to the floor.

Georgiana soon followed.

CHAPTER 24

*W*ednesday, 30 June 1812

In the three months since Lady Catherine suffered apoplexy, much had changed at the older woman's home in Kent. Her brother, the earl and his wife had hurried to Hertfordshire when they received news of Lady Catherine's collapse. When they ascertained the length of recovery time needed before Lady Catherine would be able to return to Rosings, it was revealed to her frail daughter, Anne, that she had inherited the de Bourgh estate two years earlier. Her mother, who enjoyed ruling as she pleased, failed to share this with her daughter. Upon gaining this intelligence, Anne immediately requested Richard's assistance in the management of Rosings. Thus, he sold his commission and took charge of the de Bourgh estate. And so it was—much to the chagrin of Kitty and Lydia—when Colonel Richard Fitzwilliam wed Charlotte Lucas, he wore the clothing of a squire.

For the first few weeks after her attack, Mr. Collins trod daily from Hunsford to Rosings; his time was spent in anxious suspense, convinced it would take his guidance and spiritual counsel to condole with Miss de Bourgh over his patroness's health. Moreover, Anne de Bourgh enjoyed toying with the man as much as her mother had done. Each day when he appeared at her door and inquired as to her mother's health, she would tell him only that she had received a note from her cousin Darcy but refused to share any information.

Within minutes of Mr. and Mrs. Richard Fitzwilliam's arrival at Rosings, Anne had abdicated full control of the running of the property to them, including oversight of the living at Hunsford. Mr. Collins was now subservient to the woman he had once thought to marry, and even though Charlotte Fitzwilliam was far less demanding than his former patroness had ever been, and her words and the tone were tempered with kindness, it humiliated the rector when Charlotte directed him in the care of his flock.

By the time Richard's parents left Hertfordshire, Mrs. Bennet had enough news for three weeks of gossip. For a certainty, Mrs. Lucas was the unfortunate audience she sought with frequency. Both Sir William and Lady Lucas were vexed when Lord and Lady Matlock refused invitations to Lucas Lodge, the excuse being their need to stay close to Lady Catherine and their nephew Darcy.

By the time Lord and Lady Matlock left for London, Darcy had improved enough to move back to Netherfield. Georgiana, intimidated by the presence of Lady Catherine, went with him, though she returned daily for visits with the Bennets.

He had heard a "yes" from his Elizabeth before his aunt's attack, and it was enough for him to petition Mr. Bennet for his blessing and approval. Should Lady Catherine not survive, Darcy wanted the engagement to be set before he went into mourning.

* * *

ELIZABETH WAS SEATED NEXT to him in the drawing room, surrounded by a watchful family and amused friends. Due to their passionate nature, constant chaperonage was deemed necessary. Georgiana was found likely to turn a blind eye to their expressions of affection, so she had been replaced by Lydia, who saw all, heard all, and told all. "Fitzwilliam?"

"Yes, my dear?" His love for this woman grew each day. He intertwined his fingers with hers, bringing the back of her hand to his lips for a kiss.

"What do you think your aunt is about?"

Though Lady Catherine's maid had arrived from Rosings, no one else was allowed to care for her, with the exception of Elizabeth. It had been a surprise the first time his aunt had requested his betrothed's presence in her bedchamber. At the time, Lady Catherine had been lying in bed for a week and was no longer being given medicinals that kept her silent.

It was a daily battle of wills between the two women, one old and irritable, the other young and so in love with the woman's nephew that she was willing to do whatever the doctor required to get this woman up and out of Longbourn. Of course, Lady Catherine had her strict opinions regarding appropriate treatments for her care. The physician Darcy brought from London had other ideas. Elizabeth followed the doctor's instructions in spite of any antagonism spewing from Darcy's aunt.

"My Elizabeth, I do not know. Believe me, it surprises me as much as it does you."

They had had this conversation many times over the three months since the interrupted proposal. Neither had an answer. His aunt must know she had no power to enforce decisions from her bedchamber at Longbourn. She was no longer in control, yet she fought every single minute to regain power.

"Sir, perhaps it is time to ask her myself. What is your thinking on the matter, my love?"

Darcy tilted his head to the side, amazed by the woman beside him. He admired her mind as well her whole lovely person.

He stood and helped her up alongside him. All eyes in the room immediately turned to them. "We are going to Lady Catherine."

They entered his aunt's bedchamber to find her sitting up in her bed, plaguing her maid to get rid of the tray the doctor had ordered and demanding rich, sauced vegetables and fruit tarts with cream instead.

"Nephew, why are you here? You refuse to speak on my behalf for Rosings so you may go—now!"

Having an attack which brought her close to death had not softened his aunt at all. He shook his head as he remained beside Elizabeth.

"Why, Lady Catherine, why do you request Elizabeth's assistance when you fight our betrothal with every breath you take?" Darcy's curiosity overruled his ire at his mother's elder sister. Like Elizabeth, he had to know.

"Bah! You would not understand the machinations of a woman, Fitzwilliam Darcy. Your father never did, and for a certainty, Louis de Bourgh did not—though he was, by far, a superior man."

As Darcy rolled his eyes in disbelief, Elizabeth could not help but ask. "Then answer me, Lady Catherine? Why do you demand my presence?"

Lady Catherine looked at Elizabeth from head to toe and back, disdain pouring from her hard eyes.

"You, Miss Elizabeth, are at a loss as to why I do so? I am all astonishment!" The older woman snorted, confident in her own superiority. "As long as I keep you here in my room, you are away from my nephew. You cannot entice him, nor can you distract him with your arts and allurements."

Elizabeth laughed until tears streamed down her cheeks.

"What is the meaning of this! This is not to be borne!" Lady Catherine's face turned as red as it had before her attack. Her maid immediately rushed to her with a draught which was instantly refused.

"I pray you accept my apologies, Lady Catherine." Elizabeth struggled to calm herself, leaning into Darcy as she did so.

Darcy handed her his handkerchief for her tears.

"Lady Catherine, on the first night I became acquainted with your nephew, I determined the most effective means of keeping him from interfering with Mr. Bingley and my sister Jane was to distract him into staying away from the couple in the same manner you are attempting with Fitzwilliam and me. As you are aware, Mr. Bingley and Jane will wed tomorrow; whilst my plan worked in that aspect, in another it did not."

Elizabeth waited to see how Lady Catherine would respond. She took the bait.

"How did it not work? I need to know now!"

Elizabeth smiled up to the man next to her. She loved him so.

"Since I thought Fitzwilliam the most abominable man of my acquaintance, I vowed that night to loathe your nephew for the rest of my life. In this, I failed terribly." Elizabeth continued. "In six weeks, I will marry your nephew. In spite of the bitter words that you share with me daily about the future of Pemberley or the children we hope to produce, we will be the happiest of couples."

Darcy leaned over and placed a kiss on her cheek.

"None of that! You are not yet wed." Lady Catherine was horrified at Darcy's boldness. "Let me be rightly understood. This match, to which you have the presumption to aspire, can never take place. No, never. You, Nephew, are engaged to *my daughter*. You cannot marry because honour, decorum, prudence, nay, interest, forbid it. Now what have you both to say?"

"But we will wed, Aunt." Darcy's eyes did not waver from Lady Catherine. "There is nothing you can do or say that will change the way I feel about this woman. She will be my wife."

"You are, in every way, truly abominable, Fitzwilliam Darcy." Lady Catherine sought to have the final word. It was not to be.

"I have been such, Aunt, but that is my past."

Elizabeth stretched up and returned his earlier kiss. She loved the feel of his shaved whiskers on her lips.

"No, Lady Catherine, he is no longer the abominable Mr. Darcy." Elizabeth smiled at her beloved. "He is *my* Mr. Darcy."

They walked out of the room to her bellows and cries, completely oblivious to the sound.

"I am no longer abominable, Elizabeth?"

Laughing, she said, "There is only one person in your family who is abominable, darling, and she and her vitriol are behind us."

* * *

THE NEXT MORNING, Jane Bennet became Mrs. Charles Bingley. She was a beautiful bride, though Darcy only had eyes for his Elizabeth.

Elizabeth gazed at the man standing next to the groom and knew him to be *Divinely Attractive, Stately Sculpted, and Fabulously Elegant.* She glanced behind him to see Georgiana sitting next to Richard and Charlotte, a wide smile on her face.

Since the day of Lady Catherine's attack, Georgiana had remained so close to either Jane or Elizabeth that she was like a shadow. She planned and maneuvered to leave Darcy alone with Elizabeth on every occasion possible. This put her at odds with Lydia whose job was to keep them apart. A sibling rivalry between the two never broke out into an all-out war, though both were determined to have their way.

Darcy was amazed at the tenacity of his sister, though Elizabeth was not. Miss Georgiana Darcy was much like her brother, and she loved her for it. She had blossomed into a fine young lady who was much more prepared for presentation at court than she had been before she arrived in Hertfordshire.

Richard and Charlotte invited Georgiana to stay at Rosings after the Darcy wedding in August. At Anne's insistence, they would move Lady Catherine to the dower house. She would no longer be in charge of Rosings. Should that not meet with Lady Catherine's approval, the great lady had the option of living in the townhouse in London.

After three months of constant attendance by Mr. Collins, Richard was loath to keep him on the property. He approached Anne about sending him to London with Lady Catherine should that be her choice. Anne agreed.

* * *

FRIDAY, 14 August 1812
Longbourn Chapel

.   .   .

"IN FRONT of God and men, you promised to obey me, Elizabeth Darcy." He whispered into her ear as she signed her name for the final time as Elizabeth Bennet. She was wearing the Darcy sapphires around her neck, and he could not keep his eyes from tracing their path.

"I suppose I did." She could not help herself; she kissed him on the cheek and then returned to the task at hand.

Richard cleared his throat—loudly. Although he had been married a few days past four months, he easily remembered the keen anticipation of his wedding day. He looked at his own bride. She had informed him the day before that there was reason to believe a new Fitzwilliam son or daughter would be born in about six months.

The declaration of war between the Americas in June had been an expected blow. Many of his former regiment had left in anticipation of the fighting and begged him to return to the army. Especially now, with a babe on the way, he was convinced he had served long enough. Without regret, he would not do so.

Blessedly, Lady Catherine had chosen to live in London. Mr. Collins immediately followed. For that, Richard had no reason to repine.

He grinned as Darcy leaned in to steal another kiss. Both Mr. and Mrs. Bingley and Georgiana had caught them out but seemed content to not acknowledge the moment.

* * *

"ELIZABETH," Darcy whispered, unsure if she was still awake. He brushed her dark curls away from her face, the braid long ago having come undone. Kissing her on the forehead, he pulled her closer, her legs wrapped around his whilst her palm rested on his chest. He smiled. She had earned her sleep.

He thought back to the night they met and remembered how her eyes had caught his attention. It was not love at first sight; however, he now knew his heart had been quickly engaged. They had followed a rocky path to their happily-ever-after, but they had finally arrived. He sighed deeply.

"William, are you thinking again?" Her eyes still closed; Elizabeth teased. "An abominable thing to do on the night of our wedding, do you not agree?"

He kissed her until he could barely remember his name. "Yes, Mrs. Darcy, you have married an abominable man."

ABOUT THE AUTHOR

Joy Dawn King started telling stories from an early age. However, she did not write any of them down until she was 57 years old. While living high in the Andes Mountains of Ecuador with her husband and family, she read Jane Austen's Pride and Prejudice for the first time. It was love at first page. After she was done, she longed for more.

When searching for another copy of Jane Austen's writings, she happened upon several books that offered alternative paths to happily ever after for Mr. Darcy and Elizabeth Bennet. She purchased and read as many as she could find. Finally, in early 2014, she had an idea for a story about the couple that would not go away. Thus, her first book, *A Father's Sins: A Pride and Prejudice Variation*, was born.

Since then, Joy and her husband moved back to the U.S. and plot bunnies kept hopping in and out of her imagination. Now, it's all she can do to keep up with them. But she tries.

www.ingramcontent.com/pod-product-compliance
Lightning Source LLC
Chambersburg PA
CBHW020313260626
47156CB00004B/1204